THE LIFE THAT MATTERED

THE LIFE THAT MATTERED

Book One

Jewel E. Ann

This book is a work of fiction. Any resemblances to actual persons, living or dead, events, or locales are purely coincidental.

Dedication

To my future self
Don't ever be predictable.

PROLOGUE

"CAN YOU KEEP a secret?"

Mom failed to answer her phone, the new normal I'd come to expect. It didn't deter me from calling and leaving a message. Fifteen minutes earlier, my life exploded. I needed someone—anyone—at that moment.

Months ago, I should have disconnected her phone line. No one still used landlines.

And ... she died.

Dead people didn't use phones. At least, I'd always assumed they didn't. At that moment, I felt like anything was possible. Literally *anything*.

I estimated that I had maybe ten more messages to leave before her mailbox reached capacity. Ten more messages before I'd disconnect her phone line, go through her things, and sell the house.

"My husband did something ... with another woman." I choked on a sob, as a deadly storm of emotions ripped through me. After a minute of strangled silence, I scrounged a tiny shred of composure and continued. "And I think I've known the truth. But I couldn't say anything because it took away his pain—at least temporarily. It's better than the alternative, right? I mean ... I thought he was dying. Part of me wanted to tell him that I knew. I hate secrets. But I feared what he might do if he found out I knew, or how it would break us if I was wrong and accused him." I wiped a few tears that forced their way free because I couldn't erase the memory of the gun in his hand and the hopelessness on his face.

"And the worst part? I can't tell my best friend. I can't tell anyone ... so I'm telling you because this insane part of me thinks you might have connections." I chuckled. "Afterlife connections. Spiritual connections. Supernatural connections. I'm not really sure because I still can't believe this is happening. I don't actually think *he's* crazy. But, Mom ... it's pretty fucking crazy. Him *feeling* her. It's not right. It's not fair."

I closed my eyes. "Sorry for the language. But I fear—" Another sob exploded from my chest. "I fear it's too late."

Rubbing my swollen eyes with the heel of my hand, I blew out a slow, shaky breath. "I'm not myself at the moment. Anyway ... Dad's good." I searched for *anything* to take my mind off the gun and those three terrible words he'd said to me. "Katie's pregnant, but I'm sure she already told you that. I haven't mentioned the affair. After her two miscarriages, I refuse to do or say anything to cause her more stress. As for me ... I'm pretty sure we're done having kids. Two is enough. Although, I thought a surprise could come along. Did I mention our sex life has been better since he's *been* with her? Weird, huh? At first, I thought it was just guilt and silent remorse, but I honestly think when he leaves her, there's this tiny window where he's not physically in pain. So, we have sex. And it's intense. It's mind-blowing."

I sighed into the phone. "A little surprise is no longer a possibility. I officially hate surprises. And…" I closed my eyes, seeing the gun and that look—irrevocable despair "…I think it's too late for new beginnings. Today I saw the end." I let a few more tears come to life before pulling back my sleeve to glance at my watch. "I love you, Mom. I miss you. And if you don't have any connections to help my situation, don't feel bad. I'll figure something out. Just the possibility that you're listening is enough. Today I miss you more…" the next round of emotions burned my eyes "…than I have in all the months you've been gone. Today I j-just really n-need my mom."

*Falling in love tomorrow is
such a waste of today.*

CHAPTER ONE

Six Years Earlier

THIRD WHEEL.
    Tagalong.
    Odd woman out.

For two years I played this awkward role. When did I lose my self-respect?

"I love Canada," my best friend, Lila, declared as she helped me pack for our threesome trip to Vancouver—tagalong me, Lila, and her fiancé, Graham Porter.

Porter Realty.

Porter Investments.

Porter Communications.

Porter Arena.

Senator Alfred Porter.

Representative Grant Porter.

Mayor Isabel Porter.

The Porters had a presence and financial investment in everything. They represented the one percent, and they did it in style.

"I'm glad Graham has meetings, so we'll get to hang out without me feeling like I'm cock-blocking your fiancé." I zipped my suitcase as Lila plopped down onto my bed.

"Stop it with the third wheel thing. We're all friends. We were all friends before anything romantic started between Graham and me. Well, except for that part where I hated him. Anyway, he likes you better outside of the bedroom."

I laughed, acknowledging the truth with an easy nod. Graham was my best *guy* friend.

When he found out my parents couldn't afford treatment for my father's failing kidneys, he arranged for his family to pay for everything, *and* he made sure Dad received the best doctors. My father owed the Porter family for his extended life.

The Porters owned the building where I had my bath shop—Clean Art. The Porters owned the bank where I had my business loan. They pretty much owned everything and a piece of everyone I knew. That was okay. They were good people. Most of them.

I collapsed onto the bed next to Lila and grabbed her left hand, still in awe of the diamond on her ring finger. "He's going to make you quit your job and pop out babies, but not before he makes you remove that barbell from your tongue."

Our friendship traveled many paths with interesting stops for things like piercings and tattoos. As soon as we could legally rebel, we did. Lila pierced her tongue. I put holes in my belly button and eyebrow. Then we inked our skin. Lila splurged with a full-winged tramp stamp, while I demonstrated my geek side with a carbon atom tattoo on the inside of my left wrist.

She giggled, yanking her hand from my grip. "Stop! No, he's not. He loves my independence, and his penis loves my piercing."

I wrinkled my nose. "Eww …"

GRAHAM FLEW TO Vancouver three days earlier, so I had Lila all to myself for the flight and the drive to the hotel—Porter Suites. Imagine that.

"Baby!" Lila hurled herself into Graham's arms as soon as he opened the door to the suite.

He winked at me over her shoulder.

"Graham Cracker." I rolled my eyes.

After Lila rushed past him, he tipped the bellboy, watching him retreat toward the elevator for a few seconds before returning his attention to me. "So you don't have to listen to her scream." Graham handed me a keycard.

"Hmm … she's never mentioned screaming. You must be referencing a movie, not actual events." I plucked the keycard from his manicured fingers.

"I'm throwing my hat in the gubernatorial race next year. You realize you'll have to address me with a little more respect when that happens."

I brushed past Graham in his pinstriped suit, potent cologne, and over-gelled coal hair—parted perfectly on the side like the preppy guy he'd always been. Lila glued herself to my existence in kindergarten, but Graham wormed his way into our circle of friends in college. He campaigned for the role of my boyfriend for two whole weeks.

Flowers.

Expensive jewelry.

Plagiarized love letters—mostly William Wordsworth and Lord Byron.

I refrained from calling him out on his romantic poems and sonnets because the thought did count, although he lost a few points by assuming my love of science meant I knew nothing about literature.

We discovered our attraction wasn't as physical as it was born of our mutual love for sports. My vagina stood in the way. He thought our shared interests plus his owning a penis and my owning a vagina equaled a match made in heaven.

As for Lila ... well, she hated him for years.

"This place is quite fancy-pants, Graham Cracker. Or should I start calling you Governor Graham Cracker?"

The suite showcased a stunning view of the coastal mountains and water's edge from the top level of the hotel nestled in the heart of downtown Vancouver. I suppressed a gasp to prevent feeding Graham's ego. In fact, I went out of my way to bulldoze his ego at every opportunity.

"Why don't you head down to the spa, Evelyn? Get a massage, maybe have them do something with your hair." He eased his tall frame into the leather armchair and pulled Lila onto his lap, kissing her neck and groping her boob while looking at *me*.

Asshole.

My nose wrinkled while Lila tried to shoo his hand away, but Graham ignored her. "What's wrong with my hair?" I ran my fingers through my pin-straight hair that stopped midway down my back.

"It's fake blond. Not sexy blond like Lila's hair." He buried his nose in her hair and sniffed.

Fine. I'll admit Lila's wavy blond hair looked a bit healthier than mine. She turned heads with a chic blend of gold and copper lowlights because Graham sent her to the most expensive salons. However, I happened to like my platinum blond hair. Sometimes I liked it with colorful streaks. Sometimes I liked it with my natural, dark blond grown out a few inches.

It was hair. Why not get creative with it? Lila lost her carpe diem with her hair. She used to possess more flare BG (Before Graham). He liked her fitting in with his conservative family. She liked his relentless pursuit of her. Who wouldn't like to be the center of someone's world?

Lila's beauty deserved all the admiration. Hell ... I admired her all the time. She knew I envied so many things about her, like her curves. Whereas, I resembled a boy who hadn't reached puberty yet.

No butt.

No boobs.

If it weren't for my hair, I could've passed as a four-teen-year-old boy.

"I love you, Grammy Gram Gram." I pinched his cheek while blowing Lila a kiss. "Try to give her a real orgasm."

Graham narrowed his eyes at me while Lila snickered,

turning to nuzzle his neck. She'd mastered the art of ignoring our banter.

Smart woman.

The truth? Graham and I should have never dated. We were destined to be friends—giving-shit, banter-driven, sports-loving friends. When Lila went through many years of her Graham-is-a-spoiled-rich-kid phase, I liked Graham. We hung out in college while Lila studied because she took school seriously, while Graham and I bet on college football and basketball.

After we graduated, Lila traveled for several years. I worked some odd jobs that didn't actually require a science degree before deciding I wanted to make body products. Graham accepted his rightful seat helping run the many family businesses while being groomed for a position in politics. When Lila returned from her worldly travels, Graham wasted no time going full-on over-the-top Porter-style campaigning for her affection. And they lived happily ever after. At least, that was the plan.

I skipped the massage and wandered a few blocks away from the hotel with my reminiscent thoughts keeping me company on my lonely outing. A whimsical wood sign for a bubble tea cafe caught my attention. The instant I opened the door, I began to salivate. Really, what *was* that smell?

"Welcome." The brunette with braided pigtails smiled at me from behind the counter while sliding hot buns onto wood serving trays. The quaint, eco-chic cafe had odd-shaped, old-wood tables, a few bookshelves, and lots of places to plug in computers while sipping bubble tea and salivating over hot buns in unique flavors like matcha, dark chocolate, and tomato basil. A perfect find for me that morning.

"I'll have the berry blend bubble tea and a lemon coconut bun."

"Those have five more minutes in the oven. Are you okay with waiting?"

Waiting for hot-out-of-the-oven buns? Yeah, I had all day. Hot lemon coconut buns had to be better than the champagne and sex going on back at the hotel.

"Five minutes is just fine." I set my money on the counter while she made my tea.

Turning, I scanned the place for somewhere to sit, but early birds occupied all of the tables. Hoping someone would leave soon, I sipped my tea and waited in the far corner by the bookshelves filled with tea pots, books on tea, bubble tea straws, and other tea paraphernalia. When braided pigtails called my number, I took my tray with the hot bun on it and inspected the table situation again.

"Do you want your drink and bun to go?" another girl behind the counter asked.

"Yeah, maybe." My lips twisted to the side.

"There's a chair right here. I'll be done soon."

I turned toward the male voice.

A handsome Asian man, sitting at a small table by the window, gestured to the empty seat across from him.

Curiosity formed a smile on my face.

Attractive stranger. Quaint cafe. First day in Vancouver.

Who could say no to that? "Thank you."

He nodded before returning his attention to the book cradled in his hands. A real physical book. Not an e-reader or laptop. He must have been from another planet. My scientific brain had always suspected life beyond Earth.

I stared. It was hard not to stare, even with the sweet lemony bun aroma wafting toward my nose. The generous stranger owned a kind, bright smile, *and* he hailed from planet Paperback Books. Did I mention his sharp jaw line and high cheekbones? It was all too much.

Mischievous eyes conveyed an unspoken pleasure. They dared me to reveal my own level of happiness and curiosity.

The hair though ... seriously ... The. Hair! Jet black. *So* thick.

It looked like a missed attempt at parting it on the right—the opposite of Graham's gel-suffocated Ken doll look.

"Haven't seen you here before," he murmured just before sipping the coffee in his right hand while keeping ahold of his book with his left hand, leaving his gaze on the pages.

"Sounds like a backward pickup line." I used my fork and knife to cut the bun in half.

He shot me a furtive glance. "Ah, you mean the tried and true, *Do you come here often?*"

I grinned, peeking through my eyelashes as I kept my chin tipped toward my food. "It *has* stood the test of time." *At least, on my planet.*

"Well ... do you? Come here often?" He leaned back

in his chair, sliding his bookmark between the pages before setting the book onto the table and resting that hand on his leg. His other hand cupped the mug of coffee. The guy looked like he should be on a billboard for something really sexy. Cologne? Jeans? Underwear? Allergy medication? Erectile dysfunction? Nah ... surely not. He was the epitome of put together—light gray suede boots and perfectly fitted faded jeans. His cream shirt hugged his torso just enough to let the world know he worked out, but he kept it partially hidden under a gray notched-collar peacoat and a deep red checked scarf as if he didn't need to flaunt his physique.

If I hadn't resembled an upside-down mop wearing a sweater, leggings, and boots, I would have flaunted my physique. I struggled to properly match said sweater, leggings, and boots.

Back to book guy. Did I mention he seemed tall? I couldn't tell for sure from his seated position, but he had to spread his legs beneath the table to accommodate my legs without us bumping knees.

"Mmm ..." I hummed my utmost appreciation for the exquisite bun as I shook my head. "No. I don't come here often because I don't live here. But if I did..." I rolled my eyes back in my head "...I'd be here every single day. This is *so* good."

His smirk greeted me when I recovered from my food orgasm. "Where do you live?"

"Colorado."

"I see. Did you come to Vancouver just for the buns and bubble tea?"

I breathed a guileless laugh. "Subconsciously, I think I did."

He continued to inspect me with bright eyes while maintaining a pleasant smile.

When my pulse picked up, because that was the effect he had on me, I cleared my throat and slid my attention to the window. "I'm here with my best friend and her fiancé. He has business meetings. It's a free trip for me, so that's cool. Right? And Lila, my friend, likes the company." I blotted my mouth, most likely covered in powdered sugar.

"Where are your friends? They're missing out on hot buns."

"They needed some *alone time*." I smirked. "So I ventured out. I'm Evelyn, by the way."

"Ronin," he said just before taking another sip of his coffee. Large hands. He *had* to be tall.

I had a thing for tall guys with slight accents who knew how to read.

"Do you live here?" I stirred my tea with the wide stainless-steel straw.

"Just for one more day. I've accepted a job … in Aspen."

"Shut up." I narrowed my eyes. "You can't be serious."

"Ski patrol."

"Really?" I cut another bite of the bun with my fork and knife. It would have been easier to pick it up and eat it with my hands, but … handsome stranger. "I live in Aspen."

"Small world."

I tilted my head, searching for warning signs—a flicker of danger in his eyes or the twitch of a wolfish grin. My love of horror movies seeped into my real life, distorting my judgment and imparting irrational fear into random thoughts.

"So what do you do in Aspen?" he asked with a slight accent. French? I couldn't tell, but I wanted him to keep talking, even if he was a stalker.

"I sell guns. And own them. A lot of them. And I'm a really good shot." See? Who says that? Me, horror movie lover … as I imagined his face covered in paint like The Joker or Pennywise.

Both of his eyebrows arched. "Okay. I didn't see that coming."

I chewed a bite of the bun, studying him. He didn't look like a serial killer. Wasn't that the most common sign of one? Since killers didn't have a look, the most notorious ones were typically normal looking—sometimes even good looking. They excelled at disarming unsuspecting women.

"I'm not a gun person, so I don't know any intelligent questions to ask about your job. Except maybe … how did you get into guns?"

I scratched my cheek and grinned with a wrinkled nose. "I don't sell guns. I'm just testing stranger danger. Do you like clowns?"

A pleasant grin slid up his face. "Clowns are fine. I suppose." He chuckled.

Wrong answer. But everyone was entitled to their

opinion.

"I own a bath and body shop. I make all of my own products. I'm a chemist who really wanted to be an artist. So, this combines both worlds."

"But do you own a gun?"

My lips twisted, and my eyes narrowed. "It's Colorado. The probability of me owning a gun is high. Let's just leave it at that."

"Fair enough."

I didn't own a gun. Never had. Wouldn't have had the first clue how to use one.

"So … ski patrol?"

"Yes. It's what I've been doing for years." Definitely a French accent. What was it with guys and accents?

"Your accent …" I tapped my finger against my bottom lip.

He took a sip of his coffee. "My father is from Chamonix, France. My mother's family is from Malaysia, but she was born in the United States, as was I. We moved to France when I was one, and that's where I grew up. My father is … *was* an Olympic skier."

I blinked several times, pausing my straw at my lips. "Wow! I'm utterly boring compared to you. Bet you're glad your coffee's almost gone, so you can go hang out with more worldly people."

Ronin chuckled—deep and smooth. "You make soap. Tell me more."

"You don't have to sound interested. We can talk about the weather. I hear rain is expected over the next few days."

He drummed his fingers on the table. "Bar soap? Liquid soap?"

I stole another bite of the warm bun, chewing while trying to hide my grin, gazing out the window at the traffic crawling along the street. "Both. And bath bombs, scrubs, lip balms, facial creams, and toners …" I blotted my mouth with my napkin. "It's really an endless list."

"Fascinating."

I coughed a little laugh. "It's really not."

"No?" He ran a hand through his hair and scratched his neck. It tightened his shirt a bit more across his chest. "I find it all very intriguing."

Ronin possessed a special charm and way above average looks. Okay … he was flat-out sexy. The heat in my cheeks probably made my thoughts all too transparent.

"To me," I conceded, "it *is* interesting and fun. I genuinely like my job. I'm not sure my parents imagined my degree leading to my owning a bath shop, but they're happy that I'm happy."

"I can relate. My father imagined me chasing his gold medals in skiing. I loved watching him ski. And I, too, love skiing. However, I was always more fascinated with the men and women who brought injured skiers down the mountain than the exuberant victors crossing the finishing line in record time. The only clock that interested me was the one that meant saving a life. That's what I do now. I've worked in several countries as ski patrol. And I've spent many summers working as a paramedic with fire and EMS."

Hot buns. Yummy bubble tea. Sunny and fifty-five

degrees in beautiful Vancouver. And an Asian Frenchman who liked saving lives. Short of Graham giving Lila a dozen orgasms … there's no way Lila's day beat mine.

"I don't suppose you'll marry me, will you?" My mouth twisted into a smirk before I laughed—a hearty laugh so he saw my humor, my joking personality (I was ninety percent joking).

"Probably." He shrugged one shoulder.

Dead.

In that moment, I died.

He did *not* just say that, did he? I was joking. Yes, he was joking too. That meant we were two strangers who found joking about marriage completely acceptable. That had to be a small percent of the population. Less than two percent?

We exchanged looks that neither of us could hold for more than a few seconds without averting our gazes.

What was that?

What the hell just happened?

"So …" I stood on my wobbly legs. "I should get back to the hotel. Thanks for sharing your table with me."

Ronin unfolded his body from the chair, proving my theory—he was tall. The whole damn package.

"It was nice meeting you, Evelyn." Ronin glanced at his phone and slipped it back into the pocket of his wool jacket. Then he grabbed his book and opened the door for me.

"Thank you." I slid past him, accidentally—or not so accidentally—brushing against him. "What did you do here?" I wasn't ready to say goodbye. Nor did I want to sound desperate, but I was sure the hypothetical marriage proposal already blew my cover.

"Which way?" He jerked his chin toward the right.

I pointed to the left, the direction of my hotel.

"Ski patrol in Whistler. I fly out of Vancouver tomorrow for Denver."

We strolled down the sidewalk, hands in the pockets of our jackets, taking our time. I craved all the seconds I could get with my new friend. At the stoplight, I frowned at my threadbare leggings and pilled, black sweater jacket.

Five years of scuff marks painted my charcoal boots.

No makeup.

Also, as Graham so kindly pointed out, my hair was not shampoo-commercial worthy.

Ronin didn't seem to care—after all, he could've made up any excuse to hop in a cab or walk in the opposite direction, yet he didn't.

"What does your father do now?" I asked.

"He's retired, so he travels a lot with my mom. She's a designer and owns a clothing line. It's a small line with a limited market, but she's doing exactly what she loves. Her best friend is her business partner, so it affords her time to travel with my dad. I can't keep up with them. I think they're in Kuala Lumpur right now, but I'm not entirely sure." He chuckled. "Do you live close to your family?"

"Yes. My parents live in Denver. My sister and her husband live in San Francisco, close to my dad's parents. And my grandma, my mom's mom, moved into an assisted living facility six months ago in Aurora. I moved out of my apartment last month and into her home, an actual log cabin in Aspen. My grandfather built it. I'm sure it could be worth a lot of money, but my grandma wants me to live there. It's important to her to see it stay in the family."

Ronin bobbed his head several times. "I like that. It seems like our generation doesn't really value things like log cabins built by grandparents. I heard the value of a lot of antiques has gone down because we just *don't value* them like generations before ours."

"I can see that, and it is sad." I pointed to the entrance of Porter Suites.

We stopped under the awning.

"Nice hotel." His eyebrows lifted a fraction.

"My best girlfriend is marrying my best *guy* friend. He's a Porter—I thought the most sensible one of the bunch, but now he's talking craziness about getting into politics. I'm not sure he'll keep a level head if that happens. But … I'm giving him the benefit of the doubt. Maybe he's just a great guy—albeit a really rich guy— who wants to be a public servant." I shrugged, slipping my hands back into the pockets of my jacket while blowing hair out of my mouth.

"Graham Porter."

I twisted my lips, nose wrinkled. "How did you know?"

"No …" Ronin jerked his chin, gesturing over my shoulder. "I mean he's coming out of the hotel."

My head whipped around as the lovers emerged from the door held open by the doorman.

It wasn't surprising Ronin recognized Graham and his fastidious, tabloid-worthy appearance.

"We're going shopping. Coming, Evie?" Lila held out her hand to me, but then she stopped, letting it fall to her side as her gaze snagged on my tall, new friend. "Hello …" She smiled, showing me a quick where-are-your-manners look.

"Ronin, this is my friend Lila and her fiancé, Graham. This is Ronin. We just met over buns and bubble tea."

Lila chuckled, reaching for Ronin's proffered hand. "Buns and bubble tea. We'll chat about that later, Evie. Nice to meet you, Ronin."

"You too." He flashed her a warm smile.

"Hi. Nice to meet you." Graham shook Ronin's hand too.

I waited for Graham to make some snide remark about me, just to embarrass me, but he didn't. Grammy Graham earned extra points for being on his best behavior. Maybe his leap into politics had already matured him. He was thirty-six going on fifty.

"You should invite Ronin to dinner." Lila looped her arm around Graham's arm.

Ha!

There was a wedding proposal and a bit of hardcore swooning on my part, but dinner with *my* friends felt exponentially more intimidating than a hypothetical wedding proposal.

"Um …" I glanced up at Ronin.

"Sounds good to me."

Lila excelled at making me think I couldn't find dates

without her expert help. She was my pimp. Just when I thought I'd found a guy all on my own, she swooped in and arranged a date. Had I not been so elated, I might have been pissed off at her.

"Me too." I smiled at Ronin.

"Great!" Lila tipped her chin up, her grin beaming with pride.

Yeah, yeah ... you're an awesome best friend.

"What time, babe?" She tugged on Graham's arm to get his attention.

"Six." He glanced at his watch.

"Where?" Ronin asked.

Lila gestured toward the hotel. "The steakhouse in the hotel. Graham says it's phenomenal."

"I'll be back around six." Ronin winked at me. "Have fun shopping."

My eyes widened, smile embarrassingly too exuberant, as I held my breath to keep from squealing like a seventeen-year-old girl who just got asked to prom by the hottest guy in school.

"See you soon!" Lila waved as Ronin stepped to the curb and slid into the back of a taxi. "Breathe! Oh my god ... breathe, Evie." She pressed her hands to my face, eyes wide with excitement for me.

"Are we shopping, ladies? If not, I have business I can do." Graham waited at the back of the black SUV with a driver holding open the door.

"Shopping, babe." Lila took my hand and pulled me into the back of the vehicle.

Graham rolled his eyes at me as I bit back my smile.

CHAPTER TWO

"WHOA, *EVIE!* YOU are hot!" Lila flipped her champagne blond hair over her bare shoulder, looking rather hot herself in a simple black cocktail dress.

Graham was … Graham. Always in an expensive, tailored suit and freshly gelled hair. That night he chose a basic black suit. What was wrong with the one he had on earlier?

"It's not too much?" I wrinkled my nose.

"Yes. It's too much." Graham smirked. "I spent way too much money on it."

"I didn't ask you to buy it. You just like to throw around your money so the world feels indebted to you. I'm going to give the dress to Lila after tonight, so you'll have one less thing to hold over my head." I sashayed to the elevator, brushing my hands over my rhubarb V-neck wrap dress with kimono sleeves. The flowing material softened my teenage-boy figure. As we stepped onto the elevator, Graham eyed my hair.

Asshole.

"I feel like the bird's nest is no longer the trend. Am I wrong?" He cocked his head to the side.

JEWEL E. ANN

Lila elbowed him in the ribs. "It's a messy bun, and it always looks good on Evie."

Once.

I had sex with Graham *once* in the two weeks we dated—if you could call it dating. We were under the heavy influence of alcohol. Lila knew. Hell, I called her the second I left his apartment on campus. She responded with, "Eww … come home and shower right away."

The flowers, jewelry, stolen poetry … all led up to a night of passionless sex. It felt like having sex with my best friend, and that felt wrong. We crossed a line because I had a vagina and he had a penis. Just because you can … doesn't mean you should. Wise words I learned a little too late.

Many years separated us from that epic mistake. I knew he loved my best friend, and they had a strong physical chemistry. Still … Graham gave me the I've-seen-you-naked look like it was something to lord over me. Yes, he'd seen the goods. That didn't give him the right to judge them for the rest of our lives.

"Oh my god! There he is," Lila whispered when the elevator doors opened to the lobby just as Ronin strutted with jaw-dropping swagger toward the steakhouse.

"*Oh my god?* Clearly, I didn't fuck you hard enough earlier," Graham grumbled.

I grinned, biting my tongue. Fine. Graham had seen my goods, but his fiancée drooled over the goods of *my* date. That magically made up for the visions in Graham's head that I would never be able to erase.

"Whoa …" Ronin stopped on a second glance in our

direction. His head jerked back as an appreciative smile slid up his chiseled face. I felt a twinge of disappointment that he unknowingly submitted to Graham's starchy dress code for the night by wearing a blue suit. However, his red tie damn near matched my dress and that thrilled me.

Don't get me wrong; he was hot as fuck, just like the look he gave me as we stepped off the elevator.

"Evelyn…" his gaze swept along my entire body, more than once "…you look incredible." He held out his hand to take mine.

Okay … this is happening.

Seven hours earlier, I had met this stranger who looked like he had just stepped off an international modeling stage, and in a blink of time, he wore a suit and a grin that dirtied my thoughts.

Graham offered Lila his arm like she was lucky to be on it, also, so he could use his hands for texting. "Good to see you again." My starchy Graham Cracker nodded at Ronin just before leading us to the restaurant. He earned more points for treating my date with a lot more respect than he gave me most days.

I received points because Lila was so enamored with my date that she couldn't even articulate a greeting beyond a dreamy smile and some drool.

Okay, not really, but I knew that look. It was usually the one she gave Graham. Lila glanced over her shoulder at us, gaze flicking to our clasped hands. It made my cheeks burn. Lila grinned at me. That made them burn even more. She knew me too well, so of course she knew I was seconds away from sweating through that dress, even

25

with the chill in the hotel lobby.

The night turned into a dream. The four of us just ... clicked. Come to find out, Ronin *was* a part-time model for five years in France. He even modeled a men's clothing line designed by Graham's aunt, who probably knew Ronin's mom.

Perfection stole the night.

Expensive wine.

Course after course of the best food.

Laughter.

Engaging conversation.

It was quite possibly the most fun I'd ever had.

As people packed into the restaurant, it became harder to hear, even though we were contributing to the noise as much if not more than anyone else. Ronin occasionally leaned toward me to hear my words. When he did, he rested his hand on my leg ... the part of my leg exposed from the slit in my dress. Maybe it was the wine, but every time that hand rested on my leg, it felt a fraction of an inch higher with a tighter grip.

"I need the ladies' room." Lila set her napkin on the table.

"Me too." I scooted back in my chair.

Ronin stood and Graham quickly followed suit.

Holy. Shit.

Lila and I shared a quick look.

Our dates *stood* for women. Talk about good upbringing ...

Honestly, I'm not sure Graham would have stood had Ronin not initiated it.

I smiled up at Ronin through my wine-glossed eyes, feeling a bit wobbly on my heavy legs.

"Got it?" Amusement lit up his face as he steadied me with his hand on my lower back. That sexy grin disintegrated my already thin and delicate panties.

"Mm-hmm." My teeth trapped my lower lip to hold in my giggle. I might have been a little tipsy. A lot horny. And hot. Hours of his hand making a return trip to my leg raised my body temperature to roughly the sun's surface.

"I've got her." Lila hooked her arm around mine. She wasn't in any better shape, but we hoped that two half-drunk women could make it to the ladies' room with the grace of one sober woman.

"Oh my gosh ... EVIE!" Lila grabbed my shoulders as soon as we slipped into the ladies' lounge just outside of the room with the sinks and toilets. "He's perfect! I like him. Graham likes him. He's *perfect!* And that accent. I got so pissed that Graham kept interrupting. I could listen to Ronin read a dictionary. And don't you dare tell Graham I said that. You have to marry Ronin. I mean ... not until after my wedding, of course. But he's the one!"

She knew everything—almost. I spilled the details on our shopping excursion. His ethnicity, his famous father, his clothing-designer mother, and the fact that he had a flight the next morning to Denver.

"I know. I know ..." I plopped into a velvet chair and grabbed the skirt of my dress, fanning it to release some heat, but everywhere his hand touched remained ablaze.

"You're going to make the most beautiful babies with

beautiful Asian skin and hair, dark eyes, and they'll speak French like their grandpa." Lila grinned, hitching her ass to the arm of my chair.

"They'll have half of my genes too."

She sighed. "Maybe they'll be recessive genes."

"You're awful."

She laughed, hugging me. "Kidding. You're the most beautiful … special really … beautiful person I know."

"Wow! You're more drunk than I am."

"Probably." She forced herself to stand again, teetering on her high heels for a few seconds before zigzagging toward the toilets.

We finished the night with dessert and more wine. Before Lila attempted to dry hump Graham's leg, he excused them from the table, taking care of the bill with a simple nod to the waiter.

"Do you golf, Ronin?" Graham asked, sliding his arm around Lila's waist to steady her.

"Sometimes." Ronin finished his glass of water.

"Call me when you get settled. We'll play."

Ronin raised his empty glass before setting it down. "I'd like that."

Okay … when did they exchange numbers? What went on while we were in the ladies' room?

"Be good, Evie." Graham winked at me, pulling drunk Lila away from the table.

What's that supposed to mean?

"Sounds tragically boring," Ronin said.

I returned my attention to him and the grin on his face after they disappeared around the corner. "What does?"

"*Good* Evie." He leaned back, looking entirely too cool. Too put together. Too damn sexy.

I grabbed my water and gulped it down. It's not that I had any intention of having sex with Ronin that night (outside of my head, of course). The last time I had too much to drink and hopped into bed with someone, it was Graham. Look how that turned out. A cautionary tale.

I flooded my system with as much water as possible to cleanse my thoughts.

"I have an early flight tomorrow morning. Can I escort you to your room?"

"Escort? Sounds like navigating to my room could be dangerous on my own. Is that what you're implying?" I chuckled, pulling my phone from my purse to check the time. It was one-thirty in the morning. I cringed, making a quick inspection of the abandoned restaurant. The wait staff wouldn't kick Graham Porter's friends out no matter the time.

"Your friends left you in my care. I feel responsible."

I peeled my ass from the chair, already feeling more sure on my feet than Lila. "But *are* you responsible?" As Ronin loosened his tie like it was ridiculous to have one on after midnight, I snagged my clutch from the table.

"Responsible? Yes. Well-behaved? Sometimes." He grasped my hand like he owned it.

Again, I felt it in places that a responsible person should not have felt it. "So a sometimes-well-behaved man is escorting me to my room?" I followed him to the elevators, handing him my room card to gain access to my floor.

He didn't let go of my hand. Not in the elevator. Not down the short hallway to my room. Not when we stopped at my door.

"Tell me about this?" He twisted my left arm, exposing my carbon atom tattoo.

"It's carbon."

Ronin chuckled. "Okay. What's the significance?"

My eyes narrowed. "What's the significance? Um … only the main element in organic compounds; therefore it's essential to life on Earth. So … pretty significant." That came out on way too much instinct and possibly way too many hours in a lab. Closing my eyes, I shook my head. Rolling my lips between my teeth, I stifled a laugh.

"What?" he asked on a slight laugh of his own.

"Wow! I just … went there. Couldn't play it cool for two seconds before defending carbon's role in the world like the science geek I was when I picked out the stupid thing and the science geek I clearly still am."

"*Science isn't sexy*" was an original Lila Mason quote and a hard concept for me to remember, not that she had any room to speak. Before she decided on the winged tramp stamp, she seriously considered a long math equation straight down her spine. At the time, she had an insane crush on her multivariable calculus professor.

"Your geek side is adorable."

My cheeks bloomed with heat. "Thanks. Obviously, it's effortless too."

Ronin grinned. "Please thank Graham and Lila again

for dinner. I've enjoyed every second of this evening."

I returned a slow nod. He *still* held my hand in his left hand and my keycard in his right hand. I wasn't drunk, barely even tipsy by that point. The wine held no blame for my desire to invite him into my room. Had I been home, I would've invited him into my house. But houses had kitchens and living rooms. Okay, my suite had both of those things too, but the large king bed monopolized the space, demanding attention. I wasn't sure I could invite Ronin into my room without doing something impulsive.

Courting and no-sex-until-the-third-date rules didn't apply to women in their thirties. That made it so tempting to give in to my impulsivity. By thirty, my parents' generation gave up on my generation going down a straight path: school, love, marriage, children. Thirty and single was the new fifty and widowed. "Poor thing ... she'll be lucky if anyone takes her."

Sex on the first date in your thirties symbolized a goddamn miracle like the lottery, not a cardinal sin with a ticket to Hell. "Yay! Someone might take her!" Their opinions were not up-to-date. The average age for my generation to get married and start a family breached thirty's door. However, my parents had two kids in school by that point in their lives, so they compared me to the past, not the present.

Still ... I smiled and took the traditional route with Ronin that night. "I had a nice time too. I hope you're not regretting this in the morning when you're dragging ass to the airport."

He winked. "I'll sleep on the plane."

"You should stop by my shop when you get to Aspen. Well, wait a week until I'm there. But definitely stop by. No need to buy anything. Just …" Enough with the rambling, I chastised myself.

"What's the name of your shop?"

"Clean Art."

He grinned. "Clean Art. Nice name. I'll stop by as soon as I get there and grab a few things to try. When you return, I'll give you my unbiased opinion of them."

No. He couldn't stop by until I was there. Soapy Sophie, my manager and sole employee, would try to steal him.

He was mine. I found him.

"Really, you should wait for me. I'll help you pick out the right products for your skin type."

"What's my skin type?"

Perfect. It was perfect.

"I don't want to say. It's terrible lighting. I'll get a closer look when I return home."

He released my hand, bent forward, and pulled his hair away from his forehead, hovering several inches from my face. "Oily? Dry? Combination?"

I returned a nervous smile, wagging my head. "It's … nice. I'll find something that will keep it nice."

His grin swelled, showing a lot of white teeth while keeping his face so close to mine I felt like it would be a waste of bending-over effort to not go ahead and kiss. I mean … he was *right* there, an evil tempter.

"Nice, huh?" he whispered.

THE LIFE THAT MATTERED

As he started to stand straight again, I grabbed his face, pressing my palms to his cheeks. "But your lips might be a bit dry." *Holy crap!* I sounded breathy.

His gaze fell to my mouth. "Is that so?"

My lips rubbed together as if a wave of self-consciousness hit them. "Happens when you're in the elements so much." My thumb brushed his bottom lip. It was barely dry. And it was probably the pad of my dry thumb, not his lip.

As my bravery dissolved, loosening my grip, he grabbed my wrist, holding my hand by his mouth. His tongue flicked out, teasing his bottom lip *and* my thumb. When he grazed it with his teeth, my lips parted, releasing an even heavier audible breath.

A prickly sensation spread along my skin while heat gathered low in my belly, up my chest, and along my cheeks.

"Sweet dreams, Evelyn." He twisted my wrist, pressing the softest imaginable kiss to the inside of it.

I swallowed, choking on my own erratic and out of control pulse. "I …" Just great. A huskiness infiltrated my words. His effect on me couldn't have been more obvious. I cleared my throat, grappling with my composure. "I should get your phone number, so you know when I'm home. For … soap." The second I said the word soap, I bit my lips to hide my grin and closed my eyes to run from my embarrassment.

Yes. Soap. Ronin was moving. Taking a new job. Settling into a new home. Yet, surely the distress over finding the right soap in Colorado kept him up at night.

33

Ronin straightened his back, wetting his lips while releasing my hand to my side. "Clean Art. Don't worry … I'll find you."

Oh god.

He wouldn't find me. He didn't give me his number because he didn't want me to call him. Right? I mean, why not just give me the damn phone number?

"I could give you *my* phone number?" I shrugged. You know … so I could obsess over why he wasn't calling me. That was always a good time.

"True. Or I could just see you soon." He opened my door with my keycard, handed it to me, and winked before sauntering toward the elevator.

My mouth fell open. No numbers were exchanged. That wasn't good. Not good at all.

Goodbye, tall, sexy, runway model who can ski and nearly make me orgasm just by biting the pad of my thumb.

I would never see him again, unless just by chance. Then it would be awkward. That, "Hey, didn't we share buns and bubble tea?" followed by fading smiles and an uncomfortable silence.

Au revoir. No … I think that was more of an "until we see each other again," which was unlikely. Maybe "adieu." If I recalled correctly (after three years of French), it was the goodbye you gave someone for the last time. "Until God." Yes, I thought it was more final.

Adieu, Ronin Alexander.

Just before I shut my door, Graham opened the door to their suite across the hallway. He'd changed from his suit to navy silk pajamas with white piping. "Thought I heard you out here."

I grinned, eyeing his getup. "I'm sure those pajamas cost around a grand, but they make you look like an old man. Where's Lila? Finishing the job on her own?" I smirked.

Graham narrowed his eyes, closing his door and crossing into my territory, forcing me to retreat and let him inside my room. I frowned. It was the early hours of the morning. My dream guy just left me. I wasn't in the mood to have a pajama party with Graham.

"I can't sleep." He gave me a matter-of-fact look.

"I can. I'm actually really good at it."

He brushed past me, flipping on the light by the king-sized bed and plunking onto it with his back against the headboard. On an exasperated sigh, I closed the door, grabbed my nightshirt, and slipped into the bathroom, sliding the door shut.

"Why did you ditch me after we slept together?"

I paused while removing my dress, narrowing my eyes at the floor, questioning if I heard him correctly. My brain had already turned off the lights. There was no way I'd answer him. I continued to get ready for bed.

"Did you have to convince Lila to be with me? To give me a chance? I wanted to do it on my own, you know? That was the point."

I rolled my eyes as I brushed my teeth. Graham's nightcap must have been laced with an overdose of insecurity. He didn't sound like a thirty-six-year-old man planning on making a run for governor. Everyone needed a dumping ground for their insecurities. I was Lila's. She was mine. But I was also Graham's. It wasn't fair that I got dumped on twice.

After washing my face, I eased open the door and yawned, hoping he'd get the hint that I wasn't in the mood for that conversation. Slipping under the covers, I snuggled onto my side with my back to him.

Hint. Hint.

He scooted down, inching closer to me so his head rested on my pillow just behind mine. "My father said you weren't good enough for me. A nice girl, but not focused."

I flipped around facing him, eyes squinted. "I don't like this bedtime story. Got a different one?"

Graham wasn't like a brother or a cousin to me because we had, in fact, had sex. We were overly acquainted friends, a different dynamic than my friendship with Lila. I'd known her longer. I would have jumped in front of a bus to save her life.

Graham? Well, I'm not sure I would have leapt in front of a bus, but I might have warned him with a really loud scream, and I would have been the first to call for an ambulance. I definitely would have donated blood to save his life, and maybe even a kidney like my sister donated to my father because she was the best match.

"I used you to make Lila jealous. I'm sorry. I think I even used you to piss off my father."

"Glad I could assist you in pissing off your father. But newsflash, dickhead, sleeping with a woman's best friend is not the way to make her jealous. Lila greeted me at the door with a can of disinfectant after I left your apartment that night. She knew you were a walking STD. And honestly, I was embarrassed that I'd stooped so low. Let myself get that drunk."

"Wow, Evie ... don't sugarcoat it."

"Coming from the guy who is ninety percent amazing to me. Really ... you're there for me when Lila's busy. You've advocated for my family, for my dad. I honestly consider you my best guy friend. But that other ten percent of the time you are a cruel asshole."

He flinched, blinking several times.

"I get it, Graham. That's why we're friends. I think I get you better than anyone, including Lila. The good in you gets suffocated by the expectations your family places on you. I'm not an idiot. Your dad still goes on and on about Lila. She has an engineering degree. I make soap. Her parents died in a car accident—that's tragic. My parents struggle to make ends meet because my dad was out of a job for so long with his health issues. And you paid for his treatment. That makes my parents poor and pathetic in your father's eyes."

"I like Ronin," he said in a monotone voice.

I coughed a laugh. "Okay then ... now we're talking about Ronin?"

"I like him. You could use someone like him in your life."

"Fine, Graham ... I'll bite. Define *someone like him*."

He reached up, pinching a few strands of my hair between his fingers, nose scrunched.

I batted his hand away.

He smirked.

Asshole.

"Well, once Lila and I get married, she's going to have a different life. Especially after I become governor."

"*If* you become governor."

Graham ignored my jab. We'd become experts at ignoring each other's jabs.

"She's going to take on a new role."

"She has a job."

He shrugged. "She'll have a different job: being the governor's wife. New duties. New friends."

"Wait ..." I laughed to keep from kneeing him in the balls for what I believed he was insinuating. "If you're suggesting Lila and I will no longer be friends if you become governor, then you're sorely mistaken. Also, there's no way in hell she's quitting a job she loves just to plan fancy dinners and attend fundraisers on your arm. No way."

"I'm not saying you won't be friends. I'm just saying she'll be much busier. Your weekly lunches might be more like monthly lunches. Your endless phone chats and incessant texting will have to scale down to quick chats on a need-to basis. Her jaunts to Aspen just to make soap with you on the weekends will have to stop. I'm saying you won't have unrestricted access to her like you have now. *Therefore ...* back to my original statement. I think Ronin is good for you. I think he could fill the void she's going to leave once we get married."

I sprang to sitting, spine straight, jaw clenched.

"Stop." Graham sat up, grabbing my arms. "You have such a knee-jerk reaction. Just ... stop. We've been friends for over a decade. You're the first to put me in my place when you think I'm fucking up my life. I'm the first person to come to your rescue when your life begins to fall apart. Like with your dad. I don't know exactly what it is between us. I don't know how I can be in love with Lila but at the same time feel so connected to you. It just is … we just … are."

Anger muzzled my words. That hurt. Graham knew how to hurt me because he knew I needed him. Or so I thought. I didn't know anymore. Something told me *Governor Porter* would no longer drive to Aspen to watch football with his buddy, Evie, while Lila read a book. He had Lila, so he no longer needed me to sing his praises. My dad had fully recovered, hopefully ending my days of begging Graham for help.

"Are you breaking up with me, Graham? Is that why you're so smitten with Ronin? You've found my replacement for you?"

"You know, Evie, if you don't stop thinking the worst of me, I'll find it hard to pardon you if you get into trouble."

"You're the world's biggest dick, Graham Cracker. Even without actually having a big dick."

"Low blow—"

Three knocks rapped at the door.

"Can't imagine who that might be." Graham smirked, climbing out of bed and opening the door.

"Are you two having sex again … without me?" Lila yawned.

"Someone didn't take her sleeping pills." Graham

39

tsked.

I shook my head. "Please tell me you're not drugging my friend."

"Not drugs, Evie. You know I would never do that." Lila shuffled into the room. "Herbs. Valerian. I've had trouble sleeping while trying to work full-time and planning a wedding." She crawled into the bed and burrowed under the covers next to me. "I didn't take one tonight because I thought the wine should do it. But then I woke up, and Graham was gone. I knew he'd be here with you."

"Well, I don't want him. You can take him."

She laughed. "I'm done with him for tonight too."

Graham collapsed onto the bed, pressing his chest to Lila's back so we were three spoons neatly nestled in my bed. "I'm feeling like a threesome tonight. Who's in?" His husky voice crushed my hopes of it being a joke.

With wide eyes, I glanced over my shoulder. Graham's hand confirmed his intent as it snaked between me and Lila, diving between her legs, rubbing her over her silk pajama bottoms.

"Graham, stop..." she breathed his name with little conviction.

My head jerked away, eyes still unblinking.

"Touch Evelyn like I'm touching you, baby."

My whole body stiffened. "No, *baby*, do not touch me like he's touching you."

Lila ran her hand down my arm which made Graham moan. It did something to me too, but I wasn't sure what.

"Evie, you *were* my first kiss," she whispered in my

ear.

My eyes nearly popped out of their sockets.

No threesomes.

No way.

We weren't those kind of friends, even if Lila and I practiced kissing on each other before we ever kissed a guy. It was science … an experiment of sorts, not preparation for a threesome.

The bed moved slightly as Graham rocked his pelvis against the back of Lila. Her breath hitched, and her hand slid to my hip, fingers digging into my flesh. She was intoxicated. The Lila I knew would not engage in such behavior.

I was … well, I was nervous and panicked, but also curious. While I didn't feel tipsy anymore, the residual alcohol in my blood had to be the reason I remained in that spot, perfectly still, instead of flying out of the bed—shocked and offended.

Lila inched her hand from my hip to my breast.

"Fuck yes …" Graham's throaty enthusiasm did nothing for me.

"Do you like that, Evie?" Lila pressed her lips next to my ear as her thumb brushed my nipple over my nightshirt.

Graham kept one hand between her legs, and god only knows where he had his other hand, but no doubt giving her pleasure. *His* pleasure seemed to come from her exploring my breast.

"Do *you*?" I muttered, not feeling it like I felt the pull in the hallway with Ronin. Not feeling it like she felt

Graham's touch.

"I ..." her warm breath washed over the side of my face, tiny little pants in response to Graham getting her off. At least, I hoped it was Graham and not me.

Was that what rich people did? Alcohol, sleeping pills, and threesomes?

I found it a little perverted, kind of gross, but still ... oddly mesmerizing like I wasn't really the one on the bed with them. My body no longer belonged to me. These three close friends entertained an odd curiosity, but I wasn't part of it. No. I remained a bystander who knew it was wrong to watch but couldn't seem to turn away.

They shifted behind me, and I closed my eyes. After all, it wasn't real. Lila guided me from my side to my back, greeting me with a glassy-eyed gaze when my eyelids fluttered open. She slid the front of my nightshirt up my body, exposing my breasts. It made every tiny hair on my body stand erect. Her long blond hair tickled my skin as she knelt beside me, lowering her head to my chest. Graham remained on his side with his head propped up on his right arm while his left hand slid into the front of his expensive lounge pants.

Oh god ...

Lila drew my nipple into her mouth, teasing it with her tongue. It wasn't bad. I'm not sure it was good either. Just different. Had it been anyone else but Lila, I would have been out of there, halfway back to Aspen already. My best friend's fascination with my breasts kept me idle, studying her, not really giving a shit about Graham getting off from the show.

Was it her altered state? Did she think of me in a sexual way in her sober state? Did it make her a lesbian or bisexual? Did it make *me* one for letting it happen?

In a sudden change of events, she teased my nipple with her tongue ring and ... well ... it sort of turned me on, but I had no impulse to reciprocate. No desire to touch, see, or taste any part of her body.

"This is insane," she slurred her words as her mouth brushed across my chest to my other breast. "Why is this so hot?" she murmured just before laving my breast with her warm, wet tongue.

I glanced over at Graham again. His jaw was slack, hand going to town, pumping his cock.

It wasn't hot. It was weird and wrong.

Wrong.

Wrong.

So. Very. Wrong.

Lila would know it in the morning.

At least that's what the my-parents-raised-me-right part of my brain said while pleading its case. The rest of my body, specifically my breasts, had a different case to plead. I couldn't take anything away from my friend; she knew what she was doing, and she did it well.

"Slide your fingers inside her," Graham's drunken eyes blinked heavily as he ordered Lila to do something I ... I just couldn't.

Nope.

Ten more piercings and a dozen additional tattoos—sign me up. That was my kind of wild side and impulsivity.

Lila's mouth feathered up my neck as her hand slinked down my abs. Her lips brushed mine. I stiffened even more, holding my breath.

Some lines weren't meant to be crossed. I couldn't shake the feeling that Lila's fingers inside of me would be *really* hard to mentally shake off as easily as her mouth on mine or her tongue teasing my nipples.

Or was it too late?

I wasn't familiar with all the acts that two people (no matter their sexual preference) considered sex. For two women, was breast and nipple play considered sex?

Kissing?

Genital rubbing?

Masturbation?

Seriously ... I had *no* clue because I never had any reason to study that topic and consider the possibilities. Until ... I found myself on a bed in a Vancouver suite with Lila's tongue doing things to my nipples—things that awakened possibilities. Would letting it go further make me feel more free, liberated?

I decided a trip to Mardi Gras to show off my tatas for some beads might be a better choice to liberate myself without risking my closest friendship. I mean ... what if Lila would have found me to be a better lover than Graham? What would that have meant for their impending marriage?

And Ronin ... what about him—all six and a half feet of my sexy new acquaintance?

Just like that ... I made my decision. I had to escape before my BFF gave me an orgasm ... which she was on her way to doing.

Really. Well done, Lila.

I rolled out of bed like a five-alarm fire and shoved down my nightshirt, turning toward the bed to give my two insane friends a very serious speech on ethics and the importance of not risking our friendship for sexual pleasure.

Too late.

Graham had his tongue down Lila's throat as they ripped off each other's clothes.

I chuckled, running my hands through my hair. "I'll give you two a few minutes. I mean … it's *my* bed. But whatever."

They ignored me, so I shuffled my feet to the door—the unneeded third wheel rolling into the ditch. After shutting the door, my back thumped against it, and I melted to the floor, hugging my knees to my chest.

"Harder, Graham!"

Biting my lips together, I cringed. How did I become their sex toy for the night? Their foreplay. And what would be said in the morning?

Over the next five or so minutes, I listened to my friends have sex—loud sex. For two full seconds—only two—I wondered if I'd made a mistake. I liked taking chances and rebelling in small ways. I liked giving the middle finger to rules when they didn't suit me. Why did I pass up an opportunity to be spontaneous … a little taboo with my friends?

Ronin Alexander. That's why.

On the miraculous chance that I would see him again

and we would get married and have beautiful babies, I didn't want a threesome tainting the memories of the day we met. I realized the moment that thought tiptoed through my mind, I was completely dismissing all other reasons like ... friendship and the fact that Lila and Graham were engaged.

As the door behind me opened, I sprang to my feet.

Graham buttoned his top, wearing a truly awful grin like the wolf that just ate every sheep in the pasture. "She's all yours again." He winked, brushing past me to the door of his suite.

My evil gaze followed him. If only I could have burned him to the ground with it, I would have. He orchestrated all of that. Manipulated her. Manipulated *me* through her. At first, I thought he would be a terrible governor, but his sexual indiscretions seemed in line with the indulgent, corrupt life of a politician.

I eased the door shut behind me and tiptoed toward the bed, hoping to find Lila passed out so I wouldn't have to deal with *things* until morning.

No such luck.

She sat up in the middle of the bed and pulled her pajama top on. Then she shimmied back into her panties and bottoms.

"Are you mad?" she mumbled with her back to me, hair a fucked-up mess. Graham did a number on her. Her voice held a lot more sobriety to it than it had ten minutes earlier.

"No. Yes. I don't know." I slid into bed, pulled the covers up to my neck, and stared at the ceiling.

"Then why did you let it happen?" she whispered.

Good question.

"I don't know. It felt forbidden."

She turned her head toward me, but I kept looking at the ceiling. "Are you tempted by the forbidden?"

"Isn't everyone to some degree?"

"I'm not a lesbian."

I laughed. "Good to know."

"It was more for Graham. He's been pressuring me for quite some time to try something new."

"Then get a different hairstyle, but don't invite other people into your bed. That's asking for trouble."

"Then why didn't you stop it sooner?"

Sitting up, I angled my body toward Lila, barely able to see her in the dark. I flipped on the light by the bed. We flinched at the brightness. "Listen, had it been anyone else, that could have gone terribly wrong for you, Lila. Seriously, how far were you willing to go? Were you going to let him put his mouth on my breasts? Were you going to let him have sex with me? Is that what does it for you? The man you love taking pleasure in another woman? It's all fun and games under the heavy influence of alcohol and whatever sleep shit you're taking." I internally cringed, remembering that she didn't take anything that night. We were all quite sober. "But..." I continued "...things get pretty real when a threesome turns into you watching Graham fuck another woman. Wouldn't you agree?"

My anger pointed at myself as much as her. But I wasn't engaged. I didn't have as much to lose as Lila did.

As I started to lecture her, more concern and regret built in my conscience. We were stupid. Really stupid.

Tears filled her eyes as she looked away and blotted the corners before a single one could creep out. "It's funny ..." She shook her head on a painful laugh. "I wanted nothing to do with him, but then you begged me to give him a chance. And the big jerk made me fall so hard for him that I hate to think how it would break me if he decided he didn't want me."

I reached for her hand, sandwiching it between mine. "Gauge your love for him by his love for you."

"That sounds selfish. Like I love myself more."

A smile stole my mouth, and I think she got my point before I said it, but I said it anyway. "Love yourself more."

After a few silent moments, Lila returned a sad smile. "Will you ever forgive me for molesting you?"

Barking out a laugh, I shut off the lights. We scooted under the covers, facing each other. "Your tongue ring though ..." I sighed.

"You liked it?"

I grinned, but she couldn't see me. "Goodnight, Lila."

I fell asleep next to my best friend like we'd done a million times over our twenty-nine-year friendship. If I was honest, the idea of something going wrong between Lila and Graham scared me to death. I would choose her; everyone knew that. However, Graham helped save my dad. He saved my family. Losing him would have felt like its own death.

CHAPTER THREE

Two weeks later ...

I LEFT MY worries over Graham and Lila in Canada—
even the weird threesome thing. Really, Lila was a
grown woman. If he became the next governor and she
willingly quit her job to support him, that was her choice.
If she chose to invite other people into their bed, again ...
her choice. I just knew it would never be me again.

Besides, they didn't invite me into their bed; they
ganged up on me in my own bed.

It didn't change my feelings for Lila. She was and
would always be my best friend, not my twin. We chose
different career paths. We had different tastes in culture,
sports, future aspirations ... and sexual *adventurousness.*

Our friendship spanned too many years of personal
struggles and laughter to let our differences be anything
more than the beauty of our own individuality.

In the back room (my lab) of my bath shop, I un-
packed a shipment of herbs while Sophie watched the
desk. September marked the beginning of holiday
preparation with limited edition scents and gift boxes.
And decorations. Yes ... it was time to start marketing for

Christmas. I loved Christmas in Aspen. It was my favorite time of the year.

The bell on the door chimed, signaling customers that we needed. Sophie chirped her bubbly spiel about the shop. I couldn't make out her words, but I'd heard them before. People loved her gleeful routine and the way so much joy flowed from the pint-sized redhead.

"Psst! My future husband is here to see you. Probably wants to get your blessing. Should I send him back so you can do that?"

I glanced over my shoulder, lifting my eyebrows.

Sophie fanned herself while mouthing, "Oh my god!" Her eyes rolled back in her head for a brief second.

A seizure?

"I'm not sure how to respond. I didn't know you had a boyfriend since the Ben incident." I used the code words for he cheated on her. We didn't talk about it. And we never said the C word.

"I'll just send him back. Then you can give me all the details later."

"Um … o—kay." It was rare for Sophie to come to work high, but that day she might have been on some-thing.

"Hey!" Ronin peeked his head around the corner.

My body shot to attention, swiping my hands along my head to tame my messy hair. It was my lab day which meant recycled hair, threadbare yoga pants, and an oversized long-sleeved T-shirt.

No makeup.

No sexy dress.

Ronin witnessed the opposite of the woman he had dinner with in Vancouver.

"Bonjour, Monsieur Alexander."

The grin on his face swelled with my greeting.

I'd been home a week. A week of jumping every time the door chimed, constantly straining my neck to look out front, hoping for my handsome ski patroller. That was the first day I didn't jump when the bell chimed because I'd given up on him, resigned that my gut feeling I would never see him again was in fact true.

It felt fantastic to be wrong, even if I looked rather hellish at the moment.

"I tried to play it cool and not show up on the doorstep to your shop the same day you arrived home from Vancouver." He slid his hands into the front pockets of his black jeans—silver jacket, black scarf, and a white beanie atop his head of thick jet-black hair.

Wait ... what?

He was what? Worried about looking too anxious? Too desperate?

Ronin inspected the shelves filled with oils and herbs. "However, I start my new job soon, so I figured my time to play it cool is limited. Once I start working long hours, I might be all cooled out. So I need to impress the hell out of you while I can."

The smile on my face took on a life of its own.

He continued, "I thought maybe we'd check out all of the great restaurants in town over the next few weeks. Shut down a few bars. Compare hot cocoa with marshmallows versus hot cocoa with whipped cream sipped around a fire. I'm sure you have some favorite trails we should hike before the first snow. And of course, I'll need to learn how to make soap. Then …"

Finally … finally he looked at me after a full visual inventory of my lab while rattling off enough stuff to make my heart stop beating.

Ronin spent one day with me, and just like that … he knew from that one day that he wanted more days. More me.

"Then what?" I whispered as he stepped in front of me, looking as tall and delectable as I remembered.

"Then we can just be past that awkward phase where people feel the need to impress each other."

I laughed, holding out my arms, my baggy sleeves hanging low, a smattering of oil stains on my white tee. "Have you really seen anyone less impressive than me at the moment?"

Ronin grinned. It was so big and delightful. "It's good to see you, Evelyn," he whispered. It sounded so seductive, so refreshing, so reassuring that the feelings weren't one sided.

I shook my head, but it didn't shake the grin from my face. "It's good to be seen." I lifted my shoulders into my take-it-or-leave-it-but-this-is-me shrug. "Even like this."

"You're like the sun, Evelyn. No matter how you try to cover it up or hide it, it's always shining." He rocked back and forth on his heels, shoulders hugging his ears with his hands still tucked into his pockets.

I would marry this boy. I just knew it.

Boy.

Yes, Ronin had this boyish charm to him. When I fell in love with him—because I was certain it would only be a matter of time—I would always remember how falling in love at any age felt like taking your first steps. Sometimes it happened slowly, and other times it took off. And all you could do was go with the momentum and hope you didn't fall too hard.

"Marshmallows." I grinned.

He cocked his head a fraction.

"Marshmallows go in hot chocolate. Whipped cream goes on pumpkin pie. Everyone knows that."

Ronin handed me his best smile. *I think.* It was really good. I couldn't wait to see more. Then I'd know if he gave me his best one that day.

"What are you doing for dinner tonight?" He nudged the toe of his black boot against the toe of my pink oil-stained Ugg.

Butterflies. Erratic breaths. Tingling. Goose bumps.

Ronin gave me *all* the feelings. If he was just a test run, a stop along the way to the man of my dreams, then said man must not have been human. Something told me the bar was not simply high; it was officially unreachable.

"I'm thinking Thai, right across the street. I'll probably be there around five-thirty. What are you doing?"

He rubbed his lips together, staring at our boots. "Same."

I nudged the toe to his other boot the way he nudged my toe. "Do you want to share a table?"

He nodded several times, keeping his gaze pointed downward. "Probably."

Probably. He said that when I joked (but only sort of) about him marrying me. I liked his almost certain response. It set my hopes high but left just enough doubt to make my heart continue to search for something resembling a normal beat.

"Do you ski?" He glanced up.

My lips curled into a grin. "Possibly better than you."

Nope. That possibility was zero, so I'm not really sure it *was* a possibility. It didn't matter. I just wanted to see the look on his face. As he let those expressive eyebrows form into curious peaks, I basked in the slight shock of his expression. For five seconds, I let him believe it—that maybe I wasn't simply a brilliant chemist cleaning the world one bar of soap at a time, that maybe I was a badass chick on the slopes.

"Really?" He stretched out the word into three syllables.

I swatted at the pesky stray hair around my face that fell out of my ponytail. "No. Not really. I'm a terrible skier. It doesn't stop me from trying. Graham and Lila love to ski, so I snowplow and sometimes slide on my ass down the runs."

"You're joking." He chuckled.

"No. I was joking about being better than you. The sliding on my ass part is one hundred percent accurate. Graham has literally taken me down the slope on his back while Lila carried my skis. And don't assume this isn't an embarrassing revelation about myself. It is because I was born here. Maybe not to an Olympic skier, but I've been on skis my whole life. My dad says I ski like a car with square tires. Sure, it's doable, but never pretty. I'm not athletically gifted at all. Which is weird because I love sports. As in … I will watch any sport. That's why Graham and I are such good friends. Whereas Lila hates watching sports, but the woman can do anything. You should see her on skis or snowboarding. She's phenomenal. It's just not fair."

Ronin maintained an unreadable expression. Was it shock in his furrowed brow? Complete disbelief? Or something else?

Oh shit!

Was it a deal breaker? Why would a ski patroller want to date a woman who couldn't ski? I overshared. The butterflies dropped dead in the pit of my stomach; their little wings tried to work against the impossible gravity of my unfortunate confession.

"I made everything in this store. Well, everything except the packaging. I even make my own essential oils. And they're very pure—medicinal. I'm an excellent chemist."

Well, there he had it. My dating résumé. Who wouldn't want to date an excellent chemist? Surely, all tall, athletic, sexy men dreamed of women wearing goggles and white lab coats.

I bowed my head, covering my face with my hands while I whispered a laugh. "I'm not bragging. It's just … *soap.* Yes, saponification is my super power. Impressed?"

"Wildly," he replied on a soft chuckle.

I giggled, letting my hands drop from my face. Ronin greeted me with a lopsided grin.

Screw it. This is me. Take it or leave it.

"Are you going to recommend soap and lip balm, or should I ask your employee out front?"

"No. I'd prefer you not talk, smile, or look at Sophie again ... ever."

"No?" Ronin followed me out front.

I shook my head, breezing past the cash register straight to the men's display. "Definitely not. She's in heat."

"Who's in heat?" Sophie asked from behind the register as I pulled products from the shelves for Ronin.

"No one." I turned with a tight-lipped smile and set the products on the counter. "My entire men's line." I wrapped the soaps, moisturizers, lip balms, body sprays, and facial scrubs in paper, then arranged them in a bag.

"Two hundred, thirty-six, seventeen," Sophie gave Ronin a total for the products.

"No!" I cringed. "He gets the ski patrol discount."

"The what?" Sophie squinted.

I took half off the total. It was still close to a hundred and twenty dollars in body care products.

He handed me a credit card.

I couldn't do it.

"We're starting a free trial program."

"We are?" Sophie asked.

I twisted my body to face her, eyes wide, lips set into a line. "Sophie, could you go in the back and finish unpacking and inventorying the herbs?"

"Are you going to explain the free trial to me later?"

I relinquished a single nod, maintaining a stiff smile.

Sophie shot Ronin a flirty grin before disappearing into the back room.

"I don't need a discount or a free trial. But that's really cool of you to offer that to ski patrol. I'll spread the word. Half off is huge."

Yes. It really was. It was the discount you gave when you didn't want to stay in business.

"The free trial is new. Maybe don't mention it until I get the kinks worked out. But I'd love to see the ski patrol use my products. So ... yeah. Spread the word on the discount."

Just like that ... the ski patrol discount became a real thing at Clean Art. Great advertising. As long as all of my customers weren't ski patrol, I'd be fine.

"There's no discount, is there?" He chuckled, trying again to hand me his credit card.

"There is now." I laughed, hugging my arms to my chest. "No. There wasn't. But there should be because I know they work hard, putting their own lives in danger to keep everyone else safe. Therefore, there is now officially a fifty-percent off discount for ski patrol."

"They do ... we do." He waved his credit card in front of my face.

I grimaced. "I can't. I can't let you pay for anything."

"Why?" He tapped the card on the counter.

"Because you already admitted that you'd probably marry me. And family gets free products. Or you can think of it as a parting gift because I bet you have no interest in seeing me again since I've mentioned marriage twice in two weeks." I blew out a long breath, releasing the residual crazy from my body.

"Family gets free products? For life?"

My cheeks burned as I bit my lip to keep from smiling too big or laughing too much. Where was he going with this?

"My mom and sister-in-law would love this. And I have two nieces. But if your men's line is as good as I imagine it is ... my dad and brother will want in on the family discount too."

Twisting my lips, I returned a sharp nod, wide-eyed and dramatic.

"Perfect." He pocketed his credit card, grabbed the paper bag handles, and then ... he leaned over the counter and pressed his lips to my cheek. "See you at dinner, *dear*." Ronin strutted out of my store.

My hand inched to my cheek where he kissed me.

It was a game. I started it, so of course I got it. But "dear?" And the kiss? Ronin took the game to the next level.

"Oh my god ... who was that guy?" Sophie peeked her snoopy head out of the back room.

"He's ..." I couldn't even formulate complete thoughts or speak them with my jaw hanging on the ground and my cheek on fire. "Mine." I scrounged a tiny grin for Sophie. "He's mine."

She did her headshake and grumbled before returning to the task I gave her.

"Please be mine," I whispered to myself with the tips of my fingers still pressed to the exact spot his lips touched my cheek.

CHAPTER FOUR

Ronin

"AM I WAKING you?"

Dad laughed. "Almost."

"Where in the world are you?" I really had no idea. My parents traveled all the time.

"Cologne."

"Germany. Nice. Is the birthday girl still awake?"

"Barely. I'll let you chat with her."

"Thanks."

A few seconds later, my mom cleared her throat. "Ronin."

"Happy birthday, Mom."

"Thank you, sweetie."

"I tried you earlier today. I'm barely making it under the wire now."

"It's just another day. How's Aspen? Have you started work yet?"

"Just some orientation. I'll start full-time soon. But I'm settled into my condo. You should come visit soon."

"Oh! Is it snowing there already?"

"No."

She grunted. "Then you know your father will not be visiting quite yet."

"Fair enough. Did Julien call?"

"Yes. He called this morning."

"He video chatted with her," Dad yelled in the background. "Showed her the water lily mobile he made for her birthday."

"Aw … sounds nice," I replied with as much sincerity as I could muster. My brother was two years younger than me. He had a wife and two daughters and a booming career as a successful artist. Some of his recycled-material mobiles hung in art museums.

I epitomized the opposite of Julien. My first real companion, a rescue dog named Rex, died of cancer. Gianna, my girlfriend of two years, left me because she thought my life was too unsettled for her relationship goals. And … I was the worst gift-giver—ever.

In my defense, it's not that I lacked the desire to be a generous person. I *wanted* to be amazing in that department. I also wanted to travel by teleportation. If I'm completely honest, I had a better chance at that than becoming the Martha Stewart of great gifts.

"It's a lovely mobile, but this call from you means just as much to me," Mom reassured me.

The truth? She absolutely meant it. My mom watched me agonize over gifts for as long as I can remember being old enough to buy gifts for other people. I missed the days of messy glitter glue and scribbled stick figures on a card made from folding a piece of construction paper in half.

She loved that stuff, still had every card Julian and I made. Of course … Julien's cards were origami cranes or some exceptional shit like that.

"I won't keep you. I know it's late there. Just wanted to tell you I love you and wish you a happy birthday."

"I love you too, sweetheart. Have you made friends?"

I chuckled. She asked me this every time I moved to a new location. And by friends, she meant had I met a woman. My usual answer was no. Then she responded with a sigh because she wanted grandkids from me so badly. My generation's lackadaisical attitude toward starting a family drove her crazy. Julien, however, also set the bar too damn high by marrying the first girl he kissed and spreading his biological seeds as quickly as possible. He didn't get the memo about our generation.

"As a matter of fact …"

"Oh, Ronin! Tell me all about her—or him. You know we don't care."

"Thanks. It really is kind of you to respect my sexual preference. However, *she's* a woman. I met her in Vancouver, but she lives here in Aspen. We had breakfast and dinner the day we met, and we're having dinner tonight. Happy birthday."

She laughed. "That's really why you called. You knew the best birthday present you could give me is this."

I silently commended her for not giving unnecessary emphasis on the word *you*.

Julien made a work of art. I met a girl.

The honorable mention son.

Don't get me wrong. Julien was amazing. I knew the

mobile had to be great. Evelyn, however, was stunning beyond words. So ... I won that round.

"Of course, I knew my gift would please you. Also, she's agreed to marry me. We haven't sorted the details."

Silence.

"Um ... wow! Okay ..."

I chuckled. "What? Isn't this what you've wanted for years?"

"Well, yes. But I just thought. I mean, you've known her how long?"

"Technically two weeks. But we've been together about eight to nine hours total." I rubbed my mouth to hide my smirk that she couldn't see anyway.

"And you proposed?" Her voice shot up an octave.

"Not exactly. She suggested it, and I didn't think it was a terrible idea."

"Wh-what exactly does that mean?"

"It means I'm joking just to get a reaction out of you."

"Oh, Ronin! You don't even have a date tonight, do you?"

I laughed. "I do. That part is true. Her name is Evelyn. She's a chemist who makes body products. She owns a store here in Aspen called Clean Art. You'd like her."

"Do *you* like her?"

"Well, I'm having dinner with her, so yes. It's safe to say I like her. Probably more than makes sense given our nine-hour acquaintance."

"She's special. I can tell. I can tell from the tone of your voice."

I ran my fingers through my hair and flipped on the shower since I took a hike after visiting Evelyn. "Yes. I think she's special." The words sounded so foreign to me. Did they really come out of my mouth? I hadn't known her long enough for my feelings to make sense, but some things didn't make sense. That didn't make them less true. Less real.

"Trust that. I know it's hard for you to trust your feelings since …" She trailed off.

Since my accident. Sometimes I felt things that weren't mine to feel.

"One day at a time. Love you, Mom."

EVELYN BREEZED INTO the restaurant ten minutes late, peeling her unruly blond hair from her face, vibrant blue eyes scanning the tables. I didn't draw her attention to me yet because I wanted a moment to just watch her—just one moment to sort out some *things* in my head.

I admired the beautiful mess, dropping her keys on the floor, fighting to slide off her pink puffy ski jacket while it simultaneously pulled on her black sweater that hung off one shoulder. When she spied me, I smiled, and she mirrored my expression.

Right there. That was one *thing*.

Her smile, an effortless light that couldn't be dimmed. It grew as we made eye contact, and it felt like she acknowledged something unspoken between us. I had no idea what it was, and maybe she didn't either. It was just a feeling.

A good feeling. I took all the good feelings I could get. Lord knows I'd had several lifetimes of the alternative.

"Hey! Mind if I sit with you?"

That was another *thing*. Her playful and flirty personality drew me into her world without even trying. I wanted to roll around in her positivity like a child in a pile of crisp leaves.

"I insist. Besides … saving you a seat seems to be my thing. Even before we met." I took her bag from her while she finished removing her jacket.

"You're such a gentleman. How un-American of you." Her lips twisted into a devilish grin.

"Hey, Ronin!"

I turned to the familiar voice. "Noah, hi!"

My boss held out his hand, and I shook it. "This is my wife, Tami. Tami, this is Ronin. He's the reason I won't have to work sixty hours a week." Noah winked at me.

Tami shook my hand. "Then it's definitely a pleasure to meet you."

"You too, Tami. This is Evelyn."

"Wife? Girlfriend? None of our damn business?" Noah shot Evelyn a smile.

"All good questions." She shoved out her hand to greet them while her gaze flitted to meet mine.

"Indeed." I returned a conspiratorial grin.

Okay, Universe, Mother dearest, Cupid, and gods of romance … I get it.

"It's packed tonight. Friday craziness and it's not even snowing yet. Tami, let's grab a drink while we wait for a table."

"You should join us," Evelyn said without a second of hesitation.

Noah and Tami shifted their attention to me, a bit of unease etched onto their faces.

I shrugged. "Absolutely."

Instead of sitting in the booth across from Evelyn, I sat next to her—a huge upside to eating dinner with friends. With every passing minute, my feelings about her solidified. The *things* multiplied. She was definitely special. As the evening progressed, I discovered Evelyn could get along with anyone. A master conversation starter. She spoke and listened with such truth. It was impossible to not feel her genuine interest in … people. Yes. Evelyn Taylor was just a great person.

Also, as dinner progressed, we navigated closer. I wasn't sure it was intentional or just natural—magnetic. By the time I paid the check, my hand rested on her leg, and her hand covered mine with our fingers laced together. Sadly, we were forced to let go when it was time to leave.

"What a great evening." Tami smiled as everyone stood.

She was right. It had been a great evening. But so was the night in Vancouver with Graham and Lila. Again, I think with Evelyn in a group, it was impossible to not have a wonderful experience.

I wasn't looking for her … or anyone. Nope. Just

minding my own business. Living my best life, an unsettled bachelor with no particular direction, no girlfriend, and no penchant for gift giving.

"It really was. I'm so glad we did this." Evelyn hugged Tami like they'd known each other for years.

Amazing.

She was that amazing.

Then she hugged Noah. He glanced over her shoulder at me, a little caught off guard at first, but his face said the same words that played in my head ... *I'm one lucky guy.*

Again, our hands automatically found each other as we walked out of the restaurant, parting ways with Noah and Tami just outside of the entrance.

"Thank you for dinner," she said, leaning into me because it was a chilly evening, or maybe just because.

"My pleasure. Where are you parked?"

She pointed to the lot across the street behind the grocery store. "Where are you parked?"

"I'm not yet. Noah picked me up from the airport when I arrived. I've been taking the bus and the occasional cab. Vehicle shopping is on my list of things to do."

"Then I'll take you home tonight."

"You will, huh?" I gave her hand a little squeeze. "That's very kind of you."

It was about a fifteen-minute drive to my condo, and she spent the entire drive telling me how she met Graham Porter. Letting me know they dated for two weeks in college and had the most regrettable sex. Then she confessed all the reasons she worried that Lila would feel trapped into the family name and politics if Graham ran for governor. I swear the woman didn't know a stranger. It felt like we'd known each other for years, taking me out of my element, bypassing the point where I'd normally say, "I had fun. We should do it again sometime." Only … sometime was code for we're done. Unless … both parties had way too much to drink. Then that led to a clumsy and oftentimes regrettable one-night stand.

I wasn't opposed to the occasional drunken one-night stand, but not with Evelyn. We weren't drunk, and I wasn't okay with an arbitrary time in the future that I may or may not see her again.

"I'll walk you to your door," Evelyn said as she turned off her Jeep.

"God …" I laughed, shaking my head. "That's messed up. Now I feel a huge urgency to get my own vehicle. I think I'll go tomorrow to buy one just so you don't ever have to walk me to my door again."

She climbed out. "I don't have to stop at your door. We don't have to play by the rules of dating. I think we're past that age. How old are you?"

I found her hand and led her to the front door. "Thirty-five."

"I'm thirty-four. Have you ever been married?"

We stopped at my door and faced each other. "No. You?"

She shook her head. "The rules don't apply once you're past thirty."

"The rules?"

Evelyn grinned. "The courting shit. The baseball game."

"The baseball game?" My head canted to the side.

"Yeah. The sexual bases? First base is kissing. Second base is—"

"Yes." I fished my keys from my pocket. "I'm familiar with the bases."

"Well, I don't know if you're a fan of baseball or not, but I am."

I unlocked my door and motioned for her to go inside.

She wet her lips and stepped into my condo without an ounce of hesitation. "You're inviting me in. So you *are* a fan of baseball."

Not so much. Skiing, football (soccer), rugby, cycling, tennis … but not baseball. However, something told me Evelyn might make me a baseball fan.

"Are you sure you're living here?" She glanced around at the sparse furnishings of my two-bedroom condo.

"I never stay in one place long. No need to own much. It's just that much more to sell or move."

Books.

I owned books and a place to sit and read them. My parents didn't believe in letting Julien and I watch television while we were growing up. Julien embraced art. I embraced fiction—mysteries and sci-fi.

"What do you consider not long?" She ran her fingers along the back of my leather recliner before dropping her bag to the floor and slipping off her jacket.

"Three to five years is a nice stay." I tossed my coat onto one of two barstools at my kitchen counter.

"Okay. So our marriage will be short." Her teeth

trapped her full bottom lip.

"Probably."

I'd dated enough women to know there existed a sequence of events that took place way before the M word should ever be discussed. I'd never reached the point of discussing the M word. Not even with my longest relationship, which lasted two years.

Two years and we didn't talk about marriage.

I was out of my realm of experience with Evelyn. We joked about marriage, but who joked about that? Then there was a baseball discussion happening, and I didn't even like baseball, but I waited with restless anticipation for Evelyn to make her point. Something told me it could be brilliant.

"Kenny was a guy I dated my first year in college. He played baseball."

I could not have cared less about this Kenny guy, but he brought her back to the baseball talk, so I folded my arms over my chest, leaned against the counter, and gave her my full attention as she walked in slow circles around my furniture. A predator with calculated moves.

Who was I to judge? I walked into her shop that day and basically said we needed to expedite our dating status—laid out my plans to eat dinner with her, close down bars, and sip hot chocolate.

"He was a solid hitter. Always got on base, but he never hit a home run. I honestly think he lacked the confidence to go for it. His coaches told him to just get on base, so that's what he did because that's what you do when you're young like that. You spend a lot of time on the bases."

Were we still talking about baseball in the literal sense?

"I think once you hit your thirties, no one should judge if you just hit it out of the park your first time up to bat." Her lips twisted as she stopped in front of me. "The goal is to hit it home. If you can do that, then why the hell not, right?"

I thought I understood the metaphor. But if I was wrong, I could get thrown out of the game.

"Can I get you a drink?"

Evelyn shook her head.

My eyes narrowed, studying her for a few seconds.

"First base is fine." She shrugged.

Fuck me …

My grin got a two-second debut before I kissed her. It was slow. A pace that set itself. Maybe she invited me to hit a home run, but that didn't mean I couldn't take my time walking up to the plate, take a few practice swings, and relish the fact that I was the star hitter that night.

The invisible crowd cheered, multiplying the adrenaline in my veins, making my heart pound in my chest. Our kiss intensified, demanding with a clear purpose. As I backed her down the hallway, I made it to second base. She moaned when the pad of my thumb brushed her hard nipple.

My mouth wanted to follow my thumb.

Two steps into my bedroom, I unfastened her jeans, and my fingers slipped deep into third base. Excuse me for not sliding into home quite yet, but Evelyn's bases were fucking spectacular.

"Yesss …" she hissed, breaking the kiss to catch her breath as she pushed my shirt up my chest.

I grabbed the hem of it, removing it in one quick stroke with my free hand.

"Seriously?" Her tongue made a lazy swipe along her lower lip as her eyes met mine and her fingers traced the lines of my chest and abs. "Now you're just showing off, Roe." Blue eyes took a few drunk blinks as I rubbed her clit.

I worked hard to stay fit. And while I'd had women admire my body before, they never did it quite like Evelyn. Her little smirk of appreciation mixed with her finger's fascination with every detail of my anatomy left me feeling on top of the world.

Keeping her hands busy counting my abs, she widened her stance a few inches. I about died when she bit her lip to accent her grin as she glanced up at me.

"I could stay on this base for hours." I captured her mouth again, swallowing her deep moan.

After she branded me with a kiss unlike anything I'd shared with anyone before her, she pulled her head back abruptly. I groaned my disappointment, pausing my fingers inside of her.

"You just have a mattress … on your floor?"

I chuckled. It was a bit strained because her hands had left my abs, deciding to work the button and zipper to my jeans. "I told you … simple life. I don't miss a lot of things that—"

Fuck … fuck, fuck, fuck!

"That what?" She smirked, lifting onto her toes to press a kiss to my jaw as her hand started to breach the waistband of my briefs.

My hand cuffed her wrist to stop her while removing my other hand from her pants. "I don't have a condom."

I didn't plan on having sex *that* night with Evelyn. That earned me extra gentleman points. However, not having *any* condoms earned me the biggest fuck-up trophy. Every man should plan for miracles.

She dropped flat onto her feet, forehead pressed to my chest as her hands fell from my pants, limp at her sides.

"I haven't played baseball since I arrived here."

No excuse. Nope ... it wasn't an excuse, more like an epic man fail on my part.

Evelyn laughed, stepping back. She zipped and buttoned her jeans before straightening her bra and adjusting her sweater. Then she picked my shirt up from the floor and handed it to me. "Let's go."

"Go?"

"Let's go get condoms. There's a store less than a block from here that's still open. We can walk."

Things ... all the spectacular *things* about Evelyn Taylor.

Yet another reason I knew something was special— different about Evelyn. I didn't hesitate for a single second. I didn't suggest another night. I didn't point out the obvious fact that we were on day two of being together and suggest we slow down.

Nope.

Jacket. Boots. Out the door.

"We should jog." I reached for her hand and started jogging as she held up her phone with the flashlight on to guide our way in the dark.

She giggled. It was a giggle that reaffirmed my life was pretty fucking incredible at the moment. I didn't want to slow down and think. If we didn't make sense … then I refused to live my life by any sort of sense or rules.

"There …" She pointed to the illuminated pharmacy sign.

We found the correct aisle. I glanced at her. She glanced at me and shrugged. I plucked a familiar brand from the shelf, took her hand, and pulled her to the checkout. A giddiness filled my belly like a young boy high on sugar that I wasn't supposed to eat before dinner. Only … Evelyn was my sugar. And maybe dinner was the morning after. If we did it—hit the home run—would we spoil everything for the next morning?

My inclination leaned toward "no." Regardless of all the threats my mom made about licorice nibs before dinner spoiling my appetite, I managed to eat every bite on my plate.

"Hey, Evie darling."

Evelyn's eyes widened at the cashier. "Oh! Hey, Donna."

The older lady smiled at me, but it faded into a neutral expression when she saw the box of condoms on the counter.

Hello, old lady stranger. I don't know who you are, and how you know Evelyn, but I'm going to see how many of these condoms I can use on your "Evie darling" before morning. And for the record ... it was her idea. I'm just playing the game.

She cleared her throat. "Did you find everything you were looking for?"

I returned a tight grin and a slight nod, internally chuckling. I wanted to say, "We were actually looking for licorice nibs, but we couldn't find any, so we're just going to have sex instead." But I didn't say that because I wasn't in the mood to chat with the nice lady. I wanted Evelyn naked in my bed ... because we were past the age of being shamed for just hitting the home run.

The thirties were good. Really fucking good.

"We did," Evelyn replied, hiding behind me with her head bowed.

I tossed cash onto the counter.

"Do you want a sack?"

"Nope. We're good." Evelyn snatched the box of condoms, shoved them into her purse, and yanked my arm.

"Evie! Your change!" Donna called as we made our escape.

"Keep it!" She laughed as we flew out the door.

"Shit ..." I chuckled, catching up to Evelyn as she sprinted toward my condo, nothing more than a dark figure with a phone light as her guide. "Who's Donna?"

"My grandma's good friend ... from church. I didn't know she worked there. Oops ..." More soft laughter erupted from her chest as her words became breathless.

When I could see my front door light, I scooped her into my arms.

"Roe!" she squealed, wrapping her arms around my neck.

The second the door closed behind us, she retrieved the box of condoms and tossed her purse on the floor. We shared the most deviant grins as I carried her to the bedroom and kicked the door shut behind us. You would have thought we robbed the store.

"What is this?" she whispered when I eased her to her feet.

We weren't drunk on alcohol, but clearly intoxicated with some *thing*.

My lips brushed hers while my fingers threaded through her hair. "I don't know." I grinned. Biting her bottom lip, I sucked it slowly before releasing it. "But I can't wait to find out."

Did she have a story? I did.

Mine involved dying and coming back to life with a new set of rules.

Hinder not the soul's intended path unto the light, lest shards of darkness shed upon thee.

I didn't want to think about those rules or any rules for that matter.

We slowed it down. It was just us. A mattress on the floor. A box of condoms. And all night.

We turned into nothing more than flesh and breath. An exploration of need.

My impatience warred with my desire to kiss her everywhere … taste her everywhere.

"Roe …" she moaned when I pushed into her.

"Evie …" I whispered over her lips before tasting her

mouth.

Her back arched away from the mattress, her firm nipples brushing my chest as I moved inside of her. It would not be a one-time affair.

One hit.

I was an Evelyn addict from one hit.

Every day felt borrowed since my accident. Every minute felt like the first and the last.

Right then Evelyn became my beginning and my end—origin and destination. And maybe ... if the impossible could find a way to be possible, she could be everything in between.

We owned the night without questioning the reason behind any of it. By morning, I woke to the condom box on the bed beside my head with a note scrawled on it.

Roe,

Had to work.

Evie xo

I grinned, rolling over to bury my face in the pillow that smelled like flowers.

"Evelyn Taylor ..." I chuckled to myself. "What are you doing to me?"

CHAPTER FIVE

Evelyn

S PENDING EVERY FREE moment with Ronin became my new pastime, interrupted only by Sunday football with Graham. Even that turned into a foursome where Lila sat next to Graham with her laptop, playing catch-up on work. Ronin pretended to watch the games, but I didn't miss him occasionally cracking open a book to sneak in a few chapters while Graham and I yelled at the refs and coached our favorite teams from the other side of the screen.

"Book nerd," I'd whisper in his ear during a commercial just before teasing his earlobe with my teeth.

"Science geek," he'd murmur in return, pulling my wrist to his mouth to kiss my carbon atom tattoo.

Once a week, we foraged for dead trees to harvest more firewood. These outings involved snowball fights and playing tag like two young kids. After taking turns splitting the wood with my grandfather's ax and piling it next to the house, Ronin started a fire in the wood-burning stove while I made hot chocolate. We piled pillows and blankets on the floor and watched the flames behind the glass door while slurping the froth from the melted marshmallows atop the steamy hot chocolate.

"You have a white mustache." He eyed my upper lip while setting his mug aside and crawling toward me like an animal on the prowl.

I shook my head, knowing exactly where his mind was going. "Nope." I swiped my tongue over my top lip several times. "This isn't happening. Sorry. I need to shave my legs."

"I'm just helping you get a little marshmallow goo off your lip." He took my mug from my hands and set it aside next to his mug.

"Then why did you take away my hot chocolate?" I grinned, crawling like a crab backward.

"Because…" he caught up to me, wedging his body between my legs, his head hovering over mine "…this *is* happening. Hairy legs and all."

That was me—as is. Take it or leave it, hairy legs and all.

He always took me as is. *Always.*

As we lost our clothes in the sea of pillows and blankets, embers crackled and "Amsterdam" by Gregory Alan Isakov flowed from the portable speaker on the kitchen counter. Ronin converted me to a lover of indie folk music. He converted me to a lot of things … like eating an apple every day and holding plank for two minutes every night before bed.

He broke all the boyfriend molds, unlike anyone I had ever known—a kind soul, laidback, a product of a culturally diverse family, and wise with the silent confidence of a true nomad. My handsome wanderer.

His biggest fault? Long showers. In all fairness to him, it was hard to put on an entire concert within the confines of a five-minute shower like I usually took—hence the hairy legs.

The first time I heard him, I recorded it from the other side of the door and sent it to Lila.

Me: I'm dating a shower singer. I can't stop grinning!

Lila: Damn! He's good. I can't imagine Graham singing in the shower or anywhere for that matter.

After sliding the phone into my pocket, I cracked open the door to his bathroom, biting my lower lip as I gawked at the blurred outline of his sexy-as-hell body. He sudsed his hair, biceps flexed as he massaged his scalp, eyes closed, and lungs belting out the lyrics to Sinatra's "The Best is Yet to Come." I learned he only sang jazz in the shower. Also, I learned if he caught me spying on his shower concert … the chase was on.

"Roe!" I squealed. Running away from his naked body (and shampoo head) chasing me into the bedroom. "The bed! Nooo!" I protested while giggling as he pinned my clothed body to the mattress with his wet torso. "You're going to get shampoo—ROE!" Wrinkling my nose, I arched my back when he rubbed suds along the side of my face, down to my neck. After he finished getting dirty with me in the cleanest way possible, leaving me naked on a mess of wet, soapy sheets, he sauntered back into the bathroom, shut the door, and started singing Sinatra's "My Way."

Weeks and then months passed, and it became impossible to remember what life was like before Ronin. It wasn't that I lacked happiness before him. I had family and friends, a job I loved, and all the best horror movies on Netflix. Wood still got chopped and hot chocolate was consumed by the fire. All the same colors painted my story; they just weren't as vibrant.

"He's taking me skiing." I frowned looking in the mirror at my soft pink bridesmaid dress while the seamstress pinned the bottom.

Lila snorted, sipping champagne, perched in a white velvet chair in the two-story library of the Porter mansion outside of Denver. "I'm jealous. Jealous that you're going skiing while I'm drowning in wedding details. And jealous that he gets to watch you slide on your ass down the mountain. Do you see the jealousy on my face?" She circled her champagne flute in front of her face as she grinned. "Besides, there's been snow on the ground for a month, and you've been dating him—or just screwing him, I'm not sure which—for three months. *Three months!* I can't believe you're just *now* going skiing with him. Graham's already skied with him twice."

"It gets worse, Lila."

The seamstress slipped off my dress and handed me a plush white robe.

"Worse?" She cocked her head to the side.

My nose wrinkled as I stole her champagne and chugged the rest of it. "His parents are coming to Aspen ... for the winter."

"Oh ... that puts a damper on your kinky time."

I rolled my eyes. "I'm not talking about that. They're staying with friends. His dad has an ex-teammate who owns a home in Aspen. A big home. Well ... not Porter big, but big in comparison to Ronin's condo and my cabin. My concern is that his parents both ski. His dad has Olympic gold medals for god's sake. And their son is dating me!"

"Oh, so you are in fact dating. I wasn't sure. It just seemed like a lot of sex. Kinky sex."

"Shut up." I smirked.

"I will not shut up. Not until you start locking your door to your house and to your lab. Four times in three months! I've walked in on the two of you *four* times! I know Ronin's bare ass better than I know Graham's. I know you call him Roe, but only in private. You moan it when his head's between your legs ... when he has you *tied up*. Seriously, I had no idea you were in to that kind of stuff."

My cheeks bloomed with embarrassment. "That happened *once*." (Twice. But what she didn't know wouldn't hurt her.) "I joked about his new scarf that seemed a mile long and asked him what he planned to do with it. Tie me up? And so he did. It was a scarf. Not chains and whips. And I'm sorry you happened to walk in on us that time. We now double-check for locked doors." Most of the time ...

New romance was the best drug, and my addiction felt incurable.

"And you can't say a word about it because you have no room to talk, Ms. Threesome."

Her face turned a bit red too. We agreed to never discuss that weird night in Vancouver, but I had to make a tiny mention of it to keep her from judging me too harshly for a few unlocked doors and scarf play.

"Four." She cleared her throat, ignoring my threesome reference. "I've walked in on you guys four times. But it's fine. If I'm honest, I have some of those images tucked into my mind, and I pull them out to use when Graham feels obligated to have sex but not in the mood to do the whole seduction act."

"You picture my naked boyfriend so you can get off?" I blinked hard several times.

Lila shrugged. "Only occasionally. You good with that?" She smirked. "I mean ... you've actually had sex with my fiancé, so can a few innocent images of Ronin pounding into my BFF really be such a big deal?"

"Depends ... am I still in the image, or do you cut me out and put yourself in the picture?"

"Nope. It's all you, babe."

On a slow nod, I returned a half grin. My breasts ... she remembered our night in Vancouver. "Then I'll allow it." My partial grin faded. "Why the hell would Graham feel 'obligated' to have sex with you? What's going on? Seriously, you haven't even made it down the aisle yet."

Lila waved me off. "It's nothing. Ninety-nine percent of the time, it's good. Amazing like it's always been. But now that he's fully committed to running for governor, he's dealing with more stress. And sometimes I feel neglected, which turns into sympathy sex. And let's just say … sympathy sex sucks."

"Unless you're imagining Ronin's naked backside."

Lila pressed her lips together, but they didn't hide her grin. "Unless that."

"Mmm. Yeah, well … I'm going to get dressed and head home. Wish me luck. I hope I don't end up on crutches for your wedding."

"Oh god! Don't say that."

I hugged my best friend and kissed her cheek. Lila was my everything. Her happiness was my happiness. Our successes and failures in life were so tightly woven together that I swore we felt each other's epic moments before actually sharing them.

"HEY, PRETTY GIRL!"

I glanced up after locking my Jeep. "Noah!"

He gave me a big hug. "I heard you're making a few runs today."

"Did you also hear I'm the world's worst skier?" I grinned when he released me. "It's been nice knowing ya. I'm sure we won't see each other much after Ronin dumps me. And he *will* dump me because our incompatibility is about to be on full display. Tell Tami I'd love to still get together for wine even when Ronin and I are no longer together."

Noah pulled off his beanie and scratched his full head of salt and pepper hair while giving me a booming belly laugh. "Oh, darling. I've seen you two together too many times. You can't fool me. I'm waiting for the wedding invitation. Break up? Yeah, right."

I blew out a long breath and slipped on my hot pink ski jacket over my white, gray, and hot pink snow pants. "Time will tell."

Yes. Time would tell.

My stomach churned, toxic with nerves, already feeling the embarrassment. Ronin met me at the bottom of an "easy" slope, wearing a grin that set my whole body aflame.

Damn!

I gawked at my sexy man in his black and red gear, polarized glasses, and mussed black hair sticking out beneath his hat.

"Evelyn …" He strutted toward me in his ski boots, a stiff but no less confident gait. Before I could spew off my last-minute pleas to make my case for canceling our outing, he wrapped me in his arms, lifting me off the ground, and kissed me thoroughly.

One of his troller buddies whistled a catcall.

Ronin grinned, ending our kiss. "How was the dress fitting?" He set me on my feet in my clunky boots. I owned my gear because Graham bought it for me years ago before he gave up on teaching me to ski. I used it several times a year to appease Lila when she wanted to drag me up the slopes for "fun."

"The fitting was fine. Do you ever have sex with me out of sympathy? Because you feel like you should maybe when I want it, but in truth you're distracted and not really wanting it?"

His head drew backward. "What on earth are you talking about?"

"Just a question." I shrugged.

"Evie …" He angled his body away from onlookers and pressed my hand to his crotch. "I'm hard as fuck just from kissing you. So, no … I've never *not* wanted to have sex with you. Why would you ask me that?"

"No reason." I kissed the angle of his jaw.

"There has to be a reason." He leaned back, tipping my chin up with his gloved finger.

My nose wrinkled. "It's something Lila said about Graham. I'll tell you more later."

Ronin screwed his lips to the side. "Okay. Later. Now we see just how horrible you are at this. Something tells me you've overplayed your lack of skiing skills."

He locked into his skis and helped me into mine.

I started to fall to the side. When he caught me, I gave him a tight-lipped grin. "You've been warned. And I'm certain after you witness this catastrophe that is me, you will never get a hard-on for me again."

"I'm going to stick my hard-on in your mouth later, if you don't stop saying stupid shit like that."

I liked Ronin's dirty mouth. I knew I'd miss it when he broke up with me in approximately thirty minutes, but I didn't say that. Instead, I shrugged a silent "we'll see." It was about fifteen yards to the lift, and I made three attempts to fall on the way. Each time Ronin hooked an arm around my waist and kept me upright. How did he balance himself and me? I usually took down anyone who tried to save me: Graham … Lila … a ski instructor they hired to teach me a few things several winters earlier.

A lost cause.

"Hey, Jim." Ronin nodded at the liftie as the moving bench scooped us up.

"Have fun!" Jim replied.

"So far so good." Ronin rested his hand on my leg and gave it a squeeze.

"You should radio ahead and tell them to be ready to stop the lift when I wipe out getting off it. Because I do … Every. Single. Time."

"Not on my watch." Another leg squeeze. He was so damn sure of himself.

I feared I would emotionally break him that day—when Superman discovered tragedies were beyond his control. And I would be one of those as soon as we reached the top.

Only … I was wrong.

At the top, he hooked my waist, literally carrying me off the lift, down the tiny slope to a small flat area before the run. A green one. Green was easy. For some people. Not for me. Ronin slid one of his skis between mine, bringing us chest to chest.

"Ready?" He kissed me, palming my ass to keep me steady.

Would it be the last time he kissed me like that? I dropped my poles and wrapped my arms around his neck.

He chuckled. "Baby, hold on to your poles. Okay?" He slid my goggles down over my eyes, and then he retrieved my poles for me.

"Duck walk like this." He pointed his tips into a V to show me, coaching me over to the start of the run.

I slanted my skis into a V. I'd played that game before. I knew the rules. I knew how it ended.

"We're just going to snowplow. Okay?"

I returned a toothy grin until the cold air hurt my teeth. He was super cute. Poor guy should have invited Lila and Graham to ski with him.

"This can't be any fun for you." I turned my skis into a snowplow.

Ronin flipped around in front of me. "Doing my favorite thing with my favorite person? What's not to love about that?"

"I'm going to ruin your favorite thing for you. And why are you backward?"

"I'm going to guide you down the hill. Catch you if you start to fall."

"You can't ski backward down the hill." I frowned.

"I can. I can do a lot of things on skis. Let's go." He coaxed me forward.

I moved two feet before I started to fall. And as promised, he had me. We did this exhausting replay halfway down the run.

"Hold up, baby." Ronin glanced toward the fence, and the skier who plowed into it. "I'm going to check on them. Move to the side and take a seat. Okay?"

"Okay."

He guided me to the side of the run. I collapsed onto my butt, skis off to my right. Ronin checked on the other skier, and several minutes later, he started talking into his walkie-talkie. I realized it could take a while, so I removed my skies. One of them wouldn't come off easily, so I twisted, pulled, and rammed my pole into it harder, and something snapped, but it finally came off.

Bye, bye …

There it went, down the slope without me. I broke the brake in the process of forcing my boot out of the binding. Classic move on my part.

"Shit." I cringed, diving for it, but it was too late.

After a few minutes, another troller arrived with a sled. They loaded up the injured skier, and the troller took him down the hill.

"Evelyn … where is your other ski?" Ronin surveyed the immediate area as he walked toward me, carrying his own skis over his shoulder.

"I think I did something to the brake when I took it off."

He slid his glasses to the tip of his nose, squinting down the hill. "Huh …" His lips twisted, and he nodded slowly, not appearing the least bit mad or exhausted like Graham did when I skied with him and Lila.

No lectures.

No eye-rolling.

Just an easy nod. A non-verbal "Okay then." Ronin spoke into his walkie-talkie again, requesting a Model 100. I had no idea what that meant. Probably a new girlfriend.

"Sorry." I frowned.

"For what?" He dropped to his knees in front of me, resting his hands on my legs.

"For the confirmation that your favorite person can't do your favorite thing."

Ronin smirked, pulling off his stocking cap. I wanted to tackle him and tear off his clothes. Seriously ... he was so damn sexy with that thick chaotic hair, those sunglasses, and a spectacular smile.

"I lied about that. You're my favorite person, but skiing is not my favorite thing. It comes in second. You do my favorite thing, and baby ... you do it better than anyone."

"Pfft ..." My embarrassment and vulnerability wouldn't allow me to entertain the idea that I was better than anyone at anything.

He smiled over my shoulder. "Thank you."

I glanced back at the woman in red bringing a toboggan.

"She okay?" she asked.

"Yes. Vanessa, this is my girlfriend, Evelyn. She lost her ski."

Vanessa laughed. "Happens."

Ronin clasped my hand and pulled me up. "Hop on, my lady."

"You're taking me down the mountain? Gah! How embarrassing." I climbed into the sled.

"Drinks later? There are six of us going." Vanessa ruffled Ronin's messy hair.

Why? Why did she touch him? And why did it bother me? I was the hug queen who thrived on human touch, always physical with my affection. But apparently, I had trouble with it after being reduced to an incompetent skier in front of dark wavy-haired Vanessa. I bet she was an amazing skier.

"Drinks?" he asked me as he secured a strap over my lap.

"Sure." I sighed, punctuating my displeasure of the situation with a frown. "That I can do."

He grinned, dropping a quick kiss on the tip of my nose before standing and locking into his skis. "What time?"

"In about an hour?"

"Great! Thanks, Vanessa."

I managed to murmur a thank you as well. Thank you for being so pretty. A good skier. And ruffling Ronin's hair. I loved it when other women ran their fingers through it.

Dammit! Knock it off, Evelyn!

We made our way down the slope, finding the runaway ski. Then we were greeted at the bottom with two more concerned patrollers.

"Lost her ski. No big deal." Ronin helped me out of the toboggan.

My ego covered its eyes in embarrassment while I put on a brave face with a friendly smile.

"Well, that was fun." I couldn't help the way my entire body sagged inward. Yes, it was possible to pout with your whole body.

"Come here. Wanna see something cool?"

I shook my head.

"Yes, you do." He propped up our skis and flipped me up over his shoulder.

"Ronin!"

"Stop pouting!" He smacked my ass while strutting about twenty yards over from the end of our run. "You like to watch, so here you go." He deposited me on my feet as skiers came down a hill dotted with sliding boxes and rails.

I grinned. Yeah, I liked to watch.

"I'm going up. Keep your eyes peeled."

"Going up? To do that?" I narrowed my eyes.

"Yes." He sauntered off without looking back.

I returned my attention to the skiers sliding along the rails and boxes, some more flashy with their turns and dismounts. A few failing to land at all—except on their asses.

About fifteen minutes later, *my* guy came down the hill.

"Slow down," I whispered to myself.

Nope. He didn't slow down. Ronin jumped onto one rail, flying off with a lot of air time, and then he was right back on the second rail. Finishing with a box, he spun once in the middle before landing perfectly back onto the run. The cockiest grin took up residence on his face as he came straight toward me.

"Stop!" I flinched, stumbling back a step as he shifted to the side, skidding to a dramatic halt mere inches from me. "Really?" I punched his arm. "You never mentioned you can do tricks on jibs."

He shrugged, removing his skis. "Now you know."

"I'm taking my loser ass home." I stomped toward my skis.

"I've got your shit, grumpy. Just head toward your Jeep."

When we reached my Jeep, I sat sideways on the driver's seat while Ronin secured my skis to the rack.

"I think it's your attitude. If you start believing you can ski, I think you'll find your body will cooperate." He removed my ski boots and tossed them in back while I slid on my snow boots.

"Yes. I think it's all in my head." I grunted a laugh, starting my Jeep.

"Want me to pick you up for drinks?"

"No." I tried to keep my bottom lip from swelling into a full-on pout. "I'll grab a ride since I don't intend to be under the legal limit when I leave the bar. And I don't want you to have to be the DD either since tomorrow is your day off."

"Cool. That means we get a little drunk together, then I fuck some sense into you for your pouty attitude. Good plan." He smothered me with a hard kiss to make his point.

"I'm not pouting." Okay, I couldn't even say it without sounding pissy. Clearly, I needed a drink or five.

CHAPTER SIX

A FTER A SHOWER, a little makeup, and drying my hair straight, I slid on white leggings, gray ankle boots, and a long-sleeved floral boho blouse. The cab arrived a few minutes early, but I was ready.

Ready to pretend I didn't go skiing.

Ready to forget my best friend thought of my boyfriend naked on a need-to basis.

Ready to drink myself into a better mood.

The bar was a quick ten-minute ride. When I walked inside, live country music greeted me just before Tami pulled me in for a hug outside of the bathroom. "Glad you made it. I'm grabbing another drink. Can I get you one?"

"Yes." I shrugged off my jacket.

"Wine?"

"Something stronger. It's been one of those days."

"Well, shit. Sorry to hear that. I'll get you fixed right up. Everyone's over at that corner table. Karaoke starts in thirty minutes."

"Karaoke?"

"Yes. The bar just acquired a karaoke machine."

I liked karaoke. Maybe the day would end better than it started.

When I glanced to the table, Ronin's eyes were already on me. His lips curled into a tiny smile as his gaze slid along the length of my body. When I approached the table, he stood because he was a true gentleman. "Take my seat. I'll find another chair."

"Stay. I'll pull this one up." Noah slid a chair over next to the empty one beside him. "Tami will want to sit by her and talk her ear off anyway."

Ronin gave me a look, the silent "is that okay" look.

"Thank you." I sat in the chair Noah pulled up. It put me at the opposite end of the table from Ronin ... and Vanessa. Yes, she was perched next to him, *right* next to him because we were all pretty crammed in there.

I'd met everyone there, so no introductions were needed, and I didn't get much more than a few nods and smiles because Vanessa was in the middle of a story.

"So it was a crazy day ..." She sighed.

I must have missed her telling the crazy part.

"But the day ended well. I got a little chuckle when Evelyn lost her ski and Ronin, being the true hero he is..." Vanessa looped her arms around his arm, giving him an endearing side hug "...had me bring him a sled to pull her down the hill."

Everyone chuckled, eyes on me and Ronin.

He winked at me. I returned my best fake smile before grabbing a menu to decide what food I should order to help absorb all the alcohol I *needed*.

"Here you go." Tami set two shots of something—I

didn't even know or care what—down in front of me before wedging between the chairs to sit down.

"Thank you." I downed the first shot.

Tequila. Good choice.

When I glanced at Ronin, he gave my drink a single peaked brow.

Yes, buddy. I'm drinking, probably more than originally planned because I don't like Vanessa sitting by you. And my grown-ass, thirty-four-year-old self shouldn't have an issue with it. But I do because it's been a shitty day. I'm human. And insecurity is a bitch I'm not immune to.

"Song choices. Sign up at the bar if you're interested." The waitress set a piece of paper in the middle of the table with a list of songs.

Vanessa plucked it from the table before anyone else had a chance to grab it. "Oh! I love this one." She pointed to a song, showing Ronin. "You *have* to sing it with me! *Please!*"

"Sure." He shrugged before taking a swig of his beer.

You've got to be shitting me.

The one thing I could do was sing my ass off, not as well as my shower Sinatra, but I could definitely carry a tune. Yet, Ronin said yes to a duet with Vanessa. I took the second tequila shot.

"Pace yourself." Tami laughed, sipping her wine.

Ronin's one-peaked-brow of concern turned into two, but I ignored him, quickly ordering more shots from the waitress. That brought him out of his chair, working his way around the table to me.

"Come here." He smiled, holding out his hand so the

rest of the table didn't question what was up.

I stared at his hand a few seconds, already feeling a buzz from two shots on an empty stomach. Then my gaze flitted to Vanessa. She watched me while sipping her beer. Placing my hand in his, I let him help me up and drag me toward the back of the bar to the one empty barstool on the corner.

"Water," he said to the bartender, lifting me onto the stool and wedging himself between my legs, hands on my thighs. "What's up, Evie?" His head cocked to the side.

I shrugged, dragging my sluggish gaze around the room. "Nothing."

"Two shots in less than five minutes doesn't seem like nothing. Try again."

I forced my eyes to meet his gaze. To meet all of him—his dark blue jeans hanging just right on his waist, black leather unlaced boots, and a fitted white button-down with the sleeves rolled up showing off his sinewy arms. And don't even get me started on how good he smelled, like pine and cedar. My mountain man.

"I like karaoke."

"Okay," he replied on a soft chuckle, handing me the water the bartender just set on the counter.

I took a few swigs before handing it back to him.

"Then you should sing."

I frowned. "I didn't know you sang, except in the shower. And now you've agreed to sing with Va-*ness-uh*"

"Va-ness-uh?" He smirked at me. "Why are you say-ing her name like that?"

"Like what?" I blew a few strands of hair away from

my face.

"Like you don't like her."

"I just met her today. Why wouldn't I like her?" Such a great question and completely rhetorical.

"Exactly. So … are you saying you want to sing with me too? We can sing together."

Too? No. Instead? Yes. But I couldn't tell him that. It would've come across like I didn't like her, which was crazy because I'd just met her. And she'd done nothing wrong. Except touch Ronin. But Tami hugged Ronin. And Lila had touched him in a friendly way, hugged him, seen him naked having sex with me.

Not helping!

"I'm not in the mood to sing." I grabbed his shirt and pulled him to me, brushing my lips over his.

"No?" he said in the same deep voice he used to whisper dirty things to me in bed. "What are you in the mood for?" He kissed me.

I wrapped one of my legs around him, hooking his leg with my foot, deepening the kiss, moaning because those two shots had stolen my self-control. That … that was what I needed. Ronin brought me back to center. He was balance and reason to my instability and doubt.

"We're up!" Vanessa interrupted, tugging on Ronin's arm like she couldn't see us kissing.

He pulled away, looking only at me. "I think I'm going to pass on karaoke tonight."

"What? No! It's one song. We're up now. It's less than four minutes. Evelyn, tell him to get his ass on stage with me. Don't you want to see him sing?"

I rubbed my lips together. Confrontation was not my thing. "It's ... yeah. Fine."

Ronin took a step away from me as Vanessa incessantly pulled his arm. "You sure?"

I smiled when I couldn't make my head submit to a nod. Well, I wasn't sure it was a real smile. It felt more like a grimace. A painful grimace.

He let her pull him up on stage, and I made my way back to the table.

"Have you heard him sing before?" Tami yelled in my ear over the start of the music.

"Yes, but just in the shower."

She laughed, jerking her chin toward the two new shots the waitress delivered while I was at the bar with Ronin. "Going big tonight, huh?"

I stared at the shots. It was fine. I didn't need them anymore. Ronin kissed me. That soothed my nerves and numbed my insecurities more than alcohol.

"Whoa! Interesting song choice." Tami rested her hand on my arm.

I glanced over at her. "I haven't heard it."

"It's..." her nose wrinkled "...sexy."

Turning back to the stage, I waited to see what she meant by sexy. Vanessa started. Her voice was okay. Then Ronin chimed in. His was better. Deep and sexy. Seductive. Or maybe that was just the words. Yeah ... it was a sexy song about *sex*!

Vanessa sang her lines, touching him—his face, his chest.

I downed one of the two shots, feeling Tami's eyes on

me, but I didn't look her way. Nope. I couldn't look at her while Vanessa tried to make love to my boyfriend in front of the packed bar.

She sang about temptation, hooked her finger into the waist of his jeans and pulled him closer.

And … I was out of there. After taking the last shot, I grabbed my handbag and stood.

Whoa! Lots of tequila. I've got this.

Tami grabbed my arm.

"I'm going to the ladies' room," I yelled.

She nodded. "Want me to come with?"

I shook my head and faked another smile. "Be right back."

My feet took me in a not-so-straight line to the bar where I handed the bartender money for my shots and slipped on my jacket in the clumsiest fashion. Risking one last glance at the stage, I made eye contact with Ronin—Vanessa grinding her pelvis on his hip and leg.

His eyes narrowed.

I hiked my bag onto my shoulder and swayed a bit as I meandered to the door. The crisp night air stole my breath, but the tequila kept me warm.

Cab. I needed a cab or Lyft. Or Uber.

Digging my phone from my purse, I tried to get the screen unlocked with my face, but it didn't unlock. I stumbled a bit. Those shots sure did their job. I tried to enter my code. But I entered it incorrectly.

"Stupid fucker …" I mumbled at my phone.

"Where are you going, Evelyn?" Ronin's voice sounded behind me.

I didn't turn toward him. My wobbly legs continued to zigzag me down the sidewalk as I fought with the code to my phone. "Home, rock star. Going home."

"How many shots have you had?" His boots scuffed along the sidewalk a few steps behind me.

"Not enough to watch Va-*ness*-uh fuck you in front of our friends and a roomful of strangers. Nope. Not enough tequila in the world for that."

"Really, Evie? 'Fucking me' is what that looked like to you? Don't you think your impression of that is a little overboard?"

"No!" I whipped around and hurled my phone at him.

Tequila was pissed off. Yes, I blamed the drinks.

"Jesus!" He bobbed to the side to keep it from slamming into his face. The muscles in his jaw flexed.

My cupped hand flew to my mouth. I couldn't believe I did that.

Whoa!

It landed on the ground, testing the durability of the case and screen protector.

I swallowed my own shock of that knee-jerk reaction and dropped my hand from my face. "I don't think my feelings are overboard. They're *mine.* You can't tell me how I'm supposed to feel about shit! Okay?"

Ronin glared at me for two seconds before turning back to pick up my phone. "You told me it was fine to sing with Vanessa."

Men. Such complete dumb fucks. Even the good ones were so incredibly stupid sometimes.

"I was practically s-seducing you on that bar stool."
My words slurred.

Oh, tequila …

"And you took that as me thinking you should go
sing with Va-*ness*-uh?"

"But you said—"

"No! Uh-uh …" I shook my head, and it only intensified my dizziness. "I was put on the spot. How stupid are
you to think I really wanted to watch that shit on stage?
You should have said no. You should have taken me home
the second we started kissing at the bar. Instead, all eyes
were on me. Insecure Evelyn. Will she forbid Ronin from
singing with Va-*ness*-uh? Is she possessive and needy? Not
okay. Not okay at all!"

*Okay, tequila. I might hate you about now. You're steal-
ing my control. You're jumbling my thoughts and loosening
my tongue.*

"I'm sorry," he said so softly I barely heard him.

I shook my head. "For what?"

He held out his arms for a few seconds before surren-
dering them to his sides. "For everything. For insisting
you ski with me today. For not asking Vanessa to switch
seats with you so we could sit together. For not taking
you home after that kiss. For getting up on that stage with
her. For putting you in that situation."

He tried to steal my fight.

"You can't just apologize for everything."

He blew out a forced breath. "Well, I am."

"No …" I rubbed my temples. "Th-this isn't over.
You can't make this right when I'm on tequila."

The ground started to move, or at least that's what my legs thought, so they stumbled two steps to the side.

"Okay, Evie." Ronin caught me and carried me to a taxi. "You can finish being mad at me in the morning."

"Put me down! You smell like her. And her makeup is on your face and shirt! Yuck! Put me down."

He didn't. Instead, he tucked me next to him in the back of the taxi, and that's all I remembered.

The next morning, I woke to an empty bed in my home—a three-bedroom, A-framed log cabin that my grandma gave me. I also woke to a throbbing head and a guilty conscience. Sadly, I remembered the worst parts from the previous night, or the previous day in general.

The covers were pulled back on the other side of my bed, so Ronin must have stayed with me. Lucky him.

I smelled coffee but couldn't bring myself to make the walk of shame quite yet. He had the day off, as did I, so there was no need to rush anything. Instead, I took a shower, brushed my teeth, and wrapped up in my plush hot pink bathrobe before padding down the hardwood floor hallway to the kitchen. A fire crackled in my wood-burning stove.

"Hey," I said, twisting my face into a cringe.

Ronin glanced up from the sofa and his book. He read all the time. Actual paperback books on everything from history to autobiographies to fictional suspense. "Good morning."

His shirtless body engulfed the length of my sofa, which wasn't fair. The urge to be mad at him clung to my ego. But there he was, shirtless, in a pair of black lounge pants sitting inappropriately low on his waist. Inappropriate because he knew those fancy carved abs and happy trail temptation were my kryptonite, which sent my thoughts into some pretty inappropriate territory—just like the tattooed symbols down the right side of his torso. He said they represented life and second chances. I felt pretty sure it was the name of an old girlfriend in a language I couldn't read.

The teapot was already hot. I tossed a tea bag into a mug and filled it with water. Warm oatmeal waited for me in a sauce pan, so I dished up a small bowl of it as well.

"You can sit by me. I took a shower last night and scrubbed all the makeup and Vanessa smell from my body," he said as I started to sit in the recliner across from the sofa.

"You should put on a shirt."

He smirked. "Is that so?"

"Yes." I chose the recliner over the sofa.

He scratched his chest, then lower … then just under the waistband of his pants.

Jerk!

I sipped my tea and ate my oatmeal while Ronin resumed reading his book.

"You make me want to stay," he said without looking up from his book. If I hadn't been the only other person in the room, I'm not sure I would have known he was talking to *me*.

Setting my tea and oatmeal on the coffee table, I hugged my arms to my chest. There had been this gradual shift between us over the previous weeks.

A slipping.

A falling …

I'd watch TV and stroke his hair while he rested his head on my lap, reading a book. He hummed and whispered, "I love that."

I knew he loved more than that.

Whenever his schedule allowed, he dusted the snow from my car and started it for me, waiting by the driver's door with a hot thermos after I closed up shop. A grin stole my face as I took the thermos and brushed my lips over his. "I love this," I whispered.

He knew I loved more than that.

Ronin eyed me as my thoughts drifted to all the things we loved about each other. I was supposed to go see my mom and grandma that day, but … it was early. Ronin said something that couldn't go unexplained. I made him want to stay. What did that mean? Before I asked him to elaborate, I had some explaining to do too.

"I've never been jealous before," I said to nothing in particular, focusing over the sofa to the front window like he spoke to his book.

Ronin slid a ripped strip of paper—his makeshift bookmark—between the pages of his book.

"I've had other boyfriends, but I've never felt like I did yesterday. Here's the ugly truth, and I'm not one bit proud of it or even trying to defend my actions—they are on all accounts unjustified and without any defenses. A simple case of *this* human behaving badly. Yesterday, I hit a low point after I lost my ski. Then this pretty woman brought a sled so you could haul your terrible-skier girlfriend down the mountain. And she ruffled your hair."

I closed my eyes and shook my head. "Yes. It was a hair ruffling. And it's your hair not mine. But I wanted to claw her eyes out for touching you. Then she retold the story last night. And it *is* funny, but it wasn't funny coming from her. It wasn't funny to me that she took every opportunity to touch you. Granted, I don't really know her. My anger was at myself for feeling that way, for feeling like you'd see something great in her during one of my not-so-finer moments. Confidence is sexy. God knows it drew me to you because you are the epitome of confident. But last night, I was the least confident person in the bar, which made me feel like the least desirable person. And that really sucked."

Ronin rubbed the back of his neck, gaze glued to the coffee table between us, his brow a little wrinkled. "I had an accident when I was twelve. An electrical shock." He held up his hand to show me the scar I'd asked about several weeks after we met. At the time, he shrugged and said, "Just a boy being a boy."

He continued, "It caused some speech issues for a while. Kids made fun of me. It was a blow to my confidence. I felt like my friends were embarrassed of me. For months I was the least confident person in *every* room. So ... I get it."

Ronin glanced up at me while sitting up straight. "Maybe you learn to ski. Maybe you don't. I have no fucks to give about it because for the first time in a long time, I can't wait to take off my gear and find you at the end of every day. Before you, I was the first to work. The first one making tracks after a fresh round of snow. Now ... I show up on time for work. Not too early, but not late. Just on time because it's impossible to leave you in the morning. I want one more kiss. One more minute just to look at you. One more smile. One more whisper of my name 'Roe ...' from your beautiful lips. *Roe* ... no one has ever called me that. And when you say it, I feel like the goddamn king of the world. I want this, and I've never wanted anything more than seeking the next adventure. But you ... you make me want to stay."

Slipping ...

Falling ...

I grinned, easing out of the recliner. "King of the world, huh? Does that make me your queen?" Lifting a leg, I straddled his lap, forcing him to lean back.

His hands slid up my legs beneath my robe. A smile played along his lips when they reached my hips, and he discovered I wasn't wearing anything under my robe.

Slipping ...

Falling ...

"Yes ..." He removed one of his hands and pulled the sash. My robe fell open. Ronin had a way of looking at me that felt predatory. The tiny hairs along my skin stood at attention. They knew he was going to do what he wanted to me with little regard for anything—a burning house, a crushing avalanche, Armageddon. "You are most certainly my queen."

My breath caught when he sucked in my nipple, teasing it with his teeth. Teasing it *hard* with his teeth.

"Roe …" I breathed, closing my eyes, tangling my fingers in his thick hair.

He cupped my other breast, dragging his mouth across my chest, etching my skin with a day's worth of stubble. "Say it again."

I tightened my hold on his hair, arching my back. "Roe …"

"Again …" He bit my other nipple, tugging it as his hands gripped my hips to work my pelvis over his erection.

My robe slipped off my shoulders as we ground against each other. His impatience pulled a growl from his chest. I *loved loved loved* how badly he needed me like that. The hand on my breast moved between us where he yanked down the front of his pants, no underwear. I wasn't the only one dressed in minimum attire.

He teased me for a few seconds before pushing into me, tightening his grip on my hips to bring me down onto him.

"Ride me, Evie," he whispered in my ear, biting my earlobe while his fingers dug into my flesh.

Ronin said things that would have made my mom gasp in horror had she known. My mom adored Ronin. She called him the "ultimate gentleman" because she saw him hold my hand, hold open doors, and stand when a woman walked into the room. He called her Mrs. Taylor, in spite of her insisting he call her Madeline, which made her blush.

But … her face would have turned crimson for differ-ent reasons had she known the things he said to me during sex—the things he *did* to me during sex. His relentless tongue, commanding hands, and large cock had explored my body. Every. Single. Inch.

Ronin obliterated all of my comfort zones, shattered all of my preconceived ideas of taboo. He made everything feel natural because it was with him. I trusted him implicitly, which made my Vanessa reaction seem so insane.

"Roe …" I dropped my head to his shoulder. He felt right. He always felt right moving inside me. I never wanted to experience that intimacy with another man. Not in this life or any other life.

"Not yet, Evie." He stilled my hips, denying me as his tongue plunged into my mouth, making deep, hard strokes.

"Everyone decent?"

I pulled away; my body frozen like frightened prey as if our lack of motion would make us invisible. But it didn't. Lila saw us. Well, she saw the back of the sofa, so the back of Ronin's head, and the front of me. I leaned forward to hide my bared chest—that she'd seen … and tasted.

Ugh …

"Stop it!" I whispered through gritted teeth as Ronin flicked my nipple with his tongue.

"Fuck no, I'm not stopping."

There it was—Ronin in sex mode. No. Fucks. Given.

"Not … again. I was kidding! I knew you'd be decent! I knew you wouldn't let this shit happen *again!*" Lila slapped her hand against her forehead, before glancing back out the door. "One minute, Madeline."

Crap! My mom?

Lila blew out a hard breath, glancing up at the ceiling for a second. "He's physically inside of you right now, isn't he?" Lila bit her bottom lip, scrunching her nose.

I nodded, mirroring her expression, digging my fingernails into Ronin's shoulders because he was *still* messing with my nipple.

Flick. Bite. Suck. Flick. Bite. Suck.

"Get your asses to the bedroom and get dressed. Your mom *and* grandma are here to surprise you, and they are literally ten steps from your porch. Go!" She backed out and shut the door.

I started to climb off him, but Ronin grabbed my ass and stood ... still inside of me. "Put me down! Did you hear her? We have to get dressed!"

"I heard." He smirked, carrying me to the bedroom, mouth sucking along my neck.

"Ronin! Stop!"

He kicked the bedroom door shut and laid me on the bed (still inside of me).

"Roe ..." I tried hard to make my case, but he felt *so* good inside of me. "St-stop ..." If my hips hadn't worked against his so relentlessly, he might have taken my plea more seriously.

Then ... he just stopped.

My heavy eyelids forced themselves open. His head hovered over mine. I could hear chattering in the other room.

"Evie ..." he whispered, raw and gritty.

Then the voices faded. The world faded. It was just us.

Slipping …

Falling …

He brought his forehead to mine, rolling it side to side. "Evie …" He feathered his fingertips along the outside of my thighs—*not* like the Ronin who was hell-bent on not stopping just minutes earlier.

That was it. When the time came, life couldn't stop it. Like your heart would burst if you didn't share the emotions that dominated your existence. It was too much for one person to bear.

So we slipped.

We fell …

"Roe … don't say it," I whispered.

He loved me.

And I loved him.

It had never been said, but it was always there.

He pulled back enough to see my eyes, a ghost of concern sliding across his face.

"It's too late." I eased his concern with a little grin, feathering my fingernails down his back. "It's too big for words now. Don't belittle it with a four-letter word. It's too intangible. Too undefinable. Don't ever tell me what you can *show* me."

He did.

He kissed me. He moved inside of me.

We rushed nothing because nothing mattered more than us, more than what we had to say without actually saying anything at all.

CHAPTER SEVEN

"RONIN AWAKE YET?" Lila asked, wearing designer jeans, a white sweater, the perfect blond ponytail, and a shit-eating grin. "I told your mom and grandma that you were in the shower and Ronin wasn't awake yet."

Mom and Grandma smiled at me from the sofa. Grandma picked up Ronin's book from the end table, inspecting the back cover.

I returned a guilty smile, pulling my hands out of my hoodie—Ronin's red ski patrol hoodie that I stole whenever I could because it smelled like him, and it felt big and warm like his embrace.

"He's in the shower now. Hey, Mom ..." I leaned down and gave her and my grandma hugs. "What a surprise."

"Mmm ... yup. Big surprise." Lila nodded, scraping spoonfuls of oatmeal from the sauce pan. She'd been on a strict wedding diet, but she ate when she was over-whelmed. Apparently walking in on Ronin *inside of me* for the fifth time overwhelmed her.

"I'd planned on driving to Denver today to see you. Why the unexpected trip here?"

"Is … someone singing?" My mom cocked her head a fraction, eyes narrowed.

I giggled and so did Lila. "Ronin sings Sinatra in the shower. It's his thing."

"He's good." Mom shot me a wide-eyed expression.

"He is. So why the surprise?"

"It was Lila's idea." Mom gave Lila a weak smile. She thought of her as a third daughter. Always had. "Grandma hasn't seen the cabin since you moved in. I told her you had it decorated differently and that she'd love it. So Graham sent us up here on his jet. Took less than thirty minutes."

I felt honored to live in the log cabin my grandfather built. It meant Katie would get everything else from their estate when Grandma died. But I was okay with that.

Grandma nodded. "I do love it, sweetie. You've made it your own. And grandpa would be so proud of all the chopped wood you have piled outside."

"I can't take credit. It's all Ronin."

"What's all me?" Ronin made his appearance in faded ripped jeans, a white tee, and messy wet hair. "Hi, Mrs. Taylor." He leaned over the back of the sofa and dropped a kiss on Mom's head.

Mom reached up and patted his cheek. "Good morning, Ronin. You have a beautiful voice."

He chuckled while shifting a few inches to my grandma and kissing her head too. "Thank you. Good morning, Mrs. Burns."

"Good morning, sweetie." Grandma reached up and patted his wet head.

I stood so he could sit in the recliner. He grabbed my waist and pulled me onto his lap as he plopped into the chair.

"They were talking about your wood, Ronin." Lila smirked from around her spoon.

"Yes. Benedict would've been proud of all your wood." Grandma nodded.

I bit back my grin. "Ronin is good with wood. And he definitely has a lot of it."

Lila choked on her spoon.

Ronin shifted me on his lap, so I could feel his wood. "I do my best. Evelyn likes it hot, so that requires lots of wood."

I loved how my mom and grandma were oblivious to the innuendos of the conversation while Lila looked ready to pee her pants in the kitchen. My lips hurt from biting them so hard.

"Your grandfather was the same way. He used to pack so much wood. But sometimes he'd forget to cover it, and it would get wet. Of course it was always my fault. He'd make up some reason why I distracted him; therefore, it was my fault the wood didn't get covered and ended up wet."

"I can see that," Ronin said like his mind wasn't just as far down the gutter as Lila's and mine. "It's quite easy to get distracted and forget to cover the wood. If I'm honest, my wood has been wet quite often."

"And it matters if you're burning softwood versus hardwood," Mom added.

This conversation wasn't happening. Was it? How the

hell did we let it get so far? My stomach ached from containing my laughter.

"It really does." Ronin nodded.

Lila snorted, turning toward the sink and running water in the oatmeal pan.

"We like to use hardwood. Right, Evie?" Ronin squeezed my leg.

I hummed my agreement, rubbing one of my eyes like I had something in it. "Uh-huh."

"There's a lot of softwood in these parts. It never lasts as long." Grandma shook her head.

"Speaking of wood." Ronin lifted me off his lap and stood. "I should go outside and get some."

"Do you need help?" I asked, rubbing my mouth to hide my grin.

"Nah ... you have company. Besides, you helped me get wood earlier. And I can't fully express how much I appreciated it. I'll handle it this time."

"If my hands weren't arthritic and my back so fragile, I'd help you get wood, Ronin," Grandma added.

I can't even ...

Faking a cough, I held up my finger and ran to the bathroom.

Before I got the door shut, Ronin said, "That's kind of you, Mrs. Burns, but I'll handle the wood by myself."

Lila slipped into the bathroom with me and shut the door.

"Oh my god," she whispered, tears in her eyes and a hand over her mouth.

We leaned into each other to keep from falling over as

our bodies shook with laughter. It took me back to grade school and the days we'd lose control with giggle fits over something like seeing the outline of a guy's penis if his jeans were too tight.

All those years later, we still found humor in the mysterious male appendage.

"Y-your gr-grandma …" Lila cried.

I nodded, keeping my hand over my mouth.

After another minute of working the silliness out of our systems, Lila dried her eyes. Her smile faded into a different kind of smile. A forced smile. The one that was unbelievable because her eyebrows frowned.

"What?" I sighed softly while blotting my eyes with a tissue.

"Your mom told me something. That's really why we're here."

"What?"

"We're here so you can digest it and help her tell your dad."

"Digest what?" I leaned my backside against the vanity and crossed my arms over my chest.

Lila peeled one arm away from my chest. Taking my hand, she opened the bathroom door, and I let her lead me into the living room.

Mom and Grandma studied me and Lila. Their expressions faded into recognition as something silent passed between them and my best friend.

A look.

What is going on?

"Come sit, Evie." Mom scooted to the side to make

room on the sofa between her and Grandma.

Lila released my hand and sat in the recliner. The air in the room thickened, making it hard to breathe.

"Evie …" Mom took my hand and squeezed it while Grandma rested her hand on my leg. "I have breast cancer."

The room fell silent for a few seconds. I wanted Ronin to come back inside so we could talk about wood. Breast cancer wasn't funny.

Time continued to tick along while I took a moment, several moments.

Death.

No amount of optimism obscured that thought. Cancer equaled death. It was what first went through any person's mind when cancer was mentioned—like the words plane crash and mass casualties.

Only … no one says it. We find better words. There are better words than death. Like … hope.

Perspective showed up next to stick its ugly tongue out at me. Fucking perspective. I couldn't believe I had an emotional meltdown over something as immature and frivolous as Vanessa and karaoke. That wasn't real life. It was just a stupid distraction from the important stuff like Ronin falling in love with me and my mom having cancer. I couldn't stop internally berating myself. I stood in a bar, seething with jealousy, while my mom dealt with her mortality.

"Okay …" I replied, forcing courage into my voice. "So what's the plan?"

I was a scientist. I liked plans.

When my dad was diagnosed with polycystic kidney disease, I didn't take the time to ask why. The why didn't matter at that point. The only thing that mattered was the plan. We needed a plan.

"Partial mastectomy. Radiation. Hormone therapy," Mom said with her shoulders back, chin up.

I glanced at Lila.

She was my rock, and my mom knew it. That was why she told Lila before me. Grandma? Well, she was everyone's rock.

"We've got this." Lila tipped her chin up too, wearing her confidence like a badge of honor.

"We've got this," I repeated.

Mom squeezed my hand again.

"You need to tell your father," Grandma said, patting my leg.

Mom cleared her throat. I could *feel* the lump of emotion strangling her. "You will stay strong for him. He will see through me. And it's not because I'm weak or even overly worried about the possible outcome. I just know this will hit him really hard. That's why I need you to tell him, and I'll be ready with my brave face."

She needed me to tell Dad because my father was married to another woman before he met Mom. He was nineteen, and she was eighteen. Their young marriage lasted three years because she died of cancer.

To that day, he couldn't even say the word cancer.

"I'll tell him." I maintained a stoic face and pushed that same bravery into my voice—steady and sure. Later, I would take five minutes for myself to let my fears have a voice, have their moment of raw emotion. "Does Katie know?"

My sister didn't have a brave face. Katie was transparent with every emotion. She would jump to the conclusion of death in the most verbal way possible. No elephants were allowed in the room with her. Nope. Katie always put all her cards on the table, and she expected the people in her life to do the same.

"No. One step at a time. You tell Dad. Then Dad will tell Katie." Mom slapped her hands on her legs like a judge using a gavel to punctuate her ruling. "She is and always has been a 'daddy's girl.' The truth begins and ends with him in her eyes. He is her voice of reason. It has to come from him."

Her kidney resided in his body, but they had a special bond before that. As much as I loved my father, I held a stronger bond with my mom. Katie saved Dad's life. Could I save my mom's life?

"You're not dying." While I pondered all the questions, I could be resolute in my statements, just like my mom. And impulsive.

Jeez … I didn't even mean to say it aloud. It was cry or fight the grim reality.

She. Will. Not. Die.

"Who said anything about dying?" Grandma scoffed. "There's an order. No one in this room goes before me."

"Except me …" Lila stood and pointed to the front door. "And by go, I mean I'm going to check on the lumberjack and give you ladies some time alone." She winked at me. It was her you've-got-this wink. We

118

dragged each other through the trenches, held each other up. That was my relationship with Lila.

Had been.

Was then.

Always would be.

CHAPTER EIGHT

Ronín

"**Y**OU'RE NOT *GETTING wood*?" Lila asked, closing the squeaky door behind her. I shot her a quick glance before returning my attention to the view of the Rockies from one of the wooden rocking chairs on Evelyn's porch.

"No." I smirked. "I did that this morning."

Lila grunted, easing into the chair beside me, zipping her coat up to her nose. "I'm aware."

"That's why the front door wasn't locked. Before Evie woke, I came out here to chop firewood. I didn't think to lock the door again. What were the chances of you *flying* up here on a Saturday morning unannounced?"

"About as good as the chances of Madeline being diagnosed with breast cancer."

I turned, inspecting Lila through narrowed eyes.

She focused on the view, but I didn't miss the tears in her eyes. "She's my mom too. When my own parents died, Evie's parents filled that void. I mean … they've always treated me like a daughter, even before my parents died, as did mine with Evie. Madeline and Corey are going to walk me down the aisle when I get married. They are my family. I don't have siblings, and I'm not close with the rest of my living relatives."

I knew all of this from Evelyn, but I listened as if I didn't know any of it.

Lila blew out a slow breath. "Madeline told me last night. I insisted we tell Evie right away—for somewhat selfish reasons really. I needed to share the burden of pain. I needed my friend. My sister."

"I'm sorry."

Lila slid her gaze in my direction, giving me a sad smile. "Thank you. I'm so glad Evie has you. She's going to need you a lot over these upcoming months. I have to move forward with the wedding. Graham will make sure she gets to Denver as quickly and as often as possible. However, Evie handles these situations by grasping for any control she can find, which means she will pour herself into work. This cabin will be spotless all the time. Her calendar will become an obsession. She'll know the times and dates of Madeline's appointments. Her parents will get a dozen calls a day. They will surrender every tiny detail of what they're doing, right down to the last time they took a shit."

I chuckled and so did Lila.

"You do your thing. I've got Evelyn. My parents are coming tomorrow. They'll be here for several months. My mom is great at managing any crisis, so she'll jump right in and be whatever Evelyn needs her to be while I'm working."

Lila reached her hand toward the arm of my chair,

resting it on mine. "Thank you."

Rocking in my chair, I returned my gaze to the view. The pain. So much pain waited for Evelyn, no matter what happened to her mom. I knew about pain, and there was nothing I wanted more than to take the pain and bear it for her.

"Oh ... how did skiing go yesterday? She was having serious anxiety over it at the dress fitting."

I grinned. "It went well."

"She's terrible. Right? The worst skier in the world."

I coughed a laugh. "Yes, she's pretty bad, but I don't care. I swear to god her willingness to try, *for me,* put her on this unreachable pedestal in my eyes. She's fucking amazing."

"You love her."

I nodded.

"You should tell her, if you haven't already."

"She knows."

"Are you sure?"

It's too big for words now. Don't belittle it with a four-letter word. It's too intangible. Too undefinable. Don't ever tell me what you can show me.

"Positive."

AN HOUR LATER, Lila, Evelyn's grandma, and mom made their way back to Denver. Evelyn dove into washing the dishes from breakfast without saying a word to me. I dried the dishes and put them away. Next, she grabbed the bucket of cleaning supplies and marched into the bathroom.

Lila knew her friend quite well.

However, I still had things to learn about this woman who had taken my heart like said heart knew it belonged to her long before we met.

Traveling. Skiing. Caring for the injured.

Those were the things that occupied my time, motivated me, and fulfilled my needs. Love at first sight, destiny, or any fictional shit like that kept a safe distance from my existence. Then one day ... Evelyn literally walked into my life, took a seat, and gave me this grin that I felt. Yes ... I felt her grin. And while I had a gift—a curse really—for feeling things, a grin was not my usual superhuman sensation. I knew ... I just knew I was in trouble—all from a grin.

"What can I do to help you?" I stood at the threshold to the bathroom, leaning my shoulder against it, with my hands tucked into the front pockets of my jeans.

Evelyn cleaned the mirror. "Don't be silly. You have your own place. I don't expect you to help me clean mine."

"Your mom is having surgery in a week."

Evelyn stopped her motions. Surely, she assumed Lila told me.

"What can I do for *you*?"

"I'm good." She continued wiping the mirror.

"What can I do for *you*?"

"Nothing. I'm good." Her words came out thick with emotion.

I pressed myself to the back of her, sliding one hand around her waist while my other hand grabbed her wrist to stop her from cleaning the mirror. I brought that hand to her chest, hugging her. "What can I do for *you*?"

Her teary-eyed gaze looked up at me in the mirror, bottom lip quivering. "Hold me," her words broke as the tears made their way down her face.

I turned her toward me, wrapping her in my arms. There was nothing I wouldn't do for this woman. Yet, the one thing that tore her apart was beyond my control.

Nothing in a medical kit could fix it. No amount of education would find a solution. Why was it when the important people in our lives needed us the most, that was when our love felt the most empty—most helpless?

I gave her my arms. They couldn't fix anything, but maybe they'd hold her together. I was certain they were made to do exactly that. She didn't want me to say the words, but I thought them. They screamed in my head and thumped in my chest; they whispered from my lungs with every breath.

I love you. I love you. I love you.

She sobbed.

I stroked her hair.

I held her up when her legs gave out.

I carried her to the sofa and let her cling to me while she worked out a bit of reality. There was so much I knew about reality and life. From a very young age, I learned about breaths, fragility, and beating impossible odds.

When her tears ran dry, she eased her grip on my shirt and glanced up at me. "Thank you."

I returned a sad smile.

"You didn't tell me it's going to be okay." She sniffled, wiping her cheeks.

"I don't know that it *is* going to be okay."

"It has to be."

I stared at her a few seconds, contemplating my next words. When I couldn't find the right ones, I kissed her forehead.

"I should finish cleaning." She tried to climb off my lap, but I pulled her back to me, wrapping my arms around her waist, her back to my chest.

Resting my chin on her shoulder, I slanted my head to kiss her neck. "Earlier, in bed …"

"Don't say it." She leaned her head into mine.

"I'm not." I chuckled. "But would it really be so bad?"

"Save it for a rainy day."

"A rainy day?"

"Yes. When there's nothing to say because it's all been said a million times before … but you have to say something."

"Then let's go get coffee."

She turned toward me. "We have coffee here."

"True. But I like going to Grinds with you, sitting across from you at one of those tiny round tables, staring at each other through the steam of our coffees. I like the shy but flirty smile you give me. It reminds me of the day we met in Vancouver. It's when I know we're thinking those words we don't actually say."

The corners of her mouth turned up a fraction. Yeah,

she fucking loved me too, and she knew. She knew it a long time ago.

I continued, "I like the soft jazz music, background chatter, and the whoosh of steam as they froth the milk. It all feels like this perfect Evelyn bubble. When I reach across the table and touch your hand, your cheeks turn pink and it does all kinds of insane things to me. But I can't act on impulse when we're there, so it's this beautiful, torturous foreplay."

Evelyn grinned, nodding slowly. "I love going for coffee with you too. I get to stare at you and pinch myself because I can't believe you found your way to me ... to my life. And I can't believe you just said all of that like you were reading my mind. That day in Vancouver, it felt like so much more than a stop along my way. It felt like I had arrived." She glanced over her shoulder.

I nipped at her lower lip. "That's the thing about you, Evie ... I had no idea I was waiting for someone until you arrived."

"Ronin Alexander, are you a romantic? A chance meeting? A look? A *feeling*?" She turned her body, straddling my lap and interlacing her fingers behind my neck.

My lips twisted. "Hmm ... I'm not sure yet."

She kissed the corner of my mouth and whispered, "You are *such* a romantic."

CHAPTER NINE

Evelyn

"**H**EY!" RONIN WIPED his hands on a dishtowel and turned down the heat on my stove. "I got someone to cover for me today, so I could clean your house, grocery shop, and get dinner started. My parents arrived a few hours ago. They're unpacking at the Gilberts' house, and then they're coming for dinner." He pulled me in for a hug. "How did it go with your dad?"

Nuzzling my nose into his neck that smelled of the woodsy soap from my shop, I grunted a laugh. "He already knew. My mom couldn't keep it from him. I guess he made some comment about how beautiful she is, and all she could think about was the disfigurement she might have after surgery. And the floodgates opened ... she told him everything. However, he's doing surprisingly well. Very optimistic, at least that's the face he's giving us. Graham is flying them out to California tomorrow to tell Katie. I have all of my mom's upcoming appointments put into my calendar, and I talked with Sophie about covering for me more often since I'll be in Denver quite a bit."

He pressed a slow kiss to my lips. I needed it. I needed it to calm my racing mind. Mom's treatment was a marathon, not a sprint.

Ronin pulled back, brushing my hair from my face. "Today, you did your part."

I lifted one shoulder. "I think so."

"Tonight, you meet my parents. They will love you. My mom will talk a lot about grandchildren. You just have to ignore her."

I bit my lower lip for a few seconds. "What if I don't want to ignore her?" Tipping my chin up, I met his gaze.

Ronin inspected me ... maybe for a glimpse of humor or a spark of honesty. "I want one boy and one girl," he said. "Two years apart. The boy first, so he can be protective of his sister."

That was our truth.

We had known—a silent certainty—that there was something special between us from the day we met in Vancouver. Attempting to be intelligent and sane, we hadn't labeled that silent certainty as anything like fate or destiny. Not love at first sight. Not perfect timing.

For me, I felt like we were a fact—the sky was blue, water was wet, the wind blew. Ronin and Evelyn just *were*.

"I have a sister and you have a brother, but you think we can manage one of each?" I chuckled.

"Absolutely." He flashed me that irresistible smile.

I believed him.

A much-needed grin took over my face. Ronin had a

way of doing that. Grins on my face. Butterflies in my tummy. Love in my heart. "I'm good with that."

"Good. Then dinner will go well tonight."

I TOLD MYSELF I wasn't nervous about meeting Victor and Ling Alexander, but I lied.

"How important is it that your parents like me? If they don't, will you leave me?" I kept watch out the window, waiting for their arrival.

"They're going to love you."

"Of course they are, but just play along with me for shits and giggles. What *if* they don't like me? Are we over?"

"Yes," he said, adding wood to the stove.

I turned, jaw unhinged, eyes wide. "You can't be serious?"

Ronin closed the stove door. "No." He chuckled. "I'm not serious."

"Every lie is actually a truth in a parallel universe."

"You believe in parallel universes?" He brushed wood dust from his hands and jeans.

"I'm a scientist, so a lot of possibilities cross my mind. However, if I believed a parallel universe existed for the alternatives to *all* our decisions and lies, then it wouldn't be possible. I mean … there are potentially a lot of parallel universes, but not a quantity as large as the infinite choices we make and lies we tell every day."

"I don't know whether to be intimidated or turned on

right now." He slid his hands around my waist.

"Both would please me immensely." I kissed his neck, taking a deep inhale. "You smell really good."

"I smell like your soaps."

"Yes, but they smell even better on you."

"Evie, are you trying to seduce me seconds before my parents are scheduled to arrive?"

"No. I'm just sniffing you." I grinned, dragging my nose and lips down his neck to the exposed area of his chest where the top buttons of his shirt were undone.

"Sniffing leads to fucking."

I giggled. "No. It doesn't."

"Yes. It does. But my parents are here, so I'll wait until later to show you the connection between the two."

"Oh …" I whipped around as my heart exploded into a sprint. "They're here. Okay. I've got this. They will like me. Right? Dear god, what if they don't?"

"So much at stake, baby. My fingers are crossed on this one." He nuzzled his face into my neck as I stood at the door, ready to throw it open the second I heard their footsteps on the porch. "Here they come …" I held my breath and opened the door, shoving Ronin in their direction so I didn't have to make a self-introduction.

"There's our boy." Ronin's mom hugged him as I remained statuesque with a petrified smile pinned to my face.

"Hey, how was your trip?" After he released his mom, he hugged his dad.

Ronin got his height from his dad because his mom was maybe five-two with heels, a little toothpick with short black and gray hair and an exuberant smile. A Ronin smile.

I couldn't help staring at them, piecing Ronin together from their distinct traits. His dad had a thick beard that was mostly gray and neatly trimmed, perfectly accenting his strong jaw (like Ronin's) and full head of hair, a mix of gray and brown.

"Mom, Dad ... I'd like you to meet Evelyn. Evie, these are my parents, Victor and Ling."

"So nice to meet you. Please ... don't stand outside. Come in." I opened the door wider.

"Such a pleasure to finally meet you, Evelyn." Ling came in for a hug. A big, firm hug. "Ronin talks about you nonstop. We knew we were going to experience something special meeting you."

Special? How was I supposed to live up to those expectations? Ronin made dinner, cleaned my house, and excelled at normal conversation that didn't involve saponification or parallel universes. He skied and sang karaoke. And he was one of those really talented people who could tie a cherry stem with his tongue. He could do a lot of talented things with his tongue.

Again ... soap girl here.

They were in for a real treat. That was for sure. On the flip side, he talked about me "nonstop," and that made *me* feel quite special at the moment.

Victor leaned down, pressing his cheek to mine for the customary French air kiss greeting.

Muah. Muah.

"Such a pleasure." He stood tall again, eyeing me with

contentment.

"The pleasure is all mine. Please let me take your coats, and then make yourselves at home."

We sipped wine by the fire. Victor and Ling sat on the sofa, close together with his arm around her, while Ronin guided me to sit on his lap in the recliner. It was intimate and felt like him telling his parents a lot about us without saying anything. I knew this because their faces beamed in a way that was in fact *special*.

Ling and Victor shared the details of their most recent trip. They lived the life I dreamed of living—retiring with a man I loved, traveling the world, but having children to anchor us in life. Ronin talked about *me*. My chemist skills. My lovely store. My friends who were getting married. The cabin that my grandfather built for my grandmother.

"When is the wedding?" Ling asked.

Children. Ronin warned me she'd want to talk about grandchildren. I wasn't prepared for the wedding conversation. We used to joke about it, but that hadn't happened for some time.

"He hasn't proposed. *Not* that I'm waiting or expecting him to propose. We've only known each other for three months."

Only.

Who was I kidding? It felt like forever.

I knew since the first day we met that I wanted to marry him, but they didn't need to know that. Or did they? That would have made them happy ... right? What about Ronin? That was a lot of pressure.

"But if he proposed—" I tried to continue.

"Evelyn ..." Ling smiled. "I was referring to your friends' wedding."

"Oh my gosh." I covered my face with my hands and shook my head. "Wow! I just made things awkward."

"February fifteenth." Ronin saved me with the correct answer, but it was too late. Everyone in the room knew what my thoughts were on him proposing to me ... eventually.

"Lila wanted a summer wedding." I jumped in with the details, a diversion from my miscue. "Her soon-to-be mother-in-law wanted a date that didn't interfere with *her* complex social calendar. Don't get me wrong, I like Helene under controlled situations, but she stole this wedding from my best friend—both of my best friends."

"Both of your best friends?" Ling's head canted to the side.

"Yes. Lila has been my best friend since ... well, forever. We met her fiancé, Graham, in college." I grinned. "Lila couldn't stand Graham in college, but I bonded with him over sports. We'd bet on sports, watch all the games, and call each other to discuss players, recruits, and trades. We still do. Lila has no interest in sports. Had I not stayed friends with Graham all these years, they wouldn't be together. Graham grew up while Lila traveled after college. I guess timing is everything."

"You have a lot invested in this relationship." Victor raised his brows.

"I suppose I do. When they fight, I hate taking sides."

"But you always take Lila's side." Ronin kissed my

shoulder.

"I do. Even when she's wrong. Graham knows I will always choose her. He also knows I'll always be his advocate, working hard to make peace between them. Graham and his family have done so much for me and my family over the years. They paid for a lot of my dad's medical treatment when his kidneys started to fail. They made sure my parents didn't lose their home during that time. And two years ago, when the landlord of my building decided to not renew my lease because he wanted to tear down the building to put up a hotel, Graham's family bought the building just so I could keep my shop. A terrible financial decision for them, but Graham always has my back."

"I can't wait to see your shop." Ling smiled.

Ronin cleared his throat. "Don't expect her to show you how she makes her products. There are too many proprietary secrets."

"Not true." I glanced back, giving Ronin a grin that was also a scowl. He knew the reason he'd never seen me make a full batch of soap was because he was responsible for too many ruined batches.

My lover thought there was time for sex between pouring layers of soap.

There wasn't.

So ... I banned him from my lab.

I smiled, batting my eyelashes to soften the blow about their child. "Your son touches too many things in my lab. However, I would love to show you my shop and how I make my products."

"Let's eat." Ronin lifted me from his lap, whispering in my ear, "I touch *you* in your lab."

I grinned, lifting my hand to his head and sliding my fingers through his hair as he nipped at my ear. His parents eyed us, and their expressions said it all. They liked what they saw. I passed the test. It would have crushed me to have my parents love Ronin so much and then feel any less adoration toward me from his parents.

We ate.

We laughed.

I fell deeper in love with Ronin by falling in love with his parents. He fit into my life. I fit into his life.

He never mentioned my mother's cancer diagnosis, and I appreciated him leaving that to me. It was still raw. When I dwelled on it, tears rushed to the surface. However, it was a chance I took as we settled back into the living room to enjoy hot drinks by the fire after dinner.

"Listen ... I want to let you know that my mother was recently diagnosed with breast cancer."

Concern etched Ling's and Victor's faces.

Forcing a smile, I took a deep breath. "It will be fine. My mother is very strong, both physically and mentally. However, my time will be divided in the coming months between her, my shop, and the wedding. If you could indulge Ronin by skiing with him, that would be fantastic. I fear my schedule won't allow much time on the slopes."

"Oh ..." Victor nodded. "That can be arranged. Now his text makes sense."

"His text?" I canted my head.

"It's late …" Ronin tried to stand, but I leaned back into his chest as we shared the recliner, attempting to pin him to it with my weight.

Victor's gaze slid to Ronin for a second.

"Don't look at him." I moved my head to block the line of sight between the two men.

Victor eyed Ling. "He asked us to refrain from suggesting you go skiing with us. I assumed it was because you weren't a skier, which surprised me since you live in Aspen. I couldn't imagine Ronin dating someone who didn't ski. Now I realize it's because of your mom." His eyes narrowed. "Correct?"

I slid off Ronin's lap and stood between the sofa and the recliner, next to the coffee table. Victor and Ling gave me their attention, but after a few seconds, confusion floated across their faces. Since … I didn't say anything.

What was there to say?

I opened my mouth to defend myself, but no one was attacking me. Why get defensive?

That insanely-jealous-woman-at-the-bar-with-karaoke-Vanessa wasn't me. Well, she was me. She was me before I knew for sure that Ronin loved me. But right then, in front of his parents, I knew. Vanessa wasn't my competition. I'd won.

He loved me.

This is me. Take it or leave it.

I smiled, but before I could say my truth, Ronin's hand cuffed my wrist as he stood and turned me toward him, putting my back to his parents. "Evelyn is a horrific skier, but she tries." He slid his hands along my neck to keep me focused on him. "It doesn't matter. She's going to marry me. She said as much the day we met."

It took me three weeks to learn how to ride a bike, while my friends did it in three minutes. However, it took less than a second to fall in love with this man. I knew this because I couldn't remember the moment I fell for him which meant ... I had loved him forever. Probably in a parallel universe.

Déjà vu. Destiny. Kismet. Serendipity.

They were all just fancy names for justifying fate when in actuality *we had* met before. We fell in love in a different world. I got to live more than one life with this man. That was some cool shit. And I believed that cool shit with complete conviction.

"Roe ..." I whispered. Even if I could play in my head the mind-numbing explanation that was us, the fact that he didn't analyze us, where we met, how quickly we fell in love, and the improbable sanity of it all ... was enough to drive a lump into my throat.

He invited me into his life ... with witnesses. It didn't get any more real than that.

He smiled.

That was it. Ronin smiled at me. One look was all it took. One look was all it ever took. We were so much greater than any words.

"Evelyn's going to marry me. Maybe not until her mom is better. Maybe not until Lila and Graham are married. But she's going to marry me. She's going to have my babies."

How did he make it so public and incredibly intimate

at the same time?

"Right, Evie?" he whispered.

An unexplainable warmth wrapped around my body.

"Probably." I smiled.

"Probably ..." he echoed just before kissing me.

CHAPTER TEN

C ANCER.

The holidays.

Wedding mania.

Thanks to Ronin and his parents, I remained in one piece with Christmas a week away and the wedding just on the other side of the new year. Guilt plagued me. I just wanted the wedding to be done.

Over.

Photos and memories tucked away for anniversaries and sharing with their children.

Terrible. Just terrible of me.

My best friends' big day felt like an obstacle, not a joyous event. I couldn't help it. My mom had been so sick from the chemo, even with antiemetic medications. It wore on my dad to see her hit the extreme lows. It was painful to witness. We knew he replayed in his mind the events that led to the death of his first love. Jumping from chemo vomiting to bridesmaids' luncheons was almost too much to balance.

"Only one of your teams won."

I smirked, wiping down the counters to my lab as a

familiar voice bragged behind me. "I've been distracted."

"Nope. You don't get to play the cancer card. Only your mom can play that card."

Rolling my eyes, I turned toward Graham. He was in Aspen to do a little playing of his own on the slopes, hence the absence of his tailored suit. Casual Graham still dressed in obnoxiously expensive clothes, but they at least reminded me of the guy I knew in college—dark jeans and a white tee, which probably cost more than I made at my shop on any given day, and a gray button-down under his unzipped black ski jacket and white scarf.

His hair danced out of control like he ran short on gel. I always liked messy-haired Graham, a rare sighting. Apparently, future political candidates required a perceived perfection right down to the hair on their heads.

"Thank you." I had a million feisty comebacks to give him about my poor performance on picking winning teams that year and my "playing the cancer card." However, I didn't speak them because Graham did what he'd always done—showed up for me in the biggest way imaginable.

Paying for medical bills before they ever reached my parents' mailbox.

Arranging my transportation via private jet from Denver to Aspen several times a week.

And this … talking about sports when it was the last thing on my mind, but knowing it was what I needed.

I dropped the rag while dissolving the distance between us. My arms slid under his jacket and around his warm torso, my cheek finding the familiar comfort of his chest.

"Thank you," I repeated on a long sigh. "Thank you for being my favorite Graham Cracker."

"How's she doing?" He returned the embrace and kissed the top of my head.

"She hates the chemo. Wants to just stop it, but she knows it's her best chance at beating this. And she'd rather deal with the physical pain than let my dad think for one second that she's giving up." I stepped back, finding a small smile to give Graham as I leaned against the counter with my hands resting on the edge of it. "How's Lila? I left a message with her earlier, but I haven't heard back from her."

Graham twisted his lips and scratched his chin, brow a bit furrowed. "Hmm ... I wouldn't know. She was supposed to go to lunch with my mom and Aunt Charlotte, but she canceled because of a business meeting."

I couldn't read his expression, so I cocked my head and crossed my arms over my chest. "Are you bothered by that?"

He chewed on the inside of his cheek for a few seconds. "I let it slide today."

"W-what?" I coughed on a laugh. "Let it slide?"

"We're not married yet. She should have rescheduled the meeting, so she didn't leave my mom and Charlotte waiting for her at the tea room."

"Well, I'm sure that means she was running too late to make it at all. And I'm sure she felt bad. But Lila is driven. She's good at her job. You said that's one of the reasons you fell in love with her. It doesn't make sense that you're acting like she will have to give that up when you get married."

"I'm not saying she'll have to give it up. It just won't be able to be her priority. Today, she made it her priority. When we're married … she'll have to reschedule meetings instead of missing luncheons with important people."

"It was your mom and aunt. I'm not implying they're not important, but—"

"Then what the fuck are you implying?"

Whoa!

My jaw hung in the air for a few moments. What was up with him? We used to laugh at his mom and Aunt Charlotte, poking fun at their "rough lives" of luncheons and how often they scolded grounds keepers for cutting the hedge shrubs a half inch too short. Graham said he would take his place in the family business, but never be cut-throat like his dad. And he wanted to marry Lila *because* she wasn't a lunch-at-the-tea-room kind of girl.

Comebacks lined up on the tip of my tongue, each one fighting to be heard first. I didn't let them speak. The Porters owned me and my family. Even if they never said the actual words, I knew the score.

The Taylors: nothing. The Porters: everything.

"I'm implying that Lila is under a lot of stress, and since you haven't spoken directly with her, maybe you should give her the benefit of the doubt. She loves your mom and Aunt Charlotte."

Truth.

Lila made a shocking transformation—hating all the Porters and everything they stood for when we were in college, to embracing their family because she fell in love with Graham. She was a better woman than I was. If they hadn't owned my family, I would not have felt the need to have lunch with his mom and aunt just because Graham and I were friends. Lucky for me ... Ronin's mom, Ling, was amazing, and I loved having lunch with her any day.

"Sorry." Graham exhaled, dropping his gaze to his feet. "I didn't mean to snap at you. Maybe I'm feeling my own wedding stress too."

"Go home. Take Lila to dinner. Remember all the reasons you begged me to make her give you a chance." Boy oh boy ... did he ever beg—promises of treating her like royalty, a priceless piece of art, making it his life's goal to make sure she was *always* happy. Of course, all of this came after I told him she would never change her mind about him, no matter how many good words I put in on his behalf. My lack of confidence in his wooing capabilities seemed to feed his cause.

However, even if I didn't say it to his financially generous face, I had every reason to be mad at him for treating Lila like a property that he was on the verge of purchasing. Newsflash, women didn't have to wear pantyhose anymore or fight for their right to vote. We sure as hell didn't have to give up our careers just because a guy put a ring on our finger. I didn't care if he ran for *president*. His life and career would never be more important than hers.

He straightened his scarf. "I didn't *beg* you. I didn't need your help."

I gasped, head jerking back. He knew that was bull-shit.

Graham waved his hand as if to avert my reaction or attack I started to mount in my head.

"Anyway ... she did buy some new lingerie. I suppose dinner would be a fair trade."

I laced my fingers behind my neck to keep from wrapping them around his neck. "Screw you, Graham Porter. I'm taking my friend back. If dinner requires her to dress in silk and spread her legs for you, then you don't deserve her. Go buy yourself a whore for the night."

"Jesus, Evelyn ... I'm kidding." He held up his hands in surrender.

Rubbing my lips together, I shrugged. "So am I."

"Really?" He narrowed his eyes. "Because it didn't sound like you were kidding."

"Were *you* kidding, Graham? Really?"

There it was ... the crux of our friendship. He was marrying my best friend, and my instinct to protect her was fierce. He begged me for help, whether he cared to admit it or not. So I begged Lila to give him a chance. And now they were getting married. I felt like their happiness would always fall back on me, the glue that stuck them together. Unfortunately, I felt stuck in the middle, wondering if I messed up.

He slid on his gloves and smirked. "Of course, I'm kidding. I don't ask her to spread her legs. I usually just bend her over a chair."

No. No. NO! He did not say that.

Honestly ... I had no comeback to that, but I hoped I

could get the awful image it evoked to vanish from my head and never return.

"I didn't come here to talk about Lila."

I returned to my cleaning tasks. "I can't talk sports. My mind isn't there right now."

"Ronin saved a man's life today."

"What?" I glanced over my shoulder, not sure I heard him correctly.

"We were waiting for a table at the lodge. An older guy behind us collapsed. Stopped breathing. Ronin did CPR until the ambulance arrived. I think he saved the guy."

"He's a paramedic."

Graham gave me an eye roll. "I know. It was just weird to see him in action. He didn't hesitate. But then he couldn't stay for lunch. Said he didn't feel well. Have you heard from him? He didn't exactly look well either."

"No ... I haven't." I plucked my phone from the opposite counter. No missed calls. No texts from Ronin.

"I'm sure he's fine. Probably just the effects of the adrenaline. I just thought I'd mention it before heading back to Denver. And in spite of what you think, I also just wanted to say hi to my best friend."

My head inched side to side. "I'm not your best friend. Heath, Eric, Wade ... they're your best buds. I'm just your cupid."

"Heath, Eric, and Wade are functional idiots. *You* are my best friend. And it has nothing to do with Lila. We were friends before Lila would even look at me, and we will be friends when both Lila and Ronin leave us for better human beings."

"Fuck you." I chuckled as he pulled me in for one last hug.

"I'm nearly married. Our fucking days are over, Evie. Sorry."

I giggled. Somehow, we made it. After the epic mistake of thinking we could be more than friends, we managed to persevere. The fact that we immediately joked about it, like the "oops" that it was, was what held our friendship together. And maybe ... just maybe our drunken intimacy actually cemented our friendship forever. We knew every detail about each other. No secrets. All had been bared.

CHAPTER ELEVEN

AFTER SEVERAL FAILED attempts at contacting Ronin, I skipped out early and left Sophie to close up shop. When I arrived home, Ronin's Outback wasn't parked in the drive, so I headed straight to his place.

"Roe?" I whispered, tiptoeing into his bedroom. He rarely slept at his place. Yet, there he was in the dark, curled into a fetal position on the mattress, still on the floor.

"Go home, babe. I don't want you to get sick," he said in a strained voice.

"I want to help." I sat on the edge of the mattress, the light from the hallway giving me a slight glimpse of his twisted face.

"You can't." His hand, pressed flat to his chest, curled into a fist as he swallowed hard. Sweat beaded along his brow while his shallow breaths chased one another. "Please ... please go, Evie. AHHH!"

I jumped as his hands clawed at his scalp and his back arched. My heart pummeled my ribcage, and tears burned my eyes. It wasn't right. It wasn't a normal pain, even for some virus or other bug he might have picked up.

"Roe ..." The tears fell fast and hard as my hand hovered over his arm, too afraid to touch him and cause him anymore pain as his body thrashed. "Roe, you're scaring me. I ... I don't know what to do. What hurts? T-tell me w-what to do!"

He didn't.

All he could do was flail in pain. I didn't know that side to Ronin. He was my rock—more than a rock. He was an unmovable mountain. But ... my mountain crumbled right in front of me.

"Ronin, stop! Tell me what to do!"

"Fuck!" He rolled away from me.

I grabbed my phone and called 9-1-1.

"9-1-1. What is your emergency?"

"Send an ambulance! M-my boyfriend is in terrible p-pain, and I don't know what to do."

I knew she was asking me questions, but I couldn't hear her past the pounding of my heart screaming at me, telling me to help him.

I muttered a few barely coherent replies as the room spun.

Yes, he was breathing.

No, he wasn't responding to me.

Evie.

Evie.

Evie ...

Each drumming beat said my name. Do something! But what?

They were on their way. The door was unlocked. I dropped my phone and kneeled on the bed, stroking his hair as he moaned like a tortured animal.

"Shh … they're coming. Just hold on … they're coming." I didn't think he heard me, but I said the words anyway. I repeated myself again and again, trying so hard to convince my heart to calm down. He would be fine. He *had* to be fine. I *arrived* that day in Vancouver.

A destiny.

Fate in perfect form.

We were meant to meet that day, and not for him to leave me. He couldn't leave me. I think I'd known for months just how vulnerable my heart was to my feelings for Ronin. Sometimes we knew things that we never acknowledge until it was pulled—ripped—from inside of us. If I lost him, there would never be enough stitches to put me back together.

The door creaked open. Voices sounded. Footsteps pounded closer.

I held my breath. The slightest movement threatened to shatter my existence.

My tears dried while I unblinkingly stared at Ronin. They tried to ask him questions. Someone said something to me. I attempted a nod, but I couldn't. I couldn't move until they fixed him—fixed him and gave him back to me. That was their job, right?

My job was to love him like no one had ever loved him before. I would do my job, but they had to do theirs first.

Him.

I wanted to spend the rest of my life loving him. Not a memory.

Retrieving my phone from the floor, I followed them out of the condo and called his parents before driving to the hospital.

Victor and Ling made it there before me because I had another breakdown in the car after I parked in the lot by the emergency room.

Roe ...

He yelled when they took him away. And they took him away quickly. I *felt* their urgency rip through my heart.

Ling glanced up at me when I entered the waiting room wearing my bravest face. I wore it for my dad when he had his kidney transplant, and I'd been wearing it a lot during my mom's chemo appointments.

Holding her hand out to me, Ling smiled. It was sad. She didn't need to pretend that it wasn't really bad. I felt certain the haunting cries from Ronin would stay embedded in my heart like shards of glass for eternity.

"Have they figured out what's wrong with him?" I asked, sitting next to Ling as Victor typed something into his phone.

"No." She had this odd expression. It was pained, yet eerily calm.

How was she not freaking out?

"I didn't know what to do. I was so scared. He told me to go home because he didn't want me getting sick, but I don't think what he has is contagious."

"You did the right thing." Ling squeezed my hand. "Now we wait."

I released her hand to send Lila a text.

THE LIFE THAT MATTERED

Me: Ronin is in the hospital.

Lila: Oh my god! Why?

Me: He's in a lot of pain, but we don't know what's wrong with him. I'm so scared.

Lila: He'll be fine. I'm on my way.

Guilt nibbled at my conscience. She didn't need one more thing to take up her time, fill her mind with more stress and worry.

Me: No. Don't come. I just needed to tell someone. Since you pray, I thought you could say one for Ronin.

Lila: Already said a prayer for him. And you.

It wasn't that I didn't pray. I was raised with religion, but my overly curious, scientific mind made it hard to keep the faith. I liked data, testing, proof ... or at least a good probability. After years of lost or wavering faith, I didn't feel confident that *if* there was a god, she would listen to my prayers.

Yes, my god (imaginary or not) was a woman.

I said my own prayers too. The unfaithful prayers involved a lot of groveling and apologizing.

If you exist, I'm sorry I lost faith. Blind faith is really hard for me. On the off chance that this unconditional love thing of yours is real, maybe you can forgive my skepticism, and do me this tiny favor of saving Ronin's life. Thanks ... or Amen.

And then ... we waited.

ONE HOUR LATER, a doctor came out to tell us they hadn't found anything, so they were running more tests. I got a little testy about their lack of figuring things out, while Victor and Ling maintained slightly sad yet eerily calm demeanors.

Two hours later, my best friends appeared around the corner of the waiting room. I jumped out of my chair and flew into Lila's embrace as Graham gave me a sad smile over her shoulder.

"I told you not to come." I hugged her like she was next on the list of people in my life to have something go wrong with her.

"You're the most important person in my world. Of course, I came."

Graham didn't show an ounce of offense from Lila's words. And he shouldn't have been offended. He knew the bond I had with my best friend was unbreakable.

"Thank you," I whispered on a wave of emotion, just as I released her. Batting away the tears before they fell, I cleared my throat and met Graham's regretful gaze.

"It's not your fault." I dug through my emotions, looking for that brave face again. It had slipped off when I hugged Lila.

Graham returned a hesitant nod.

"There was no way for you to know how bad he felt. When I got to his house, he tried to convince me to leave. You did your part by telling me. Thank you." I stepped into Graham's embrace.

"Is there anything I can do?" Graham kissed the top of my head.

Money. He was asking if he could pay for something. He must have been emotionally stunted in a way; it's wasn't that he didn't care. He just struggled with the fact that sometimes there wasn't anything you could do about certain things, no matter how much money you had to throw at a situation.

"You turning around and bringing Lila to me is *everything*."

Graham released me, delivering a hesitant nod.

Lila and I took seats in the waiting room while Graham fetched coffees and food for everyone. His need to feel like he was doing something was admirable and sweet. Sometimes Graham Cracker showed his vulnerability, and it came with a side of generosity. He felt bad for not seeing that Ronin was in such bad shape when leaving the lodge before they had a chance to eat lunch. I was positive Ronin did everything he could to hide the level of pain he felt.

"You can see him now." The same doctor gave us her best comforting smile. "He's in Room 212 on the second floor. We're keeping him overnight just for observation. We didn't find anything of concern with the test results. And he's feeling much better now."

"Did you give him something?" I asked because he was dying … it sounded like he was literally dying at his condo and when they loaded him into the ambulance. That wasn't nothing. That wasn't something that should have come back negative in testing.

"No." She rubbed her lips together and shrugged. SHRUGGED!

"So you don't know what was wrong with him?" I asked with heavy incredulity in my words.

She shook her head. "Not at this point." Really, kudos to her for being honest and not giving us some made-up bullshit generic answer. But how could she not know?

"Let's focus on the fact that he's feeling better." Ling took my hand and kissed the back of it.

I knew I'd be a much different mother than her—the kind that freaked out over cuts and scrapes, the kind that grabbed doctors and shook them while yelling, "How can you not know? It's your job to know!"

When we got to Ronin's room, he was sitting up in bed. And fuck me if he wasn't wearing that same eerily calm but slightly worried smile. It must have been genetic.

I stayed back, waiting for Ling to run to his bed and embrace him with a deep sigh of relief. She didn't. Maybe she was waiting for me to have my turn. I didn't question it any further. I simply threw myself at him, burying my face in his neck.

"Oh my god … I was so scared."

He hugged me with weak arms, which told me *something* was wrong with him. "I'm fine, baby. I'm fine."

"But …" I pulled back, shaking my head. "You weren't fine. You were in terrible pain. I heard you. I saw you. That wasn't nothing. They have to keep looking. Something is—"

"Evie, Evie, Evie …" He pressed his palms to my cheeks and smiled as I blinked back my tears. "It was probably just a migraine. I'm fine."

I covered his hands with mine. "A migraine? That ..." I eased my head side to side, eyes squinted. "Do you get migraines?"

He never mentioned them before. And I'd never had one that I knew of—maybe a bad headache with an illness or too much stress, but not a migraine. I'd heard they could be painful, debilitating, and scary. But ... Ronin was a strong man. I was supposed to believe the death scene that played out at his condo was a migraine?

"Not often." He gave me a half shrug, releasing my face.

Why was everyone shrugging like it was no big deal? I wanted to scream. Just remembering what happened at his condo had my heart racing again and my breaths quickening.

"You need to rest for a few days. No work." Ling sidled up to him on the other side of the bed, taking his hand.

I made a mental note to get on my computer and search up migraines as soon as I got home. If that was all it was, why did he need to rest for *a few days*?

"I shouldn't have let you leave the restaurant," Graham said to Ronin.

Lila hugged Graham's arm, comforting him. We didn't get to see vulnerable, guilt-ridden Graham all that often.

"It wasn't your fault. I honestly didn't realize how bad I felt until I got home."

"You saved that man's life." Graham shook his head

slowly as if he had nothing but admiration for what Ronin did.

Ronin and his parents exchanged a look. I narrowed my eyes at him. When he returned his attention to me, the look vanished.

"I'm a paramedic. It's my job." A slight smile turned up his lips.

No more shrugs. No more weak smiles. Everyone needed to stop pretending what happened was no big deal.

"Surely they gave you something for the migraine," I said.

"No. It uh … went away just as quickly as it came on. By the time they finished running tests, it had eased up. Now, I'm just a little tired."

"We'll let you rest." Victor, who had been very quiet through this whole thing, finally spoke up.

"Rest, Ronin." Ling kissed him on the cheek and left the room with Victor.

"Let us know if you need anything." Lila gave him a hug.

"Thank you. Maybe take Evelyn to dinner. Get her a glass of wine."

They chuckled.

I didn't see the humor. I hadn't overreacted. Why was everyone downplaying and completely dismissing what happened just hours earlier?

"We'll take care of her." Graham reassured Ronin.

"Can I have a minute?" I gave Lila and Graham a tight smile.

"Graham and I will meet you downstairs. Take your time." Lila took my hand and gave it a quick, reassuring squeeze.

I waited until they left the room, keeping my back to Ronin a few more seconds after the door closed. With my scattered emotions, frazzled nerves, and racing thoughts, I needed a moment, a few breaths to formulate the words I wanted to say to him.

"Look at me," he said, just above a whisper.

Closing my eyes, I took one last deep breath and turned toward him.

"I'm fine." He held out his hand.

I stared at it for a few seconds.

"Evie …"

Biting my lips together, I shook my head. "I'm not buying it." Ignoring his proffered hand, I hugged my arms to my body.

A crease formed between his brows. "Buying what?"

"The migraine."

"They found nothing. Speculation is all we have. And I'm feeling better, so what does it matter?"

"It's serious." I swallowed past the lump of alarm and disbelief in my throat. "You have something really wrong with you like cancer, and you've known it. You told the doctor to tell us the tests came back negative and maybe they did for everything but … cancer."

Ronin shook his head. "No, Evie. I don't have cancer." Again, he extended his hand toward me, but I stayed just out of his reach.

"It's okay." I cleared my throat and tipped my chin

up. "I know you think I can't handle it because of my mom and the wedding chaos, but I can. I'm stronger than you think I am. Maybe I can't ski, but I can handle bad news."

"Evelyn …" He pushed himself up so when he bent forward his hand could reach my wrist, and he pulled me to him.

I sat on the edge of the bed while he held my hand and brushed his knuckles along my cheek with his other hand. "I know you're strong. And if I had cancer, I would tell you. I would let you micromanage my treatment, my meals, my sleep schedule, and my exposure to environmental toxins."

My eyes couldn't help but roll at his words, his reference to everything I'd done for my mom since her breast cancer diagnosis.

"Don't roll your eyes at me, Miss Taylor. I'm not making fun of you. In fact, I'm quite envious of all the attention your mom has gotten from you. And over the next few days I'm taking off to recover from whatever this was … I expect nothing short of your undivided attention. You'll need to feed me, bring me hot tea and my favorite book. Bathe me …" He smirked. "Yes. You'll definitely need to bathe me."

Ronin tried his best to be fun and cute. He tried his best to ease my worry by dismissing the events of that day, but my gut rarely lied. It told me I hadn't seen the end of whatever it was that landed him in the emergency room. However, with a doctor's list of negative test results accompanied by a shrug, I had nothing to go on at that moment.

"I'll take care of you." I leaned toward him, resting my cheek on his chest as he stroked my hair.

"Thank you," he whispered on a sigh.

CHAPTER TWELVE

Ronin

"YOU'RE HOVERING." I grinned at the page in my book, feeling the gravity of Evelyn's gaze on me as she peeked around the corner to the bedroom. Three *long* days passed under the wide umbrella of her worry. I anticipated more bathing and less studying, less frowning, less wrinkled-nosed concern.

"Just seeing if you got out of the shower okay. You didn't sing today." She slipped into the bedroom, her bedroom. I wasn't sure why I still kept my condo, maybe for times I needed to suffer in solitude.

"Had you been in the shower with me, then you would have known the answer to that. You might have screamed the answer to that. And I would have sang for you."

Her cheeks turned the perfect shade of pink as she climbed into bed. I lifted my arm to let her snuggle into me, and she draped a leg over mine. Her mind refused to let go of the events that led to my days off work. My mind didn't care about that. It was too busy planning how I would get her out of that bulky sweater and fitted jeans.

"I have to go to Denver tomorrow for my mom's treatment."

"I'm going back to work, so the timing is good."

Her finger traced the tattooed script along the side of my torso. "What do you think happened to the guy you saved in the restaurant?"

"He died."

She twisted her head to look up at me. "How do you know?"

I masked the tension—the truth—behind gritted teeth for a few seconds, regretting my knee-jerk response to her question. "Just a feeling. Most people don't make it out of the hospital after their heart stops ... even if we successfully resuscitate them. I don't *know* that he died. It's just ... a feeling."

That wasn't a lie. I had distinct feelings, or lack there-of, that told me he died. Not right away. His heart started beating again, but it didn't do more than prolong his pain, offering temporary hope to his family.

He died. The ringing in my ears vanished, and the pain *died.*

"Graham thought the CPR did something to you ... like hitting a low after an adrenaline high."

"Yeah, maybe."

"Has that happened before? I mean, surely you've administered CPR before, either as ski patrol or for sure in your EMT training?"

"Yes. I have. But every time is different. I don't know

what happened. I'm just glad that I'm feeling better."

I lied to the woman I loved. Maybe it was for the best that we didn't say the actual words. Maybe I didn't deserve to love her if I couldn't let myself trust her with the truth.

Hinder not the soul's intended path unto the light, lest shards of darkness shed upon thee.

The man at the lodge collapsed.

The familiar voice whispered to me.

I made a choice—a choice to be a hero or a coward.

Hero. I always chose hero.

With every compression, the ringing in my ears intensified.

The paramedics took over. I stood, breathless, watching them load the man into the back of the ambulance, watching them prepare to shock his heart again.

One, two, three …

I counted, waited for the ringing to stop or the pain to begin.

"Me too. I'm so glad you're feeling better." Evie kissed along my bare chest. "Is there anything I can do for you? Lunch? Want to watch a movie? The sun's out. We could bundle up and sit on the porch for a little while, get some fresh air."

I threaded my fingers through her hair without saying a word. Blue eyes made their way to me as her lips paused at my sternum. A look … that was it. Not a smile. Not a word. Not a flinch. She saw it in my eyes.

The need.

The desire.

The wavering edge of control.

Her long lashes brushed her cheeks with several slow blinks before she wedged her body between my legs and kissed her way down my abdomen, letting her tongue tease along my muscles to the waist of my jogging shorts.

Was it wrong of me to want this from her, given everything she had done for me?

I didn't know. All I knew was she did it better than anyone, and I wanted it pretty fucking bad.

Her fingers curled into the material of my shorts, and she slid the front down just enough to release my cock. I drew in a slow breath and blew it out just as slowly as my lips parted—as *her* lips parted—taking me into her mouth.

Fuck …

Nothing felt quite like the slide of her tongue, the warmth of her mouth, the look in her eyes just before they closed—heavy and drunk.

Mine.

I'd suffer a million eternities of that unexplainable pain if it meant Evelyn Taylor would never look at another man … let her mouth do to another man what it did to me.

Mine.

Could she be mine if I didn't give her all of myself?

Her hands inched up my abs, fingers digging into the hard muscles. She hummed with her eyes closed. I grimaced, biting my lower lip as I gently fisted her hair with my right hand while my left hand claimed a handful of the sheets, my control slipping as the need to rock my

163

hips off the bed, sliding deeper into her mouth, warred with my instinct to not hurt her.

My instinct won. It always did with Evelyn … at least it did that day. But I wondered if there would come a day that my mind would lose control of my physical needs. Needs that weren't really mine.

Would my *feelings*—my life—ever really be my own?

Evelyn

"WHERE ARE YOU going?" Ronin reached for my hand as I climbed out of bed, but he was too slow.

I glanced behind me. Naked, ratted hair, and thoroughly fucked.

The unapologetic slide of his gaze along my body as his hand slid beneath the sheets between his legs contradicted my assessment of *thoroughly,* at least on his part. There was no question about his stamina … he was ready to get back to work.

"If you get yourself off, I'm going to feel like a failure in bed." I lifted a brow, plucking my clothes from the floor.

He grinned, dragging his gaze to meet mine. "Sorry." His teeth scraped along his lower lip as he homed in on my abs. Ronin liked my navel ring. "I have an incurable desire for you."

"I'm sure a baby in my belly someday and stretch marks marring my skin will cure it."

On a laugh, he released himself and propped his head up on his bent arm. "Don't count on that. But since you mentioned it … let's set a date."

"A date?" I called from the bathroom.

"A wedding date."

"Maybe we should set a date for you to properly propose to me." I smiled at myself in the mirror.

"Okay. Tonight."

I shook my head, pulling on my jeans. "I need a manicure, and I'm not sure I can get one today." Manicures didn't matter. He liked talking about marriage (yes, I know I started it), but talk was just talk. Until he bended a knee and said something that brought me to tears, I refused to do anything more than play our little game.

"Tomorrow?" He tried again, his voice a little muffed.

"I'm not sure what time I'll get back from Denver. And again … manicure."

"Christmas?" He sounded farther away, maybe the kitchen.

"Too cliché."

"Evelyn, you're being difficult."

I combed through my hair, rolling my eyes. All he had to do was toss me over his shoulder, carry me to an altar, and say I do. The excruciatingly painful circus that was Lila's and Graham's wedding planning had turned me off to the idea of a "wedding."

If I could have blinked and been Ronin's wife, I would have. The health scares with my parents made me value life. Not the circus.

"I'm not being difficult. I just think I'm worth something that feels more real than random mentions of

JEWEL E. ANN

marriage and wedding dates. A proposal. Nothing grand. I mean…" I laid my brush onto the counter "…at least bend a knee and mold a paperclip into a circle, or—"

Oh my … god.

As I stepped out of the bathroom, my heart stopped.

Rose petals everywhere. Every color of rose imaginable. It was as if he took several trash bags full of rose petals and scattered them everywhere. I couldn't see the bedding or the wood floor and rug because … petals … petals … petals. Where did he get all those petals?

The room smelled like roses.

Lavender used to be my favorite scent, but that day changed everything. Roses would forever make my heart skip, gallop, and melt into Ronin Alexander's hands.

In the middle of the rose petal sea, Ronin waited for me.

On.

Bended.

Knee.

His hair was a mess, just like his wrinkled white tee and gray jogging shorts. He looked out of breath, nervous, but hopeful. Like my future.

Oh …

And pinched between his thumb and finger was a diamond ring.

Ronin swallowed and cleared his throat. "I'm fucking out of breath from doing this in under sixty seconds—and we owe Noah and Tami for the delivery. But here goes everything. You've seen my condo. The sparse amount of clothes in my closet. You know I could eat oatmeal for breakfast every morning and a bowl of soup for dinner every night. I'm a terrible gift-giver and a terrible planner. I don't value *things* that much. And I've been content with my small family and ever-changing circle of friends who come and go from my life as I drift from one place to another.

"I wasn't looking for anyone the day you walked into that cafe in Vancouver. But since that day *all* I can do is look at you. My mother once said I'd find something … some-*one* who would make me forget my purpose in life. Break my compass. Jumble my thoughts. And steal my heart." He shook his head. "I didn't believe her."

I smiled through my tears, warm on my cheeks and salty as they slid over my lips.

"She was right. I can't think straight. I have no clue where I'm going. And if you hold out your palm, you'll see that pulsing thing that used to reside in my chest is now sitting quite contentedly in your hand."

"Roe …" I swallowed my sob, taking a step toward him.

"Will you marry me, Evelyn Grace Taylor?" He took my left hand and slid the ring onto my finger because he knew the answer long before he asked the question.

Ronin kissed my finger over the ring, and then he looked up at me. "Will you?"

I grinned, wiping more tears with my right hand. "Probably."

His grin matched mine as he stood and kissed me, lifting me off the ground. A breath later, my back hit the bed as petals scattered everywhere right along with our clothes.

CHAPTER THIRTEEN

A MINISTER FRIEND of my grandma's married us a few days later on Christmas morning. Just us, Ronin's parents, my parents, and my grandma. It felt bittersweet to get married without my two best friends there, but we didn't want a wedding, and we didn't want to wait.

I knew Katie would be pissed off, and Lila would feel like I trumped her big day by squeezing in my own wedding—well, really just a marriage. So we vowed to not tell Lila and Graham until they were married and past the honeymoon phase. I wanted Lila to have her fair share of attention and marital bliss.

It snowed that morning, so I insisted we slide our jackets on over our clothes—my simple white sheath dress and Ronin's black suit—don our snow boots and get married in the clearing just beyond the wood pile. It felt like we got married in a snow globe. It really couldn't have been more perfect.

"I promise to find you in every life … in every universe." I smiled, blinking the snow from my eyelashes.

Ronin grinned. "I promise to carry you down every mountain."

THE LIFE THAT MATTERED

Everyone chuckled at Ronin's humor.

He squeezed my cold hands. "And shelter your heart, keeping it warm and safe next to mine in this life ... in every life ... and every universe."

We said everything without ever saying those three words. There would come a day when we would need them. And saying them would mean everything. It would be a profoundly important moment in our lives. Maybe a last straw, a final breath, or maybe a new beginning. A spark of hope in the desolate dark.

"I now pronounce you husband and wife. Ronin, you may kiss your bride."

He slid his hand along my cheek and brushed his lips over mine. Before kissing me, he whispered, "Evie ..."

I grinned, letting my mouth ghost over his. "Roe ..."

On the most perfect Christmas ever, my instincts were confirmed. I had in fact ... *arrived*.

Seven weeks later ...

I GAZED AT my secret husband sitting next to my parents in the front row of the church. He winked at me, his secret wife, as I stood next to my best friend, the most beautiful bride ever to wear a wedding gown. Lila and Graham shined. It wasn't the million-dollar wedding, the celebrity guest list, the string quartet, or even the five-carat diamond he slid onto her finger.

It was all the years of friendship. Graham's steadfast love for Lila. When most men would have given up, he didn't. And when Lila let him into her life—her heart—she was all in. Her love for him equaled his love for her. No two people had ever seemed more fated.

Well ... until I walked into a bun and bubble tea cafe in Vancouver and met the son of an Olympic Frenchman and Malaysian fashion designer. In his words ... an ethnically diverse ski bum.

The groom kissed the bride.

My mom (working hard at kicking cancer's ass) grabbed my dad's hand as happy tears filled her eyes. On the opposite side of them were two empty seats with roses on them, for Lila's parents, stripped too early from our lives after that fatal car accident. Somewhere, somehow, I had to believe they were watching with tears in their eyes and smiles on their faces. Their beautiful daughter had grown into a successful engineer and married a man who adored her.

And just like that ... life was absolutely perfect.

"It's over!" Lila declared on a huge sigh as I held her dress so she could pee before the reception. "I'm so fucking glad it's over. Ya know? The past several months have been hell. I was getting to the point where I just wanted to sneak off and elope, giving the rest of the uppity Porter clan the middle finger. I hope we can settle into a normal marriage where we only have lunch with his family once a month. Is it wrong that all I want is to have Graham to myself for a while?"

Her confession left me speechless. I thought she wanted the big wedding. Sure, I knew it was stressful, and Graham's mom and aunt were driving her crazy, but elope? That was my MO.

"You're joking." I handed her a wad of toilet paper as she tried to find her bared crotch, buried beneath layers of expensive satin and lace, to wipe herself.

"No. In fact, if you want some advice from your best friend, run off and just marry Ronin. Don't have a wedding."

"I did it." Those three words flew out so quickly; I wasn't even sure if I said them. But no one else was in the lounge with us, the fancy lounge in the *guest wing* of the Porter mansion. Wow! I didn't realize how badly I needed to tell her, until it catapulted from my tongue.

"You did what?" She stood and I guided her forward to keep her dress out of the toilet. After washing her hands, and maybe forgetting that I said those three words, she turned toward me. "Did what?"

Nope. She remembered.

"I uh …" Maybe it wasn't such a good time to confess. The lineup of second, third, and fourth guesses congregated at the door to my conscience, waiting to offer alternative explanations for my comment. What if she wasn't serious? After having my nipple in her mouth months earlier, I found myself second-guessing all her words, their meanings, and her intentions.

"A million people are waiting for us. Out with it, Evelyn."

"It's nothing." I shook my head, looking over her shoulder to check my hair in the mirror. It was still in a lovely messy bun (Graham's favorite). Toasts, dancing, and too much drinking wouldn't bode well for it, but I'd deal with that later.

"I said you should elope, and you said, 'I did it.' But you couldn't have meant you eloped, so what did you do?"

Geesh, she was relentless. Were we still talking about that? How could her mind snag on something as frivolous as my three-word confession on her wedding day?

"Ronin and I got married on Christmas."

No big deal. I said it with a breeze, like requesting someone pass the salt.

"Oh my gosh!" Her instant excitement fell dead at my feet, replaced with a confused expression. "Oh ... you mean you're *getting* married on Christmas. Right?" Her eyes narrowed as her head cocked to the side.

"*Got* married. On Christmas. Two months ago. I didn't want to spoil your wedding or take the spotlight. And we didn't want a wedding. We just wanted to be married. So we did it. We had a minister marry us right outside of my house with my grandma, parents, and Ronin's parents. Afterwards, we had a holiday brunch with them. They left. And we spent the rest of the day in bed—Mr. and Mrs. Alexander." I gave her a toothy smile.

Lila? Well, she didn't even blink.

I deflated and grimaced. "Please don't be mad. I wasn't going to tell you until all this wedding stuff was over and just a distant memory. Then you suggested we elope, and I've been dying to tell you because the day was so bittersweet without my best friend there, and—"

Lila took two steps and pulled me in for a really tight hug. "I hate you and love you. I'm proud of you and pissed off at you. But ..." She held me back at arm's length. "Our friendship will survive this betrayal. And you're the only one I trust to help me piss tonight, so I can't unfriend you yet."

I bit back my grin, giving her the moment she needed to act upset with me. "And we're secret lesbian lovers. Without me in your life, you'll never have a quality threesome again." I shrugged.

After several blinks from her stoic expression, she turned toward the mirror and checked her makeup. "You know ... I never bring that up. In fact, it was my idea to never bring that up again. Yet, you seem to slip it into certain conversations which makes me think you liked it more than you'd ever admit. Were you..." she looked up at my reflection in the mirror and smirked "...close to orgasming that night? Did my mouth on your breasts ... my tongue ring flicking your nipples feel good, Evie?"

Delivering my own smug smile, I let her have her moment. After all, it was her day. "No *woman* has ever made me feel the way you did, snookum."

"Is that sarcasm?"

"You have guests waiting for you." I opened the door. "Oh!" I jumped, not expecting Graham to be *right* there on the other side of it.

"Evelyn." He smiled like the Devil himself. I'm not sure I had ever seen such a deviant expression on his face. "I need a minute with my wife."

That made me smile. *Wife.* I liked hearing him refer to her as his wife. "I suppose you've earned it. By the way ... I'm married."

I waited for his eyebrows to shoot up his forehead.

"I know." He glanced over my head at Lila, and his smile doubled.

He knew?

What!

Ronin couldn't keep the secret. Traitor.

"Of course, you did," I grumbled. "Don't be long. Your mom will have a coronary if things don't stay on schedule." I made my way toward the reception, texting Ronin.

Me: I can't believe you told Graham we got married!?

Ronin: Why would you say that?

Me: Because when I told him, he said he already knew.

Ronin: I didn't tell him. But clearly you did. He simply played you. He's good at that.

I grumbled, shaking my head. How was I supposed to respond to that?

"Evelyn, dear. Have you seen the bride and groom?" Graham's mom, Helene, asked as I reached the bottom of the stairs to the foyer.

"Yes. I just helped her in the ladies' room, and Graham showed up as I was leaving."

"Be a dear and tell them we're ready to have them seated for the first toast."

I nodded, trying to be a *dear*. She hated me. Never understood why Graham kept me as such a close friend— me and my sick, broke parents.

"Thank you." She spun on her high heels and mounted her high horse to ride off and rule her rich little world.

The door to the lounge slash bedroom suite was still cracked open like I left it minutes earlier. I eased it open a few more inches. Then I froze, my mouth agape nearly as wide as the door.

"I own you now," Graham murmured next to Lila's ear as he fucked her from behind with her leaned over the back of a winged-back chair. Clearly, he wasn't lying about that. Her dress was bunched at her waist, his pants pooled at his ankles. What looked like remnants or shredded pieces of her panties littered the floor a few feet from them.

"Say it, baby." He bit her ear as his hands cupped her breasts, pulled free from her strapless gown.

She arched her back, releasing tiny grunts. I couldn't read the expression on her face, the clenched teeth and cringe. Painful pleasure? Just pain? "You own me."

"You like me in your ass, don't you?" He released her breasts, one hand grabbing her chin as he devoured her mouth, his other hand fishing beneath the front of her dress. She cried into his mouth as he plunged his fingers into her, filling her—owning her—in every possible way.

Lila's knees started to buckle.

Before they had the chance to look back at me standing in the doorway, completely bewildered by not only what I was seeing but what he just said to her, I took a step backward.

ASS?! He's in her ass?!

I slid around the corner into the hallway, my cupped

hand immediately flew to my mouth to keep from screaming as Ronin surprised me with his presence like Graham had done earlier.

He narrowed his eyes while mine couldn't possibly get any wider. I shook my head frantically to keep him from speaking. Ronin's confusion deepened, but he didn't speak. Instead, he shifted to the side to glance into the bedroom.

Ronin looked … and looked. Eyebrows creeping up his forehead with realization. A slight smile formed along his mouth as his head cocked to the side, studying them.

Did I want him watching my friends? Seeing Lila exposed like that? Would he think differently about them? It wasn't exactly newlyweds making love. Graham occupied his wife in every possible place she could be *occupied*.

I tugged on Ronin's arm. He took a few steps back, so we were hidden behind the corner. The grin on his face continued to work its way up his face like bread dough rising in a warm room.

"How long have you been watching them?" he whispered.

My head jutted forward, eyes open as wide as they could open. He thought *I* was watching them? I was, but not on purpose. It was an accident.

He, however, spent way too long checking out the situation.

I pulled him down the hallway into another bedroom. "I wasn't watching them."

"No?" Ronin nodded slowly, rolling his smirky lips

between his teeth.

I didn't appreciate his disbelief.

"Helene sent me to get them. I encountered the *awkward* situation. It took me a few minutes ... er ... *seconds* to realize what they were doing. As soon as I did, I turned around to leave and there you were."

"I see. Well ... Evie, I can tell you what they're doing. Or even give you a hands-on demonstration. It would be my pleasure."

So much embarrassment rushed up my neck into my cheeks. I felt certain I might set off the fire alarms.

"Graham ... please ... Graham ... GRAHAM!" Everyone at the reception must have heard Lila scream. Not moan. She screamed.

I covered my mouth. "Oh my god! He's hurting her!" As I turned to stop Graham, Ronin grabbed my arm.

"Evie ... they're having sex. You clearly haven't focused on your own screams during sex. She's fine."

"I don't sound like that!"

"Care to let me prove you wrong? Shut the door, Evie."

Okay. I'll admit I was vocal sometimes. But that sounded like the scream of a woman being murdered, not a bride on her wedding night. Well ... it was late afternoon.

"Ronin, I'm serious. He's in her..." my nose wrinkled "...ass."

"And?" Ronin gave me a look.

I frowned, knowing what it felt like to be *owned* like that. "It wasn't on our wedding day. And you were gentle."

"And you still screamed my name."

I fought what I thought I knew and what I feared, hoping they were not one and the same.

Ronin sighed, nodding toward the hallway. "Go check on her if you're worried. I'll meet you downstairs."

I trapped my lip between my teeth. The screams stopped. I didn't want to check on them, but better me than Helene. On a huff, I tiptoed toward the other room. "Lila?" I called as a warning before I got to the door.

Graham sauntered out of the bedroom, tucking in his crisp white shirt, sporting that same stupid grin he wore on that regretful night in Vancouver. "Evelyn, you should have joined us."

My nose wrinkled. "I'm married."

Graham shrugged, leaning down close to my ear. "So am I. What's your point?" He brushed past me toward the stairs.

I had a long lecture for him. When Graham got too high on himself, his job, his wealth, or his dick … I had to put him in his place. However, the only place anyone needed to be at the moment was the reception.

Lila glanced up from her disheveled dress, trying to tuck her breasts back into the bodice of it.

I rolled my eyes and gestured for her to turn around. Unzipping her dress, I helped adjust it from behind while she put everything in front back in its place.

"Are you going to be able to sit down for dinner? Or will you need a high-top table?"

"I take it you've been up here for a while."

I cleared my throat, ignoring her question. "Do you need to use the toilet again? Are any bodily fluids leaking from any of your ... orifices?"

Gross? Yes.

But sex had its not so glamorous parts, and I had a feeling Graham didn't wrap it up before *owning* his wife.

"That's disgusting, Evie." Lila glanced at me over her shoulder with a sour look on her face.

"Yes or no?" I kept a straight face. I wasn't trying to be anything or do anything but help my friend get to her really expensive wedding reception without smelling or feeling like a sperm receptacle.

She blew out a hard breath, eyes averting to the side as she returned a single nod. I unzipped her dress and helped her step out of it. Then she waddled to the toilet, sliding a hand between her legs. Men had it so fucking easy.

Without exchanging any more words, I helped her get dressed, and then fixed her hair and makeup. That's what friends did. They overlooked embarrassing situations and had each other's backs.

"Did he hurt you?" I had to ask, just before we got to the door that led to the reception in the Porter's private art gallery. It killed me to ask her, but I wouldn't have forgiven myself had I not said something.

Graham loved her. I knew that. I really did. But her cry still echoed in my ears. Ronin was wrong. There was no way I sounded like that.

"Evie ..." Lila turned toward me, taking my hands in hers. "Graham would never hurt me. How can you even ask me that?"

"Because I heard you scream, and it sounded bad. Not like you were enjoying it." God ... I felt stupid and embarrassed having that conversation with her.

Her grin didn't help my situation. "There's a reason why we're friend soul mates, Evie ... you always have my back. Literally." She winked and blew me a kiss before making her grand entrance into the gallery of people waiting for the bride.

I rubbed my forehead. Lecturing her on any sort of taboo sex would have been very hypocritical of me. I knew what I had done with Ronin.

But fuck ... I didn't scream like that. Only victims in my horror movies screamed like that.

The rest of the evening rebounded back to the same kind of perfection as the wedding. I expected nothing less with three wedding planners and an endless budget.

"You're mine on the dance floor, Evelyn." Graham held out his hand to me.

Ronin nudged me off his lap. "Go show him your moves."

I begrudgingly accepted Graham's hand and looked over my shoulder, sticking my tongue out at Ronin.

He laughed, sipping his beer.

"I requested this song just for us." Graham pulled me into his arms, gazing down at me with all kinds of mischief.

Rob Thomas, "Lonely No More."

I suppressed my scowl, pretending I didn't get the significance of the song even though I knew. It was the song that played on MTV the night we surpassed the legal limit and had sex. Quite fitting since, aside from the alcohol, the only good reason we had for testing our friendship with a stupid decision like sex was sheer loneliness.

"Thank you." Graham kissed the top of my head as we attempted to slow dance to a song that wasn't really a slow dance or a dancing song at all.

"For what?"

"Lila."

I swallowed my tiny lump of regret, still hearing her scream from earlier. "You're welcome. If you hurt her, I will kill you."

Graham chuckled. "I'd expect nothing less of you."

We swayed together as the song played on, Lila on one side of the room shooting me a big smile and Ronin on the other side of the room chatting it up with my parents while also giving me the occasional wink and grin.

As the song came to an end, Graham gave me one last hug. A tight, sincere hug. "I love you, Evelyn, more than you could possibly know."

Peering up at him, I didn't even try to hide the tears in my eyes. I loved him too. There was really no good reason why we didn't end up together other than that *thing*. I believed for two people to fall in love there had to be a lot of definable things like common interests, goals, and the obvious attraction, but also the *thing* that couldn't be defined. It had no label. It was just an invisible component of a relationship that made it work— that part of you that physically felt empty without that other person.

"I love you too, Graham. But I love Lila more … and so should you."

He kissed my cheek, letting his lips linger against my skin as if it was some sort of goodbye. "Agreed," he whispered. "We love Lila more."

CHAPTER FOURTEEN

Two years later …

GOVERNOR GRAHAM PORTER.

It's not that I didn't think he'd get elected. Money and influence mattered. No one had more money and influence than the Porters. Hoped … that was a better word. I'd hoped that he would choose a different path, more for Lila's sake than his wellbeing.

"He asked me to quit my job." Lila helped me package the bars of soap in my lab, and by helped, I meant she did it while I sat on one stool with my feet up on another stool because they were achy and swollen.

Three weeks to go until my due date. A boy … we were having a boy, just like Ronin wanted. A boy then a girl.

"He married you." I thought back to the day of their wedding and the situation I encountered that would forever be burned into my memory.

What Graham said to Lila.

The bloody shrill of her screaming his name.

"But in spite of anything he's ever said to you, he doesn't *own* you. Not your decisions and not your job."

He didn't own her ass either (without permission and lube), but I didn't go there.

With her back to me, she continued packaging the bars of soap. I didn't feel bad letting her do all the work. My little lab was a sanctuary for her. She visited when she needed a time-out from life. There was something therapeutic about making soaps and turning herbs into essential oils. Maybe the scents that infiltrated the air calmed her. They always calmed me.

"When he's happy, I'm happy. That's not wrong, is it?"

I thought about her words for a bit before answering. "No. It's not wrong unless he can't say the same thing about you. It's beautiful that you feel so connected to his happiness, that it fulfills something in your own life. I feel that way about Ronin. But I know he feels the same way about me. Hell, that's one of the reasons we're even married. He was a carefree bachelor who loved to travel the world, living job to job. I was a game changer for him. He wanted to be with me and share in my life and my happiness more than he wanted to continue down that same uninterrupted path. My happiness matters to him."

"I'm happy." She shrugged.

"You haven't quit your job. If you quit tomorrow, will you be able to say the same thing in six months? And if you quit, are you doing it because it's what you want or what Graham wants?"

"Both. I told you. He said it would make him happy to have me experience this with him, being by his side like a partner. He's serving the people. He has the opportunity to do great things and make a difference. Why wouldn't I want to do this with him?"

I chuckled. "I don't know. Why wouldn't you? And for the record, Lila, it's *me*. You can speak freely. You can be selfish. It's not wrong to choose your dreams over public service. I make soaps. Sure, they keep people clean, but I'm not exactly saving lives, feeding the hungry, or housing the homeless. Should I feel bad about that?"

"Maybe." She turned toward me, leaning against the counter. Her lips turned up into a small grin. "Maybe you could do more, Evie."

The wheels in my head spun because our conversation punched me in the gut with a solid dose of reality. I needed to do more. Maybe plant a tree for every gift box I sold. Or for every bar of soap someone purchased, I could donate a bar of soap. Something … I needed to do something that felt bigger than myself or my customers. The ski patrol discount (yes, that happened) wasn't enough.

"You're right. I'm going to do more. But I'm not going to close my shop to do it. I love my shop and my customers. I love what I do. So I'm going to figure out a way to do more by using what I love as a vehicle for change. Maybe you could do something with your job."

"Graham wants us to work together. And he's governor now. He doesn't have an engineering degree."

"But he owns businesses. You could work together in a way that incorporates both of your strengths—"

"Evie …" Lila smiled, easing her head side to side. "I appreciate where you're trying to go with this. It's why we're best friends. But I'm okay with changing directions in my life. Graham won't be governor forever. This is where our lives have taken us right now. I don't think it's wrong of me to seize the opportunity to use my new position to make a difference."

She made it sound so right. I just wasn't sure if those words were truly hers or regurgitated from Graham's mouth.

"Then I support your decision ... unless the next thing you're going to tell me is that you won't have time for me or to be an aunt to this little baby boy in my belly."

"Don't be saying stupid shit like that. You know I'm going to take every opportunity to spoil my nephew."

"But are you going to give your nephew a cousin?" I tilted my head to the side.

Lila's brow tensed a bit, just for a second, but I didn't miss it. "Eventually." She smiled, but it didn't quite reach her eyes. "I think Graham would die if I got pregnant now."

"Why would you say that? He's ecstatic about this little guy coming soon." I rubbed my belly.

Lila's gaze shifted to my hand. "Because that little guy won't wake him up in the middle of the night or demand my attention. Graham likes things a certain way right now." She laughed. It was an odd laugh. Maybe a sad laugh? Definitely a dark sarcasm. "If I'm honest, I might be quitting my job just to take care of him."

"He can wipe his own ass like a big boy. Don't be ridiculous. Do I need to have a talk with him? It's been a while since I put him in his place. Sometimes, Graham needs a kick in the teeth to bring him back in balance and remind him that he's not the center of the universe no matter what sort of entitlement his parents bestowed upon him."

"He's done a lot for you. I'm not sure kicking a gift horse in the teeth is a good idea." Lila lifted a single eyebrow.

My parents … I would never be free from everything Graham did to help my parents through their health issues. My dad had a working kidney, and my mom was cancer free with her eyes focused on remission. But that wasn't everything. Graham owned the building where I had my business. Not because it was a great investment on his part; he did it to keep Clean Art in its spot, to prevent the original owner from tearing down the building.

"So …" I blew out a long breath. "Governor's wife. Ambassador to all things great for the state of Colorado. You must be so excited."

A grin crawled up her face, finally reaching her eyes. "Yes. I'm going to change the world. Or at least do good for 5.6 million people in the world. Anyway, I have to get back. Graham wants me showered and ready for bed by seven tonight since he doesn't have any meetings."

"Showered and ready for bed? Seriously? Is that his way of scheduling sex with his wife?"

Lila pulled on her white wool coat. It screamed expensive. It made her look rich and very important—even if beneath it she wore leggings and an old sweatshirt.

"He's busy all the time. If something's not on his schedule, then it doesn't exist. I'm fine with it. At least it's ..." She rubbed her lips together as if she had said too much. Her gaze focused on her leather handbag and her phone that she dug out of the side pocket.

"It's what?"

"Nothing. The plane is ready. My driver is out front. I have to run." She kissed me on the cheek while resting a hand on my belly. "Give Ronin a big hug for me."

"Elbow Graham in the ribs for me," I shouted after she was already halfway to the door.

TWO WEEKS LATER, we made our way to the hospital's birth center at three in the morning after a sleepless night of contractions. My midwife told me to relax at home. There was no need to labor at the birth center any more than absolutely necessary. Still ... this was our first child. We were a little nervous and a lot anxious. I'd heard too many stories about not making it to the hospital in time. And while I loved Ronin and trusted him with my life, it was early March in Colorado, and I didn't want to have our baby in the back of a car.

"Call my mom and Lila." I tugged on Ronin's sleeve as he helped me follow the nurse to our room. My contractions were less than four minutes apart and lasting close to a minute. And they hurt. A LOT!

"I already did. They're on their way."

"We should have called them earlier. They're going to

miss it."

"Maybe. But we won't miss it. At least I'm not going to miss it. I don't know what your plans are."

The nurse giggled at Ronin's remark.

To say we called it close was an understatement. By the time we made it to the room, my contractions were a minute apart, and I had a strong urge to push.

"Push whenever your body feels ready." My midwife pulled on a pair of gloves as the nurse and Ronin helped me out of my clothes and into the soft birthing gown Lila bought me.

I cringed after a contraction that left me doubled over in Ronin's arms. "I can't push. It hurts too much."

The midwife chuckled as Ronin helped me into the bed. The nurse suggested I relax in the tub a bit, but I just wanted to lie down as soon as possible.

"Look at me." Ronin brushed my hair away from my face after I grimaced through another contraction.

I saw it ... that look. He was going to say it.

"No. Don't you dare say it." I grabbed his shirt to hold him close to me, stressing my point.

He loved me. Why wouldn't I just let him say it? Well, we'd gone over two years without saying the actual words. We said it with a look and a hundred other words strung together. But mostly we said it with a touch. Our bodies said it for us when he lost himself inside of me and when I found shelter in his arms.

It wasn't our rainy day. Not yet.

The fact that it *had* been two years made it even more special, like an aging wine. One day, we would open that bottle, and it would be something very special to be savored.

"I wasn't going to say it." He grinned. "I was going to tell you that you *have* to push. I want to meet our son. He's mine too. You've kept him to yourself long enough. It's my turn. Give me my turn."

Only Ronin could make me laugh during such physical pain. "Franz will be a mama's boy. You know this, right?"

He kissed my lips, and as I started to moan with pain, he moved his mouth to my cheek while stroking my hair. Then he brushed his lips against my ear. "I love Franz with my entire being, as I do his mother."

Sneaky … he snuck that in there without pointing the words directly at me. Real sneaky.

"It hurts!"

The midwife remained in chill mode with a smile on her face and her soothing voice repeatedly reminding me to "open up." It's not like I was trying to close my vagina. It didn't have an actual door with hinges. It was like trying to put a toddler's sock on an adult's foot. Sure … it could possibly stretch that far, but probably not without tearing it. And the sock would never be the same.

However, as I knew in the rational part of my brain, my body was designed to do this. Eventually, it wasn't up to me. I couldn't *not* push anymore. When I made peace with that little biological phenomenon, Franz Benedict Alexander came into the world weighing six pounds, seven ounces.

Franz was Ronin's German grandfather's name,

which had plenty of perfect meanings like Frenchman and free.

Benedict was my grandfather's name, the lumberjack who built my home.

Lots of solid testosterone in our son's name.

"He's perfect, Evie ..." Ronin almost made it. Almost ...

A single tear escaped as he kissed Franz's tiny head while I cradled him in my arms.

My tears were too many to count. A million was my best guess.

The midwife and nurse meandered around the room doing post-delivery things to me and Franz without actually taking him from my arms. Within minutes, a lactation consultant joined us to make sure he attached to his food source.

Everything ... everything was perfect.

Several hours later, we had company, just family—my parents and grandma and Lila and Graham. Ronin's parents were scheduled to arrive in two days. Franz insisted on coming out a week early just to mess up their plans of being there for the birth.

"Evelyn." My mom tried to cry even more tears than I had cried. She wanted to live long enough to meet at least one grandchild.

I had no doubt she would live to meet all of her grandchildren and maybe a few of her great-grandchildren. My mom embodied the true meaning of strength and perseverance.

"Meet your first grandson, Franz." After being alert

for two hours following the birth and eating like a champ, he had drifted off to sleep in Ronin's arms.

With a bit of reluctance, Ronin handed our son over to my mom. God, I loved how he instantly bonded with Franz. It made me fall for him all over again. It made those three unspoken words multiply with meaning and emotion.

"Congratulations. He's beautiful." Lila kissed my head and squeezed my hand as she looked adoringly … maybe even longingly at Franz.

"Thank you." I squeezed her hand back.

"Congrats," Graham mumbled without looking up from his phone screen. He wore a gray suit and perfectly knotted tie. The reality of his new position hit me for the first time as I glanced at his security detail stationed by the door.

"How's the new job?" Ronin asked Graham, resting his hand on Graham's shoulder.

He took two seconds away from his phone to smile at Ronin, which was more than he gave me—his friend of more than a decade.

"Good. I feel pulled in a million directions." He glanced back down at his screen.

"Nice of you to come, Governor Graham Cracker." That finally brought his attention to me.

He smirked. "Governor Porter to you."

"I would never invite a politician to visit my newborn son just hours after delivery. So you'd better have more to offer than a smirk and starchy suit and tie." I held out my hand.

Graham sighed, relinquishing his phone to the inside pocket of his jacket before taking my hand and giving me a hug. "Are you still taking care of *our* Lila?" I whispered in his ear.

He pulled back a few inches, inspecting me with slightly narrowed eyes. "Yes. What are you getting at?" Graham glanced over his shoulder at Lila who had her attention focused on Franz.

My question held no implication other than a simple reminder that I gave him Lila. Yes. That was how I remembered things. I just wanted to make sure that *Governor* Porter hadn't forgotten that his most important job was loving my best friend. The greatest gift anyone had ever given him came from me. I gave him Lila.

"What?" Lila caught his gaze on her. Then she looked at me with confusion on her face.

"Just making sure Governor Porter is treating his First Lady like the queen she is." I winked at Lila.

She didn't wink back.

He didn't show any emotion. Instead, he released my hand and fished his phone out of his pocket again. "Ten minutes, then we have to go," he said to Lila.

I waited for her to roll her eyes or tell him there was no way they were leaving in ten minutes. They just got there. *Who flies to Aspen for a ten-minute visit?*

She didn't roll her eyes.

She didn't argue.

"Okay." She returned an emotionless nod to Graham before shooting me the most pathetic fake smile I had ever seen.

Like I had done so many times before, I thanked god I didn't end up with Graham. I wasn't submissive enough to live under his shadow of control. I didn't think Lila was either. I thought she would complement him, put him in his place, and build him up when he needed to exert his independence from his family. Since his family liked her, I thought she was the perfect person to do that.

Maybe I was wrong.

CHAPTER FIFTEEN

T WO.

   I stuck two candles in the birthday cake. Where did the time go? How was it possible that our little guy was turning two?

"You're not crying, are you?" Ronin asked, sliding his hands around my waist and kissing my neck.

My teary gaze lifted from the cake, focusing out the window at our family and friends building a snowman out front with Franz. It was all he wanted for his birthday. A snowman. Man ... I loved that kid so damn much my heart always teetered on the verge of bursting.

It was another perfect day in our life together. Well, almost perfect. Graham and Lila couldn't make it. They didn't make it to a lot of things. Since they got married, my friends took on a new life that didn't involve us quite as much. Ronin saw Graham more than I did. They skied several times during the winter and managed to play golf once a week during the summer.

Lila took the role as First Lady and ran with it. I was so proud of my friend for walking away from a profession she loved to embrace her own civic duty. She wanted to make a difference in the lives of the great people of Colorado, and she did. Sadly, that meant I saw her maybe once a month, relying on quick phone calls and texts as our new form of communication.

"I'm not crying. It's just dry in the house. Did you refill the humidifier?"

Ronin made me turn toward him. "Yes. I did."

I nodded, averting my teary-eyed gaze. "Good. That's good."

"He's two, not twenty." Ronin slid his hands into the back pockets of my jeans and pulled me closer to him.

I held out my arms because my hands were a little sticky from frosting the cake. "It's not that. It's how bittersweet everything has become in our lives. It's the change. It's Lila and Graham being too busy to make it to the party."

"It's life, Evie. He's *The Governor*. He was supposed to ski with me last week, but he had to cancel. I didn't take it personally. And neither should you."

"I'm not." Well, I sort of wasn't. I knew Graham and Lila weren't missing any birthday parties for Graham's family. I hated feeling like we were growing apart. Family wasn't supposed to grow apart. It was stupid of me to fix up my best friends, like putting all my eggs in one basket. It felt like I was losing them at the same time.

I sighed, licking the frosting from one of my fingers. "They're not even done rolling the first snowball for the body. They're going to be out there for a while. I should throw in a load of laundry since I have a few spare minutes."

"Or …" Ronin grabbed my wrist and sucked on the finger that was just in my mouth.

"Or?" I questioned with raised eyebrows.

"I could fuck my wife."

I coughed on my next breath. We were married with a child. We made love. We didn't "fuck." Where did that come from?

Ronin kissed along my arm. "Franz is always in our bed. We have very quiet sex *with* him in our bed. I have to make the tiniest movements as to not wake him. And while we manage to get the job done when the stars align, I miss *fucking* my wife."

"Roe …" I whispered a little out of breath as he sucked the frosting from my other fingers.

"I miss that too." He grinned, releasing my finger. "I miss you moaning 'Roe …' as my tongue makes its first swipe between your legs before I finger you to your first orgasm, lick every inch of you, then give you a second orgasm with my cock pounding into you over and over."

"Roe …" I closed my eyes, fighting my weak knees. His effect on me hadn't worn off. If anything, the lack of his dirty mouth had only intensified its ability to make me want him so badly.

"Do you miss that too, Evie?" He palmed my ass and jerked me into him.

I nodded a half dozen times while making a quick glance over my shoulder. They were just completing the first snowball for the snowman. As soon as I turned back to Ronin, feeling a bit unsure if we could do it and be finished before anyone came back into the house, he kissed me so hard my lungs burned for air.

I missed kissing him like that. The urgency. The bite of his needy fingers digging into my flesh. He lifted me up, so his erection wedged between my legs as he carried me to the bedroom. He kicked the door shut and reached around to lock it.

Good boy ...

We tore off our clothes in record time ... some of them actually getting torn, like several buttons on his shirt and my thin, white cotton panties.

He pushed me onto the bed and attacked my mouth and neck, working his way down to suck and bite my nipples causing me to yell his name.

God ... I hoped no one sneaked into the house unexpectedly.

He didn't stay in one place long before kneeling on the floor, jerking my hips to the edge of the bed, and draping my legs over his shoulders while burying his face between my legs. His tongue relentlessly probed inside of me as he hummed like a starving man eating for the first time in weeks.

My body contorted and twisted as he kept my hips pinned to the mattress, slaying my efforts to hold off, ripping an orgasm from me then plunging his cock into me before I could see clearly again or find a single thought to make the slightest protest.

Then ... he fucked me. And I liked it.

No. I loved it. I *needed* it. He was right. After two years of silently tiptoeing through sex with a sleeping child a few feet from our naked bodies, I needed to be taken the way he took me when we first met. Until the padded headboard thrummed the wall, I'd forgotten how it felt to get tipsy from oral sex and completely intoxicated by him fucking me so hard it felt like we were in another dimension.

The hard, concentrated expression on his face as he moved above me.

The slap of our skin.

The taste of sweat.

And the explosion … the string of swear words … and his body collapsing onto mine, pulsing with labored breaths.

"Oh … my … god …" I whispered on a heavy breath, completely exhausted and drunk on Ronin Alexander. "That was …"

Ronin nodded with his face buried in my neck. "Yeah …" His hot breath washed over my skin. "It sure as fuck was."

That day … it was the day we conceived Franz's little sister. It was also the beginning of a lot of ends that we never saw coming.

CHAPTER SIXTEEN

I MISSED THE days of taking the Porter jet between Denver and Aspen. Three hours in the car with two kids wasn't the highlight of my day.

"Oh …" Mom answered the door to their three-bedroom ranch in Littleton, a suburb of Colorado. "I thought you were coming alone."

"You said it was important."

A theatrical smile took over her face as she gazed at three-year-old Franz standing next to me with a backpack full of toys and books and his nine-month-old sister, Anya, asleep in her car seat straining my right arm.

"But I said we should speak alone."

I pushed my way past her so I could set the car seat down. "I thought that was code for chatting while Dad ate lunch at the diner with his cronies. I have two kids, a working husband, and a business. Today is my day off which means it's Sue's day off."

"Did you check with Lila?" Mom closed the door and helped Franz wiggle his backpack off his back. "Hi, sweetie." She kissed him on his head.

I chuckled. "No. I didn't see if the governor's wife

had time to babysit today. I don't see Lila that much anymore. We chat for maybe ten minutes on the phone each week, and I send her pictures of the kids, but other than that …"

"Life changes." Mom gave me a knowing, sad smile.

"It does." I slipped off my shoes and lugged Anya's car seat into the living room while Franz shuffled down the hallway to the spare bedroom that doubled as a toy room for him.

"Hey, honey."

I turned toward Dad's voice as he came around the corner from the kitchen. He handed me a cup of tea.

"You're here." I took the tea. "Now, I feel like you're both ganging up on me. Is this an intervention? I know … I could use a haircut, and my house is a disaster."

"No intervention." Dad took a seat on the sofa next to Mom as I sat in the oversized chair with Anya's seat on the floor next to me, gently rocking her to keep her napping as long as possible.

"What's up?"

"The cancer is back," Dad said, reaching over to take Mom's hand, giving it a squeeze.

I shook my head. "What? No … I mean, how can that be right? Your tests and scans have been clear."

"That was six months ago." Mom put on a brave face even though her knuckles were white from clenching Dad's hand so tightly.

"So …" I focused on Anya. Young and innocent. She represented life. I needed some *life* in my life at that moment. "Six months. It can't be that bad. What are we talking? Surgery? Some radiation?"

"It metastasized to my brain. I had some symptoms, but nothing that felt that alarming since everything did seem fine after my last checkup. But honestly, we wonder if they missed something at that checkup."

"Symptoms?" I asked.

"Headaches that would sometimes make me nauseous. Memory issues that I just attributed to aging. Dizziness that I thought was from the headaches. But last week I had a seizure."

"What? How am I just now finding out about this?"

"Because once we found out what had caused the seizure and other symptoms, we had some choices to make. And they're not easy choices." Mom talked about her cancer like it wasn't hers. She had always acted like it was happening to someone else. Always so matter-of-fact.

"Treatment choices?"

They nodded.

"So what's the game plan? I can see if Ling and Victor will come help with the kids so I can be here for your treatments. Have you told Katie yet? She'll want to fly out and stay for a while too."

"We're using money from your dad's 401k and going to Italy."

My head jerked back. "Before the treatment? Don't they want to get started right away?"

Dad gave my mom a quick glance and blew out a slow breath. "Your mom doesn't want to go through the treatment. It will only help with some of the symptoms.

At best, it may give her six extra months. But in exchange, she'll be sick from the chemo. Even her doctors feel the best option is to enjoy what time she has left with family."

Emotion burned my eyes.

My mom ... she was dying. Yet, my heart broke for my dad. His strength amazed me. How could life be so cruel to allow cancer to take both the women he chose to love in this life?

"What about experimental treatment? I can talk to Graham and—"

"Evelyn." Mom rolled her lips together and shook her head. "It's time. And I'm ... I'm okay with it. I've spent the past week coming to terms with it."

"Wow ... okay, well ..." I looked up at the ceiling while tears blurred my vision. "What if I'm not okay with it? What if *I* can't come to terms with you giving up? Do my feelings not matter? Katie's feelings? She won't be *okay* with this at all."

"We told her last night." Dad leaned forward, resting his forearms on his knees. "We called her. And she accepted the fact that it's your mom's decision. It's her body. It's her life."

I grunted a breath, biting the corner of my lower lip and shaking my head. "I ..." My voice cracked. "I don't know h-how I'm s-supposed to live without you." I fell apart.

My parents made their way to me, doing what parents did best—offering comfort in the face of grief.

Maybe Katie was okay because she didn't understand like I did. I was a mom. I knew how special that bond was between a mother and a child. I knew firsthand what it was like to have another human need you for their own survival … their own existence. And I also knew that feeling never really disappeared. We *never* stopped needing our moms.

After my mind made its way to something resembling acceptance, we took the kids to lunch and the zoo. I needed to get home, but I couldn't leave her yet, so we stayed for dinner too.

"Oh look!" I held up my phone to show Franz. "It's Daddy. He's probably wondering where we are." I pressed the answer button. "Hey." I tried to force some enthusiasm into my voice.

"Hey. I see you haven't left yet. I'm not sure I want you on the road now this late at night."

"I agree. I think we're going to crash here tonight and head home after breakfast in the morning."

"So what was the urgency?"

I closed my eyes and made my way down to my old bedroom, leaving the kids in the living room with my parents. Anya was fed and half asleep in my mom's arms. After closing the door, I sat on the bed. It creaked underneath me. I couldn't remember a time it didn't creak.

"My mom's cancer is back," I said it as quickly as I could, feigning bravery in my voice even though tears instantly sprang from my eyes, and my body shook with silent sobs. So much for coming to terms with it. Clearly, it was still very raw and painful. I wasn't sure "coming to terms" with someone dying, especially your mother or a child, was a real thing. An actual power humans possessed.

"Evelyn … I'm so sorry."

I nodded and fought past the lump in my throat. Had I tried to say actual words past it, I wouldn't have been able to keep my sobs silent any longer. So I just sat there, falling apart without making a sound while Ronin waited for a response I couldn't give him.

"Are you still there?"

I had no choice. He deserved some sort of verbal response.

"Yeah …" I choked out the word.

"Oh, baby … are you crying?"

I responded with sobs—strangled, painful sobs that I couldn't contain any longer.

"Oh, Evie …" His voice and all the sympathy it carried just made more emotion pour out of me.

"Do you need me tonight? I can drive down tonight. Do you want me to do that?"

I shook my head. If only he could have seen my physical gestures, so I didn't have to squeak out the answers. "No … I'm … f-fine." I grabbed a pillow and put it over my face to silence my grief, not only from Ronin, but from my parents and Franz too.

"Are you okay to drive home in the morning?"

"Yep." Another clipped word made it out, each one clawing past the lump in my throat that had taken on a pulse of its own.

"Okay. Hug our babies and tell them I love them. I wish I was there right now to hug their mommy."

God!

He wasn't helping my situation.

"Hug your mom for me too."

"K. Bye." I ended the call, hoping he knew it was survival for me and nothing against him.

I held no illusion that my life was somehow exempt from loss and grief. Still … the pain cut deeply. There was no way to guard my heart no matter how hard I tried to see it through my mom's eyes. We wanted the people we loved to live in our lives forever.

"Mommy …" Franz knocked on the door.

I opened it, hoping in the dim light he wouldn't question my swollen eyes as I gazed into his innocent blue eyes. He was me. A crazy irony in our family. Franz had blond hair and blue eyes. I think it shocked everyone to see my genes expressed in him. Then Anya came along, the female version of Ronin with the darkest eyes and jet-black hair.

"I tired." Franz rubbed his eyes.

"Oh … of course you are. It's been a big day. Let's wash you up. I think Grandma might have a spare pair of jammies here for you."

I moved through the motions on autopilot, clinging to bedtime routine as a needed distraction. Franz nestled under the covers where the bed met the wall and wedged pillows filled the space between the two. I laid Anya in the middle of the bed and slid under the sheets beside her.

The door creaked open. "Night, baby." Mom kissed my head.

I closed my eyes to ward off the tears. "Night, Mom,"

I whispered. "I love you."

"Love you too," she whispered back, emotion thick in her voice.

I reached over and stroked Franz's back. He sighed, drifting off to sleep. Then I did the same to Anya.

My world.

Somehow, maybe just the product of sheer emotional fatigue, I managed to close my eyes and find sleep. A reprieve from the day's events.

I woke up feeling hot and disoriented. It wasn't anything new. My kids had a gift of navigating toward my body in the middle of the night. But when I cracked open my eyes, they were both still on the other side of the bed, Anya crowding Franz. I was the one who had moved toward the middle of the bed. At that point, I realized the heat was at my back. A *body* was at my back, and familiar arms wrapped around me.

"Roe …" I whispered, turning toward his chest.

"Evie …" He kissed my forehead.

"You're here."

"I'm here."

"For me …" I whispered over his lips, pressing my palms to his cheeks.

"For you." He kissed me slowly.

I nestled my face into his neck, no longer caring how much heat our family of four emitted in that room. My Roe had come for me.

"This is our world." I kissed his neck and ghosted my fingers along his bare back.

"It is." He slid a leg between mine, probably to keep

from falling out of bed.

"My mom is dying." I would have cried had I not drained the tears earlier. I think by that point I was a little numb.

"Yes. I'm *so* sorry, Evie." Ronin buried his nose in my hair.

"I can't let it shatter our world."

He inched his head side to side. "It won't. I'll hold it together. I'll hold *you* together."

CHAPTER SEVENTEEN

"**H**E'S A NATURAL!" Ronin declared, beaming with pride as the skiing crew filed into the house with their newest member—Franz.

My almost four-year-old could out ski me. Lovely.

"Mommy! I did it!" He ran into my arms.

"I'm so proud of you. I knew you'd be amazing." I kissed along his rosy cheeks and neck until he giggled and squirmed out of my arms.

"Bathroom, buddy." Ronin pointed toward the hallway, recognizing Franz's potty dance.

"Be quiet. Anya's napping."

For Christmas, Santa brought Franz skis and a snowboard. The previous year, he got a sled. I preferred the sled. It was an activity I could do with him.

"He's really good," Graham smirked, peeling off his jacket.

I didn't even care that my friend used my son's achievement to poke fun at me. Governor Porter took the day off to see Franz go down the mountain for the first time on skis. My feelings of neglect, from both of my best friends, took a back seat that day because life had changed, and Franz mattered more to me and clearly more to them as well.

"He didn't get too cold or scared or—" I started my mom spiel.

Lila wrapped her arms around me from my backside, nuzzling her cold nose into my neck as I made hot chocolate for everyone. "I played the mom role. He was fine the entire time."

"I see. Did it make you want to play the mom role in a more permanent way?"

Lila stiffened just before releasing me. "Ha!" She returned a nervous laugh, which died completely as soon as Graham looked at her.

He didn't utter a word, and I couldn't detect any decipherable expression on his face, but something clearly passed between them that was awkward and uncomfortable.

"How's *your* Mom? I sent her a Christmas gift, but never got a reply," Lila grabbed one of the mugs of hot chocolate and sipped it.

"They went to Italy. I told you that in a message I left you." I couldn't help but add the jab. Even if Lila had a long list of things she accomplished as the governor's wife, being a good friend to me wasn't on that list. Not anymore. After trying and failing to reach her numerous times after my mom shared the news about her cancer returning, I finally gave up and left Lila a message … a freaking message on her phone about my mother dying. I think I could have forgiven her for not answering my calls had she called me back, but she didn't. Her condolences came in the form of a three-word text: "I'm so sorry."

Lila ignored my jab. "Yes, but I thought it was only for two weeks." She sat on the opposite end of the sofa as Graham preoccupied with his phone.

"It was. But then Ronin's parents invited them to France for two more weeks."

She stared into her mug of hot chocolate. "Oh, you didn't tell me that part."

I tried *so* hard to bite my tongue, but I felt too slighted by her lack of acknowledging me most of the time. "Well, you only respond to ten percent of my messages, so I probably didn't figure it was worth mentioning. I'll make sure to keep you in the loop with the big things ... like when she dies."

"Evelyn ..."

I turned as Ronin said my name, a look of shock held hostage on his face. Graham and Lila had the same look.

Closing my eyes, I shook my head. "I'm sorry. That was out of line."

"A word, Evelyn." Graham stood, tugging on the sleeves to his thermal pullover.

On a sigh, I stomped to the bedroom, ignoring Ronin's eyes on me. Graham closed the door and leaned against it.

"We love Lila more. Weren't those your words?"

I grunted a laugh, gazing out the window at the snowy Rockies. "That was about you and me. *This* is about me and Lila, about more than thirty years of friendship, about my mom stepping in to love her and treat her like a daughter after Lila's parents died."

I turned, crossing my arms over my chest. "Or maybe this *is* between us, Graham. As I recall, you made it clear that once you became governor I wouldn't get to spend as much time with Lila. So here it is ... I got the news that my mom's cancer was back and had spread to her brain. I got the news that she has, at most, one year to live. And when I needed my best friend, she didn't answer her phone. When I finally gave up and left a message, she replied with a text. A fucking text!"

Graham flinched.

Biting my upper lip, I shook my head. "So are you blocking me from Lila or is she just blatantly ignoring me? Giving our friendship the middle finger? Because I'm hurt ..." I blinked several times to ward off the tears. "And I'm angry. And I just want to know why this is happening. I want to know why, when I need her the most, she's not here for me. *You're* not here for me."

"Evelyn ..." He took slow steps toward me. "I'm here for you. Do you need money? Do you need—"

I shook off his attempts to take another step, pressing my backside to the windowsill. "You are emotionally dead. I hate that I feel so indebted to you. I hate that you think everything can be solved with a check. I'm so glad I have Ronin and my kids because you are not my friend anymore. You don't understand that what I need are people who will try to fill this huge fucking void that will be left in my heart when my mom dies. A void that can't be filled with all the money in the world. And I hate that you've taken my best friend from me. I hate all of it, and I fucking hate *you* right now too."

The muscles in Graham's jaw pulsed steadily as he stared at me. Finally … finally I could see the tiniest hint of emotion in his eyes. Maybe saying that I hated him was going too far. Maybe telling Lila that I'd message her when my mom died was going too far. But as badly as words could hurt, the unspoken words hurt more. I'd rather be emotionally invested to the point of stepping out of bounds than emotionally dead. At least I cared enough to be hurt and angry … and *say* it.

I honestly felt as if Graham and Lila didn't care at all. Feeling like I'd lost my two best friends felt like its own death.

"I love you, Evelyn."

I laughed. "No. You don't. You're just proving a very important point about my marriage. You see … I've never said I love you to Ronin and he's never said it to me."

Graham's eyes widened a fraction.

"Shocking, right?" I continued, "We missed the opportunity to throw that phrase out there like the next step in our relationship. And by the time we felt the desire to say the actual words, it was too late. We'd become so much more than a common and overused phrase. And you just proved that point. You throw it out there like it can solve every problem. But after a while, people build up this immunity to those words. They lose their effect. They become a crutch when you're too lazy to go the extra mile and actually *show* someone how you feel. Show them how much you love them.

"I'm immune to your empty words, Graham. I'm immune to your money. I need more from you. And if you can't give me more, then we don't have anything left to say."

After a heartbreaking silence settled between us, Graham left my bedroom. I heard a few indecipherable mumblings in the other room, then the front door clicked shut. Several seconds later, Ronin stood in the doorway to our bedroom, holding Anya as she yawned and rubbed the sleep from her eyes.

"I know what you're going to say."

Ronin cocked his head to the side as Anya grabbed his cheeks, rubbing her hands over his stubble. "You do?"

"You're going to say I was too hard on them."

"I was going to say you stood up for yourself and your emotions, and I'm incredibly proud of you. I was going to say if they are truly your friends, they'll come around and see how inconsiderate it was of them to not be there when you needed them. Then I was going to say we should make cookies with the kids."

Didn't see that coming.

"I think I just lost both of them." I frowned.

"I think time will tell."

THAT NIGHT WE put Franz to bed, and Ronin rocked Anya to sleep while I called Lila. Screw Graham. Really, I had no feelings left to spare for him. But Lila was family. It would have broken my mom's heart to hear our friendship had been severed over something so undefinable. Also, calling her was a test. I wanted to see if she'd answer her phone, if I meant enough to her, if she held any regret.

"Hey," Lila answered in a solemn tone.

She answered. That was all that mattered to me. It meant something. A big something.

"Hey," I replied on a sigh. A little relieved. A little sad.

"Evie, I don't know what you said to Graham, but he's visibly disturbed by it."

"I don't want to talk about Graham. I want to talk about us."

"You don't know what my life is like now, Evie. You don't understand that my lack of being there for you isn't because I don't want to, it's because I have so much pressure on me every single day. And it's not an excuse for not doing more when you told me about your mom, it's just my truth."

"Well, I wouldn't know your truth or understand how much pressure you have on you because you don't talk to me. And if you're really too busy to have a conversation with your best friend, then you need to give something else up before you lose yourself completely. That should worry you more than losing me. And if Graham doesn't see it, then you need to make him see it. I worry you're losing yourself in this new role, under the high pressure of being a Porter."

"It's just … I think it's just the extra everything that comes with him being the governor. Once it's over, things will go back to normal."

"Normal? What is your normal? I'd love to have

lunch with my best friend some time to get to know her again, to get to know this new normal. I have a new normal too. Do you ever wonder how my life has changed since I got married and started a family? I realize our lives have gone in two very different directions, and there's not much relatability anymore between our lives, but there's history and friendship. There's this comfort in feeling like you can confide in this person because they know you better than anyone else. Don't you miss that? Don't you miss having that safe zone where you can truly be yourself?"

Silence took its turn on the line. It was hard to say everything because some things weren't definable. My reaction with Graham was a culmination of feeling the loss of my friends mixed with the extreme toxicity of my mom's situation. Maybe … maybe I didn't *hate* Graham, but I hated the situation. And … well, he should have shown the fuck up for me. Just once, I needed something from him that money couldn't buy. I needed him to give me back my Lila.

"Tuesday afternoon. Lunch. I'll come to you. Graham will be gone all week."

I laughed a little. "What if he weren't? Can we not have lunch when he's in town?"

"Evelyn …" Lila sighed. "I'm trying. I want this. I'm sorry that my life isn't as simplistic as you'd like it to be. But … I'm trying."

Simplistic sprinted out the door when cancer attacked my mom's brain. Lila was right; gone were the days of spur of the moment lunches, giggling over guys, and

THE LIFE THAT MATTERED

shutting down the bars because we had nothing better to do.

"Text me the time and place."

"Thank you," she whispered before ending the call.

CHAPTER EIGHTEEN

"I'M NERVOUS. THAT'S crazy. Right? Why should I be nervous about lunch with my best friend? Well, other than the fact that I'm taking two young children with me, and we won't actually get to talk that much." I brushed through my hair and applied moisturizer to my face while Ronin finished showering.

I rarely woke up as early as he did on his early days, but I couldn't sleep because I couldn't stop thinking about lunch with Lila, and Ronin tossed and turned all night.

"See if Sue can watch them," he mumbled, grabbing a towel and rubbing it over his wet head.

That body of his ... it never got old. Sure, he had a little gray working its way into his hair and beard when he let it grow, but he kept the rest of his body looking like it did the day we met.

Perfect.

"I should wake up early ... before the kids ... and watch you shower more often." I waltzed toward him, sliding my hands around his waist to curl my fingers into the hard flesh of his backside while licking water rivulets off his chest.

"Evie ..." He dropped the towel from his head, giving me a painful grimace, his voice weak, his body slightly slumped.

"Not in the mood? No time?" I smirked. "I can be quick."

My smile vanished as he stumbled a few steps to the side, grabbing the counter for support. Then it hit me. He didn't sing. In the shower, he hadn't sung a single note.

"Ronin!" I tried to grab him and slide an arm around his waist to support him, but he was nearly twice my size. "What's wrong? What's going on?"

Blinking his eyes heavily, breaths shallow, he shook his head. "I think I'm getting the flu. Several other people at work have had it." His words slurred together in two weak phrases like it took all the energy out of him to say them.

"Bed. Now." I forced him to drape an arm around my shoulder as we stumbled to the bed before he collapsed and took me down with him. He plopped one arm over his forehead, completely out of breath, while his other arm and one leg dangled from the side of the bed.

"How bad is this? And don't lie to me. Should I call an ambulance?" It had been years since the incident in his condo that led to a trip to the hospital and *no* diagnosis or one single clue as to why he seemed to be dying one minute and completely fine the next.

"No ambulance," he murmured as I tucked his arm and leg into bed. Then I grabbed a pair of briefs and worked them up his legs. He could barely lift his lower body to help me get them up all the way.

"Roe …" I whispered with my heart aching in my chest, a boulder of fear swelling in my throat as I kneeled on the bed beside him.

"I'm fine …" Without opening his eyes, he pawed for my hand, grabbing it and giving it a squeeze—a weak squeeze.

"I don't believe you." I kissed the back of his hand.

"Well…" he stifled a grunt as he rolled on his side toward me, peeling open his eyes "…you should."

I pressed my body to his as if I needed to keep him warm with it. "Why?"

"Because I'm your husband."

"And I'm your wife. I'd like to stay your wife instead of becoming a widow."

"I'm not dying, Evie. Can't I be sick like everyone else?"

"No." I kissed his chest and grinned. "You're a god. You're *my* god. Strong. Immortal."

"I was immortal before I met you." He pressed his lips to the top of my head and left them there. "You and the kids have weakened me, taken huge chunks of my heart." He paused for a few breaths. "Now I second-guess shit and worry about things like choking on grapes and exposed electrical sockets."

"I'm calling Lila and rescheduling our lunch."

"Nah-uh." He slid his hand to my hip. It felt like deadweight resting there. "You're calling Sue to see if she can watch the kids so you can have a relaxing lunch with Lila. And I …" he released a slow breath. "I'm going to sleep while my body fights this off."

"It's her day off."

"She'll watch them."

She would. I knew it. But I still hated to ask. Sue was Soapy Sophie's mom and a retired schoolteacher. Sophie hooked us up with her after Franz became mobile and I could no longer keep him confined to a carrier or bouncy seat at the shop. Saponification with a toddler running around wasn't exactly easy.

"Fine. But I'm going to ask her to come here to watch them."

"No. I need my rest."

"Well, I need to know that you're not dying while I'm having lunch with Lila. That's my final offer."

"Offer accepted," he whispered.

WE MET FOR lunch at our favorite Italian restaurant. Lila arrived first, sipping a glass of chardonnay when I arrived.

"Hi." Her sad and apologetic smile made me completely melt. One look was all it took for me to recognize my friend again. She stood and we hugged. "I'm sorry."

Releasing her, I shook my head while sliding into the other side of the spacious booth by the window. "Don't apologize. I'm to blame as well. My emotions have been all over the place since my mom's cancer returned. And then this morning, Ronin about collapsed getting out of the shower, which immediately sent me back to the time I had to call an ambulance before we got married."

"Oh my gosh! Is he okay?" She sat up a little straighter.

"I ... I don't know. I think it's just the flu or some *normal* sickness. Sue is at the house, watching the kids and keeping an eye on him."

"Who's Sue?"

I bit my tongue, taking in a slow breath. Lila was right. I didn't know her life anymore. And clearly she didn't know mine either. "She's Sophie's mom. Franz's and Anya's babysitter." She'd only been helping me out for *years*. Why would I expect my best friend to know this?

Lila nodded just before taking another sip of wine. "Well, let me know if Ronin doesn't get better soon. I want to help."

I reached across the table and rested my hand on her hand as she fiddled with the cloth napkin. "I want to help too. What do you need? What can I do to help with some of your stress?"

Grunting a laugh, she rolled her eyes. "You have a business to run, two young children, and a sick mother. I don't need your help. Really."

"How's your marriage?"

"My marriage?" She laughed. "What do you mean?"

The waitress interrupted to take my drink order. I splurged on a midday glass of wine as well.

"I mean, are you still hopelessly in love? Do you find time to be alone? Have private conversations ... have sex?"

Lila blinked at the flickering candle in the middle of

the table. "Hopelessly in love," she echoed my words. "Sure."

"Wow, what a confident answer."

"Are you? Can you honestly say after two kids, jobs, and family issues that you're still in the honeymoon phase of your relationship?" Lila canted her head, eyes narrowed in question.

"Yes. We're still madly in love. We still can't get enough of each other. Sure, making love gets a little monotonous when we're trying to get a quiet quickie in between kids waking up and coming into our room. But when we do get ten minutes alone and know the kids won't be interrupting, we still relentlessly screw like it's a sport and we're the best at it."

Lila's perfectly sculpted eyebrows climbed up her forehead. "I see. Well, lucky you for having the best of both worlds."

"You don't?"

She sipped more wine and then licked her lips. "No. I'm living the opposite life. It's rare … basically nonexistent to *make love* with Graham. He's very scheduled. He has certain needs. And my job is to meet those needs when it fits into his schedule. We don't slowly make love at 11:00 p.m. I get fucked from behind while bent over his desk between appointments. I literally get summoned for this.

"It's on his schedule as 'executive time.' And unbeknownst to me how she magically knows this, but my assistant is privy to what goes on during executive time because she waits outside with a cloth and spare pair of panties for me in her handbag. How embarrassing is that?"

I wrinkled my nose. "I guess I'd be happy that it was me ... his wife ... on his calendar for executive time instead of someone else."

Lila ignored my comment; apparently, she found no humor in it. Really, I found no humor in it either. My hands twitched with the need to strangle Graham. What the hell was wrong with him? Loving Lila more didn't involve screwing her like a job.

"Do you two ever discuss starting a family?"

Something ghosted across her face. A flicker that made my spine tingle.

"No." She gave me a nervous smile.

It gripped my heart. Something wasn't right.

"I mean ..." She accompanied a nervous laugh with that awful smile. "He knows I don't want to start a family while he's still governor. And honestly, I'm not sure we'd be the best parents."

"Lila ..."

"Don't." She shook her head. "Don't feel bad for me. We made this decision together. I wanted him to be governor as much as he did. I knew there would be sacrifices. I've made them, and I will continue to make them because it makes Graham happy. And isn't that my job? To make him happy?"

"Um ... no. We've had this conversation before. Why do you still think that?"

"Graham said it before we got married. He said we were going to live such an extraordinary life together. He said things would be easy for me; that all I had to do was keep him happy. Then he said I was already an expert at it. So basically, all I had to do was keep doing what I had been doing—what I loved doing."

"I sense things didn't go as planned."

"I just don't see him much. We don't even share the same bedroom."

"Wait … what?"

Lila shrugged. "He gets better sleep by himself. His parents haven't slept in the same room for years. It's really not that uncommon."

"So … you have what? A booty-call in his office. That's it?"

"Did you really want to spend time with me just to discuss my sex life?"

I rubbed my forehead. "No. I didn't. I … I don't know. Tell me something good that's going on in your life. I need to know my friend is happy. I need to know I didn't encourage you to marry the wrong man. You wanted kids. You always talked about having kids. So I just need to know that you're not giving up your job *and* your dreams of having a family. If Graham loves you, and I honestly believe he does, then he will want to share your dreams not squash them."

Lila traced the rim of her wine glass with her French manicured nail. "Had I not fallen in love with Graham, I wouldn't have married him. My marriage and my happiness are not on you. It's between Graham and me."

"That's fair."

She could take all the credit for her relationship with

Graham. I didn't argue. I also knew I would *always* feel like the common bond between them in spite of her willingness to let me off the hook.

"Hate …" Lila's lips twisted as she glanced up at me.

The waitress returned with my drink and took our order.

"Hate's a pretty strong word, Evelyn. He finally told me what you said. What has Graham done personally to you to warrant your hatred?"

He made my best friend quit her job. And I felt pretty certain he put his political aspirations ahead of her dreams. More than that, I felt like he took her away from me. The marriage wasn't supposed to replace our friendship. Since I couldn't prove it, and Lila seemed headstrong on defending him and the direction of their relationship, I had to let it go.

"I'll make it right." For Lila … I would make it right for her.

"Thank you." She smiled.

Right there.

That smile—the one that wasn't the exuberant Lila smile I'd always known—*that* was the reason I knew Graham wasn't keeping his promise. When you loved someone—truly loved them—you didn't take their smile.

People with broken souls didn't have real smiles. They grimaced from the broken pieces of their soul impaling their heart.

I didn't think he actually broke her soul, but I felt certain he was suffocating it with his own selfishness.

"Franz and Anya," Lila said.

226

I shifted my gaze to her. "What about them?"

"They're something good in my life. And so are you and Ronin. And when Graham is Graham … not Governor Porter, he is something good in my life too."

I held out my hand, and she reached across the table and rested her hand in it. With a single nod and my most sincere smile, I let her know that we were still us—and I would always have her back.

"We're losing Mom." Tears filled her eyes.

It was a late sentiment, but that was okay. I took it. I needed it. I needed to know that *she* had my back too.

CHAPTER NINETEEN

RONIN RECOVERED WITHOUT a trip to the doctor's office or hospital. I needed to see him get sick in a normal way and recover without incident. If he couldn't be a true immortal, I could settle for a really strong mortal with a properly functioning immune system.

Lunch with Lila put the countdown clock in motion for me to make up with Graham. I said I would talk to him, but I had no idea what I was supposed to say. So instead of insisting he meet me for lunch or showing up announced at his office, I made the ultimate gesture—the ultimate sacrifice.

I invited him and Lila to go skiing with me and Ronin.

"Why did you do this?" Ronin shot me a side glance as we pulled into the parking lot of the resort.

"I told you. I knew Graham wouldn't say no to watching me make a fool of myself. He knows I *hate* to ski, so this gesture says a lot without me having to actually say much at all."

"Nothing says sorry quite like a broken arm or blown-out knee." Ronin chuckled, opening his door and retrieving my skis from the rack.

"I have you. And you'll have my back. Right?" I slipped on my jacket and grabbed my ski boots.

Ronin locked the doors and took my hand. "Always."

We waited in the lodge for Lila and Graham to arrive. I loaded up on hot chocolate, knowing I'd freeze my ass off when we got up the mountain because I'd spend so much time on my ass.

"There they are." Ronin nodded toward the door.

I stood, drawing in a deep breath.

Lila hugged me first, and then she hugged Ronin, leaving me standing in front of Graham. He did nothing to ease the tension or make my job easy. I squirmed under his emotionless gaze, his wordless scrutiny.

"I don't hate you," I mumbled, forcing my gaze to his.

"Is that an apology, Evelyn?"

Did he have to be smug about it?

"Yep."

Gah!

I couldn't help it. Graham had a PhD in arrogance. I knew he'd take an apology as an outright admission of total wrongdoing on my part. While I was wrong to say I hated him, the emotions that led to that misstep in words were very justified. They were the day I said it. And even after lunch with Lila, I still felt some anger and resentment toward Graham for allowing so much distance—or putting so much distance—between my best friend and me when I needed her the most.

"Hug it out, you two." Lila nudged my arm.

Graham made no effort to ease my apology burden. He just stood there with no sign of remorse, not the tiniest bit of shared guilt evident anywhere on his body.

I wrapped my arms around his torso and hugged him. He didn't hug me back.

Jerk!

After releasing him, I turned and gave Lila a tight smile—an I-tried smile. Before I could take more than two steps, Graham's long arm hooked my waist, pulling my back to his chest as his chin rested on my shoulder.

"You're stubborn, Evelyn. Outspoken. Bossy. And ... stubborn. But I forgive you."

Lila and Ronin grinned at Graham's display. Everything had to be on his terms.

The hug.

The apology acceptance, even though I didn't actually extend a real apology.

"Lucky me," I mumbled.

As Lila turned toward Ronin to give him a grin, because her pleasure over Graham and I making up was obvious on her face, Graham kissed my cheek and whispered in my ear, "I miss you."

His rise to governor hadn't changed him as much as I thought it had. He still excelled at being an asshole with me one minute and reminding me why I loved him as my friend the next minute.

"I miss you too." I leaned my head against his and sighed.

"Careful ..." Lila smirked. "People are taking photos. I can already see the front-page news story tomorrow:

Governor Porter shows PDA toward his mistress in front of his wife."

"Well…" I wiggled out of Graham's hold on me. "We definitely wouldn't want that."

"Let's go! I can't wait to see what Evelyn's learned from Ronin. I bet she's going to school us today." Lila looped her arm through mine and led me toward the door.

Ronin followed behind us with Graham. They both chuckled. No one could ever say I didn't make huge sacrifices for my friends.

I made it down two runs without breaking anything, but I feared pushing my luck wasn't a great idea since I needed to be in one piece to take care of two kids and be there for my mom.

"I'm done. There's a hot drink and chocolate chip cookie calling my name in the lodge." Hugging Ronin, I buried my cold face into his warm neck.

"But you were just getting the hang of it."

I giggled. "I was so *not* getting the hang of it. It's best for me to quit while I'm ahead. Now you can have some actual fun."

"What makes you think I wasn't having fun?"

I lifted onto my toes and kissed him. "Humor me and try to have fun without me. Then we'll find a different kind of fun to have later."

"You've thrown down the gauntlet now, babe. There's no picking it back up."

"As if I would want to." Biting his lower lip, I playfully tugged it. "Go be awesome. Put Graham and Lila in their place."

"I'll do my best."

Finally, things felt right again. Making up with my friends didn't cure my mom's cancer. It didn't dissolve the stress of their jobs or guarantee that I would get to see them more frequently. Just like I couldn't rush winter or slow down summer, Graham and Lila were in a different season of their lives than Ronin and me. If I wanted to keep my relationship with them, I had to accept that.

After my cookie and hot tea, I found a comfy chair in the lodge by the fireplace and drifted off to sleep. Sue had our kids while I took a nap—a rare, yet glorious opportunity.

"Ma'am?"

I peeled open one eye, unsure of how long I'd been asleep—but it felt like quite a while. An hour or two? A man I vaguely recognized from Graham's security detail stood above me, lips pressed into a firm line.

"Ma'am, I need you to come with me."

"Where? Why?" I sat up straight.

"There's been an accident."

Sitting up straighter, I combed my fingers through my hair. "What do you mean accident?" I stood, leaning to the side to see past him, looking for Graham, Ronin, or Lila.

"I'm not at liberty to go into detail. I apologize. Governor Porter asked me to escort you to the hospital."

Sliding my phone out of my pocket, I tried to call Ronin, but he didn't answer. Then I tried Lila. It went straight to voicemail. And while I didn't expect to reach

Graham, I tried him anyway as I followed the man out to an SUV and climbed in the back as he held the door open for me.

"Evelyn …" Graham answered. "Did Barry find you? You … you need to get here." That voice wasn't my Graham Cracker's, my best friend's husband, and it definitely wasn't the governor's. The voice was too tortured, too broken, too insecure.

"Graham, what's going on? You're scaring me. Where's Lila and Ronin?" I gripped my phone tighter as I gazed out the window at the busy late afternoon traffic on the streets of Aspen.

"She …" his voice cracked.

She.

Lila.

"Graham!"

"She got off course. I … I don't know how. And she fell … Jesus, Evelyn … it's like she fell off the side of the fucking mountain. It was so far."

Biting my lips together, I swallowed hard as everything outside of the window blurred behind my tears. "Is she …?" I couldn't say it.

"I don't know. They're working on her. She wasn't breathing. Ronin did everything he could. They airlifted her out, and he went with her, straddling her, compressing her chest over and over. God … what if she doesn't …"

The line went dead. I let my phone fall to my lap, feeling numb—frozen. Maybe it was a nightmare. Maybe I was still asleep at the lodge, and the man who resembled one of Graham's security guards was an illusion. After all, Graham didn't sound like himself. It had to be a nightmare, so I rubbed my eyes and crossed my arms over my chest, pinching the skin on my arm.

Nothing changed.

I was still in the same vehicle, staring at the back of the man who, in spite of my heart not wanting it to be true, was real.

Everything was real.

Reality fucking sucked.

THE BURLY, BUZZ-HAIRED blond in a black suit drove me to the hospital and escorted me to a waiting room on the fourth floor.

"Graham."

He looked up from his hunched over position in the chair, slightly hidden by the two other security guys who stood with their backs to him. Graham didn't look like an heir to one of the wealthiest families or the governor. Stripped of his tailored suit and a solid portion of his dignity, he looked almost unrecognizable to me.

Dark jeans with wrinkles like the anguish on his face.

Black snow boots.

Charcoal thermal shirt, half untucked.

Dark, sweaty hair that looked like his hands had tortured it a million times.

But the anguish on his face was most unrecognizable.

My friend was a pillar of strength and confidence, just

like my husband—only Graham always had an aura of arrogance. That was gone. The only aura he possessed in that moment was one of devastation.

"Graham." I shoved my way between the two security guards, dropping to my knees and hugging Graham's defeated body.

He embraced me in a way he'd never embraced me before. It was desperate, fragile, and heartbreaking. "She's in surgery."

I nodded, gripping his shirt. We held each other together.

"Where's Ronin?"

"They're running tests on him."

"What?" I released Graham, scrambling to my feet.

He grabbed my hands. "Something happened."

"What does that mean?" I tried to pull away, to go find someone who could take me to my husband.

"He stopped breathing."

I jerked my hand from his grip and cupped it at my mouth. "W-what?"

"They brought him back. Then he seemed fine. So now they're running tests to figure out what happened."

"W-was he injured too? With Lila?"

Graham stared at me, more like through me, completely unblinking.

"Graham!"

His gaze jumped to mine. "N-no …" He shook his head, a complete shell of his normal self, dazed and confused. "He wasn't injured."

I pulled my other hand away from him and shouldered my way between the two men again to find a nurse or anyone who could give me more information on Ronin.

"Can you help me find my husband?"

The nurse behind the counter glanced up from the computer. "What's his name?"

"Ronin Alexander. He came in with my friend after a skiing accident. He's ski patrol. He was trying to save her, but her husband said Ronin stopped breathing." The words tumbled from my mouth without pause, leaving me breathless.

"I ordered some tests. We'll have him in a room shortly." A dark-haired woman turned to face me.

I homed in on her lab coat. *Dr. Christine Allyn, M.D.*

"Is he okay? Why did he stop breathing? Was he injured? Did he have a stroke or heart attack?"

Cancer. Brain tumor. Fatal infection.

Something wasn't right with Ronin. I knew it in my gut since that first trip to the hospital. But that was years earlier. Surely if it were something like cancer or an infection, he would have gotten much worse. It didn't make sense. Was he hiding something from me or downplaying what he perceived to be a random health crises that quickly passed without any apparent cause or explanation?

"He's stable at the moment. We haven't yet determined the cause of the incident, but we're working on it."

His. Heart. Stopped. Beating.

How was that an incident? A flat tire or tripping over uneven terrain on a sidewalk was an *incident*.

"What about Lila Porter? Has there been an update on her?"

The doctor narrowed her eyes. "I'm sorry. We're not at liberty to disclose any information about her outside of her family."

"Give her an update," Graham's monotone voice crept up behind me.

"Of course, sir." Dr. Allyn nodded before returning her attention to me. "They're working to stop internal bleeding and repair fractures in her leg. I don't anticipate her being out of surgery for several more hours."

My mind liked to visit places it didn't belong, like trying to imagine how I would ever survive if I lost my husband, my best friend, *and* my mom in the span of a year.

Death.

Why did I go there? I guess internal bleeding and re-suscitation opened the door to think the worst. While I didn't always try to think the worst, I tried to prepare for it.

"If she doesn't make it," Graham whispered behind me.

I whipped around, grabbing his shirt in my fists. His security guys took a warning step toward me, but I ignored them. "Don't say that. Don't ever say that."

I *thought* it because one couldn't control their thoughts. But I never would have said the words aloud. That was in my realm of control. Putting those words out there for the world to hear made them too real.

"You'd be it, Evelyn. You'd be the only person I have

left." Graham didn't cry, but I saw his unshed tears. I heard the weight of them heavy in his voice.

His only person? How could that be? He was the governor! Rich beyond words. And surrounded by family. Arguing these points would have played into his notion that Lila wasn't going to make it. I couldn't do that.

And ... I needed to find my husband.

Releasing Graham's shirt, I turned back toward Dr. Allyn. "I want to know the second my husband is in a room."

She returned an easy nod and kind smile. "Absolutely."

Graham shadowed me as I paced the space between the desk and waiting room.

"A truce ..." I shook my head. "An olive branch. I just wanted to make things right between all of us. How did it end like this? And ..." I stopped, looking up at Graham. "How did she get off the run? Where were you and Ronin? I ... I just don't understand."

His eyebrows knitted together. "We turned left after we got off the lift. Lila went right. By the time Ronin noticed she wasn't behind us, it was too late. The run was closed." He pinched the bridge of his nose. "It. Was. Closed. I ... I don't know why she ignored the signs ... the fencing ... but she did." He sighed slowly and heavily. "She's always said that rules were made to be broken."

On a tiny headshake, I averted my gaze to the side. "After we got our first tattoos..." I twisted my wrist and ran my thumb over the carbon atom "...we vowed to break rules that held us back from really living." Biting my upper lip, I grunted. "I'm going to have a serious talk with her when she gets out of surgery. It's time to rethink that vow."

"*If* she gets out," Graham corrected me.

If …

"Mrs. Alexander?"

I turned toward Dr. Allyn.

"Your husband is in a room. You can see him now."

"Want me to come with you?" Graham asked.

"Not yet. I need a minute alone with him."

He grabbed the back of my head and kissed the top of it. "Okay."

As I entered Ronin's room, he forced a lopsided smile. "Evie …"

"What the hell, Roe?" I took his hand and kissed his face all over before nuzzling my nose into his neck just to feel his warmth, a reminder that his heart was beating, moving blood, facilitating breaths, loving me …

"How's Lila?"

I sat on the edge of his bed, keeping a firm hold of his hand. "Still in surgery. What happened to you? What did they find out? Ronin …" My words broke as I lifted his hand to my lips. "Y-you stopped b-breathing." I couldn't stop my emotions.

"Shh …" He pulled our linked hands to his chest.

I rested my cheek next to him, counting every heart-beat.

"My heart paused for a few seconds. That's all."

"Don't …" I squeaked out as more tears flowed from tired eyes. "Don't downplay this. Someone has to explain this to me. What aren't you telling me?"

"Am I interrupting?" Another doctor peeked her head around the corner, tucking her ebony hair behind her ear, revealing her perfect brown skin and kind eyes. "I'm Dr. Waters." She held out her hand to me.

"Evelyn." I released Ronin's hand and shook Dr. Waters' hand. "Please tell me you know what's wrong with Ronin."

She returned a slight grimace, hugging her tablet to her chest. "I don't yet. Everything came back within normal range. We're going to keep running tests and go over a thorough medical history, Ronin. We'll continue to monitor your heart. If we don't see anything abnormal, you can go home in a day or so. However, I'd like you to wear a heart monitor over the next few weeks. At this point, we don't know what caused your heart to stop beating."

"How can you not know?" I stood, raising my voice because we weren't talking about a mysterious rash or a high fever.

He. Stopped. Breathing!

"Evelyn." Ronin grabbed my wrist. "It's not her fault."

Dr. Waters rubbed her lips together, waiting for the right time to speak, or maybe she was searching for the right words to say.

"If this were your husband, your father, a son, or a best friend, wouldn't you *need* to know? Wouldn't you stop at nothing to figure out why this happened? How am I supposed to take him home with no idea *if* or *when* his heart could stop again? We have two children. They can't watch their father die!"

She mirrored the anguish I felt—which was probably plastered to my face. I appreciated that, but it solved nothing. I had family and friends to offer sympathy. Dr. Waters needed to give me more. She needed to give me answers and solutions.

"This could be Long Q-T syndrome, a disorder with your heart's electrical system. It's rare, but clearly not impossible. Medications can cause this, but since you're not taking any medications, I want to look into congenital Long Q-T syndrome. Do you know if anyone in your family has had this condition?"

Ronin shook his head. "Not that I know of."

"Well, that's something we'll want you to confirm. In the meantime, I want to schedule an exercise stress test, and as I said earlier, have you wear an ambulatory monitor. If there's a family history, it's possible we can treat this with gene therapy. Again, more information about your health history and your family's will help."

"I'm calling your mom." I reached for my phone.

Ronin narrowed his eyes, not looking at me or Dr. Waters. "Okay," he mumbled.

"Why do you look confused? Or are you in pain?" I rested my hand on his arm.

After a few more quick headshakes, he gave me a barely detectable smile. "It's nothing. Call my mom. They'll happily help with my family health history."

"I want to go over your health history again with you to make sure we're not missing something." Dr. Waters took a seat on a stool next to Ronin's bed.

"I'll go out in the hallway to call your mom." I pointed toward the door.

Neither Ling nor Victor answered their phones, so I left a quick message to let them know something happened, Ronin was okay (even though I wasn't convinced of that), and I needed them to call me back.

"How's he doing?" Graham caught me just before I walked back into Ronin's room.

I shrugged. "I don't know. I mean … fine, except for that minor detail that his heart stopped. And they don't know why. Any news on Lila?"

Graham rubbed the back of his neck, dropping his chin to his chest. "Not yet. I demanded an update as soon as possible, but I have yet to hear from one of her doctors."

"Well, you're the governor *and* a Porter, so if they haven't taken the time to give you an update, it must mean they're busy keeping our girl alive. Right?"

"Yeah …" he murmured.

CHAPTER TWENTY

"WHERE ARE YOUR kids?" Graham whispered around midnight as we waited for them to let us see Lila. She made it through a long surgery, and they were moving her to the ICU.

Ronin fell asleep a little before ten with me in his arms, facing Graham in the chair by the window. I couldn't fall asleep, not with my hand on Ronin's wrist keeping track of his pulse and my eyes on the heart monitor.

"You're going to be a terrible father if this is how long it takes you to think about the kids," I murmured softly to keep from waking Ronin.

"Not my kids."

"Sue is staying with our kids. Do you think *you'll* ever have kids to worry about?"

He leaned his head back, lacing his fingers tighter on his chest. "When I didn't know if Lila *and* Ronin would make it, I thought I would be helping you raise Franz and Anya."

I opened my mouth. Nothing came out. Where were the words to respond to him? Why did he say that? It made me mad, and at the same time it tipped my world on its side. Lila and Ronin weren't dying. To be honest, I was shocked that Graham knew my kids' names besides "buddy" and "princess."

"I haven't called my parents yet. I was scared to tell them about the accident until Lila came out of surgery. And now I just … I feel like it's too late. I should wait until morning," I said.

Graham lifted his head and opened his eyes, giving me a contemplative look. Of course, I didn't have a response to his statement because it was ludicrous. He would help me raise my kids? How? As my friend? As their replacement father? As my new husband? It made me hurt all over. Any thought that involved a life without my husband and my best friend made everything inside of me ache. Maybe it was his way of showing his support. That was what friends did … they supported each other.

"Wait until morning. No need to wake them in the middle of the night. She's out of surgery, and Ronin is sleeping. My parents aren't coming until morning. Just … wait."

I slid out of Ronin's arms and sat on the edge of the bed. Running my hands through my messy hair, a soft chuckle escaped. "That's so messed up. I … I feel sorry for you. For Lila. The reason I haven't called my parents is because my mom is dying. I don't want to expedite her death by making her worry about Lila and Ronin until I know for certain there is, in fact, a grave reason to worry. But your parents … they could have been here within an hour of you telling them. This is their daughter-in-law.

You are their son. They should want to be here for both of you."

"Not everyone has your life, Evelyn."

I lifted my gaze to meet Graham's somber expression. "Do you envy my life, Graham? I mean … my dad needed a new kidney, and my mom might not be alive in a year. We live paycheck to paycheck. My Jeep needs new tires, and my washing machine is ready to give out."

"But if you called your parents right now … they'd be in their car on their way here," he said.

There it was … Graham Porter had so much, but he didn't have the things money couldn't buy. He was right. My life was infinitely better. That made me sad for Lila. She deserved a family like mine. I wanted Graham and her to make the family they both didn't have, but undoubtedly deserved.

"You can be so much better than your parents, but you'll never have that chance if you don't make your own family."

"You can see your wife now," a nurse whispered from the entrance to Ronin's room.

I turned toward Ronin, smiling at his peaceful face, his soft brown skin, and his long, dark lashes resting on his cheeks. I had the *best* life. Ronin's heart just needed to remember that and keep beating for me, Franz, and Anya. Before following Graham, I kissed Ronin on the cheek. "I'll be right back."

The glass doors to Lila's room gave us a glimpse of her before we ever stepped foot inside. Graham stopped, taking a deep breath while reaching for my hand.

I squeezed it. "We love Lila the most," I whispered.

He squeezed my hand in response, keeping his gaze on her. Nothing could have prepared me for seeing Lila with half of her face and skull bandaged, looking so lifeless. As Graham opened the door, the beeping monitor told us she was alive, but it was the only sign of life. I moved to one side of the bed as Graham took his place next to her on the other side.

"L-Lila ..." His voice completely shattered.

My hand made a fist at my mouth as the room blurred behind the welling tears. His body collapsed over hers. He took her hand with both of his, resting his forehead next to her head on the pillow. Silent sobs racked his body.

Regret curled its relentless claws into my gut, punishing me for ever doubting his love for my best friend. Everything seemed so petty compared to that moment. How could I worry about her job, her becoming a mother, her losing her independence?

Life was about breaths and heartbeats.

A smile.

A wink.

The squeeze of a hand.

Sunrises and sunsets.

The rest ... it was all extra.

When forced to choose what really matters, it all became so clear. This moment. The only moment.

I slipped out of the room, out of sight, and slid my phone from my pocket.

"Hello?" my dad answered in his middle-of-the-night

voice.

"Dad," I whispered.

"Evelyn ..." his voice gained a bit more life, a deep tone of concern. "What's wrong?"

Swallowing hard, I wiped my tears before taking a slow breath. I knew once I started to speak, everything would have to come out really quickly. "Lila was injured while skiing today. It was bad. She had surgery. Now, she's in the ICU. Ronin saved her, but then his heart stopped beating, and we don't know why. He's okay now, but ..." Covering my mouth with my hand to stifle my sobs, I fought to find another sliver of composure to keep talking. "I'm not. I'm not okay. I need you and Mom."

That was it. No apologies for waking them. No apologies for asking my sick mom to make the trip to Aspen in the middle of the night. I knew what it meant to be a parent—that unconditional love thrived on being there for your children when they needed you the most. And while I had never battled cancer, I couldn't imagine anything short of death itself keeping a mother from her child in pain.

"We're on our way."

I let the phone slide from my ear, hugging it to my chest. My heart felt ripped apart in too many directions.

My mom.

My young children.

Ronin.

Lila.

I couldn't be everywhere at once and everything to everyone. I couldn't fix all the broken pieces.

For the next twenty minutes, I stood outside of Lila's room, watching Graham cling to her like a lost child. Unchecked tears flowed from his red eyes as he kissed the exposed side of her face and whispered things in her ear. Sometimes, he closed his eyes and lifted his face to the ceiling as if praying to a god who allowed so many bad things to happen that day.

As soon as that thought crossed my mind, I realized that *if* God existed, she and her infinite power might have been the reason we were at the hospital and not planning funerals. I didn't know. But I knew how it felt to not believe in something as improbable as God, yet so desperately needing the *hope* that something was more powerful than myself and the imperfect and mortal doctors tending to my loved ones.

A miracle.

We needed a miracle. And what could be more miraculous than something all-knowing and all-powerful putting the unfixable pieces back together? So I decided to try the concept of power in numbers as I closed my eyes and asked for a miracle from a God I doubted. If her love was truly unconditional, she would not hold my wavering faith against Lila and Ronin.

I asked for more breaths.

More heartbeats.

More smiles and winks.

I asked for more moments.

Then I told Her I would let Her know when I was ready to let go. I realized it was a bold move on my part, but if there was truly something to "ask and you shall receive," then I had nothing to lose.

Not true.

I had *everything* to lose.

CHAPTER TWENTY-ONE

FAMILY.

Two days and many tests later, Ronin came home with a monitor and instructions to always have someone with him in case … well, Dr. Waters didn't say the actual words, but it wasn't hard to read between the lines.

In case his heart stopped doing its job.

"Your parents should be here in about two hours if their plane arrives on time." I handed Ronin a cup of tea as he sat on the sofa with Anya asleep on his lap and Franz next to him, flipping through the pages of a book about sea creatures.

Best. Life. Ever.

"I want at least two more." I grinned, taking my own tea to the recliner so I could just … stare at my world all cuddled onto the sofa.

"Two more cups of tea?" He brought the mug to his mouth and blew at the steam.

I smirked. "Kids. I've just been blown away by family since the accident. Our parents. Even Graham's parents shocked me by showing up an hour after they moved Lila to the ICU. Graham didn't think they were coming until the next morning. I know he hated them seeing him so broken—*weak* in his words—but that's the point, right? I mean, of course I want to have lots of days like this ... fire, hot drinks, books, and naps with our kids. I want to travel the world with them. Birthdays. Graduations. All the good stuff. We brought them into the world for all of that ... but also because no matter how strong we think we are, everyone *needs* someone at some point in their life."

A barely detectable smile graced Ronin's face. "I'll have a dozen kids with you, Evelyn."

"What's wrong?" I set my tea onto the coffee table and moved to the sofa, scooting Franz and his pile of books over just far enough to allow me to sit by Ronin. "You're in pain. I can tell. Why? What's hurting you? Is it your heart? Are you having trouble breathing? Do you feel dizzy or lightheaded?"

We had a defibrillator just feet from the sofa on the kitchen counter. I knew how to use it. Ronin had a heart monitor. Yet, I wasn't truly prepared to administer CPR or shock my husband in front of our two kids. My parents were at the hospital with Lila, planning on coming to our house close to the time of Ronin's parents' arrival.

Just a couple of hours. He had to keep his heart beating a couple more hours—forever really—but at the very least, a couple more hours.

"I'm just..." he shook his head, but it didn't erase the tension on his forehead or release the tiny creases next to his eyes "...fine. It's nothing."

Twisting my body to the side, I grabbed his face. "Don't lie to me," I whispered so Franz didn't focus in on us. "I know when you're in pain, so don't tell me it's nothing. Tell me where and how bad."

"I ache all over. But my leg especially. Can you take Anya?"

"Of course." I scooped up her limp body and carried her to the bedroom, managing to lay her down without waking her. A true feat.

"Franz, your grandmas and grandpas will be here soon. I think you should go to your room and color pictures for them." I kissed the top of his head.

He loved to color and draw. Ronin felt certain he got Julien's artistic talent.

"Okay!" He slammed his book shut and ran to his bedroom, leaving a scattering of books on the sofa and floor for me to pick up.

Ronin rubbed his right leg, grimacing a bit.

"Roe ... I'm scared." I drew in a brave breath as I sat next to him without touching him. It took lots of slow, deep breaths to keep from breaking down. Franz didn't need to see me crying. I had no way to explain it.

"Why are you scared?"

My gaze remained on his hand slowly rubbing his leg. "Because I've researched all the possible things Dr. Waters said might have caused your heart to stop beating, and none of them had body aches and leg pain as symptoms. They're missing something, and I'm so scared that they won't figure it out until it's too late."

"I don't think they're missing anything."

Jerking my head to make eye contact with him, I squinted. "Why would you say that? Unless you know what it is but you're just not telling anyone. And if that is the case, I'm going to be so damn pissed off at you for letting me go through all of this unknown, thinking the worst, angry at doctors, and praying to a God I don't believe in about a problem I can't define."

After rubbing his lips together for several seconds, he shifted his blank stare to the window, blinking a few times at the new round of snow swirling in the air. "It's hard to explain."

I grunted a laugh, shaking my head while running my fingers through my hair. "Well, you need to *try* to explain it to me because I can't keep myself from completely unraveling without any explanation."

His eyes narrowed. "Do you remember when I told you that I had something happen to me when I was younger? It affected my speech for a while, and kids made fun of me?"

It was shortly after we met. The day after the Va-ness-uh karaoke incident. Years later, I still remembered how insane and insecure I felt that night. Not a finer moment of mine. With a slight cringe, I nodded.

"What happened to me was quite significant."

How did I not ask him more about it at the time? Oh, right … I was drowning in my own embarrassment and insecurity.

"What happened?"

"My uncle was remodeling his house. We stopped by to visit him. The adults talked, except mom. She stayed busy keeping an eye on Julien. I decided to snoop around a bit. I honestly don't remember much after that, but apparently, I came across some exposed wires that were live. I was electrocuted."

"Yes." I took his hand and turned it over to rub my thumb along the scar on his hand. "But you got better."

"I did. Eventually." He curled his hand into a fist, flexing it several times. "That day … my heart stopped beating."

"Roe …" I whispered as a chill slithered along my spine. "Why are you just *now* telling me this?"

He relaxed his hand, face expressionless. Eyes vacant.

"My uncle performed CPR until the paramedics arrived. They were gravely worried that I would have severe brain damage because it took so long to get my heart beating on its own again—it took the paramedics a long time to get there. As a result of the accident, I had speech issues for many months."

"But you got better." That was my line, and I would repeat it a million times if that made it a fact.

"Sort of …" He wouldn't look at me. Something outside or years away from that moment held his attention.

"You don't think so?" I cocked my head to the side. "You think your heart issues stem from that accident? Do you think it's possible it damaged your heart or its electrical system somehow?"

"No."

I froze, opening my mouth to say … what? I didn't know. *No.* How could he say no? It made the most sense. "Then what's your point? What's the connection?"

"It's funny…" he rubbed his temples a few times, inching his gaze to mine "…you don't believe in God, but you're open to the idea of parallel universes."

"Well …" I said slowly. "One is based on faith, and the other is based on scientific probability. But if it matters, every time you get sick, I pray. At the hospital, I prayed for you and Lila. I like the *idea* of God even if I can't wrap my head around it. What does this have to do with you and your heart?"

"Unexplainable phenomena and unprovable ideologies." His eyes searched mine. For what? I didn't know, maybe a flinch of disbelief or a glimmer of understanding.

I neither understood nor disbelieved. But *unexplainable phenomena* was a pretty weighty thing to throw out there—and an unacceptable answer to my question. What did it have to do with his heart?

I shook my head. "Stop spoon-feeding this to me, Ronin. Just say it. Your ambiguity scares me."

"I had a near-death experience."

That qualified as an unexplainable phenomenon. It also earned us a few minutes of silence, a few more minutes for him to gauge my reaction.

I didn't give him anything. It explained his resistance to tell me, but not its impact on his heart. "So … like going toward the light?"

"I don't recall a light. Just a voice."

"Maybe it was one of the paramedics or the doctors at the hospital."

"No." He shook his head without a blink of hesitation.

"Okay. What did the voice say?"

"It said I was safe. I said I didn't want to be safe."

"Why would you say that?"

"Because I've always dreamed of being a superhero." Ronin grinned, eyes trained to his hand rubbing slow strokes along his leg.

It wasn't his best grin. I could tell *he* wasn't feeling his best. Still, it was something, and I needed something. "You have?" When I thought I couldn't possibly love him more … there I was, loving him more. "How did I not know this about you?"

He lifted a single shoulder. "It stops sounding cool once you're an adult."

"What did the voice reply?"

"It asked why? I said I wanted to save lives."

"You're my superhero. And you're definitely Lila's."

"Maybe." He frowned. "But it comes with a price."

"Your heart issues?"

"Not exactly. More like extreme empathy. The voice restored my heartbeat, but only after I agreed."

"Agreed to what?"

"It's hard to explain. Not necessarily a proverb, more like an unspoken law of nature. Honestly, it feels more like a curse. I was twelve. The words meant nothing. The choice to live meant everything. So I agreed."

"Do you remember it? The proverb or curse?"

"Yeah. It said, 'Hinder not the soul's intended path unto the light, lest shards of darkness shed upon thee.'"

The kitchen faucet dripped. I hadn't noticed it before. A lot of sounds came to life between Ronin's proverb and my inability to respond. The tarp covering the woodpile whipped in the wind, clapping against the side of the house.

Creaks from the logs bending like the joints of a ninety-year-old.

The howl of the wind carrying smoke out of the chimney.

"You think I'm crazy?"

That wasn't the word. Not crazy. We'd spent five years together. I'd seen his crazy, and he had seen mine.

"No. Science doesn't know a lot about near-death experiences. And when they think they have an explanation for one near-death experience, there are ten other cases defying that explanation. Clearly, it's not something that can easily be studied. It's frowned upon to purposely take a human to the edge of death, push them over, and then try to resuscitate them to test their out-of-body perception." When all else failed, I wore my geek hat and droned on like the world's most boring professor.

"That didn't answer my question." Ronin frowned.

"I did answer it. No. I don't think you're crazy. I just don't understand what this means." I closed my eyes, rubbing them with my fingers while forcing a breath through my nose.

"It means I'm not supposed to bring the dead back to life."

I paused my fidgeting, letting my hands slide down my face. "You know this for a fact?"

"It's what I've been told. And it's been my experience."

"Told by whom? And what experience?"

"Look!" Franz ran out of his room, holding up two colorings. "Shh …" I held my finger to my mouth, but it was too late. Anya's fussy cries filled the air.

"Let me see those, big guy." Ronin held out his hand.

I stood, backing up a slow step at a time, focusing on *everything* about my husband—his forced smile, his strained voice, his pale face, and his drowsy eyes. Before I could say another word or make eye contact with him, Anya let out a louder cry. After that, everything fell into an unstoppable chain of events.

Anya.

Poopy diaper.

Franz needing a snack.

Graham calling to give us an update.

My parents arriving.

Ronin's parents arriving.

He left me with a mind-blowing confession, a revelation too unreal to sort out and make sense of it. I had so many questions, but life took center stage, allowing us no time for more answers.

On autopilot, I tossed together ingredients for a pot of chili, threw in a load of laundry, and absentmindedly nodded when someone spoke to me. Yes, I knew Lila was doing better, but at the same time, she was in more pain because they were weaning her off the stronger pain medications. Everything my mom and dad shared from hours earlier at the hospital, I already knew because Graham texted me several times an hour.

I watched Ronin, slumped into the corner of the sofa,

pretending to engage with the kids while my dad rubbed his hands together over the wood stove, sharing his thoughts on the Denver Nuggets with ... I wasn't sure. Victor had drifted off to sleep in one of the recliners, probably not a fan of the Nuggets or basketball in general. Sometimes Ronin and I would make eye contact. He knew I saw his pain. I knew he saw all the unanswered questions running rampant in my head.

"Would you like me to get Franz ready for bed?" Ling asked as I put away the last dinner dish and tossed the towel on the countertop.

It took me a few seconds to respond. Everything felt heavy: my limbs, my eyelids, and my thoughts—sluggish and unfocused. I needed sleep. But yes, my kids needed to get to sleep as well.

"That would be wonderful. Thank you."

"Franz, show me your favorite jammies," Ling said with Franz's level of enthusiasm.

Before he could scramble to his feet to follow Ling, Anya cried from her bedroom.

I flinched, my gaze darting to Ronin. My mom had taken Anya to her room to rock her to sleep.

"She's teething. I should give her something." I yawned.

Before Ronin could return a full nod, his gaze redirected toward the hallway, eyes widening as he pushed himself off the sofa. My gaze followed him ... as if in slow motion. At least, that was how I always remembered that moment.

Anya, stumbled down the hallway with her already

unsteady toddler gait, a trail of blood from her head to her jaw. My mom … nowhere in sight.

"Anya!" I rushed to her right behind Ronin.

He picked her up as if nothing in his body felt pain at that moment—the power of adrenaline. Then he inspected the cut on her head as she reached for me. I didn't think it was possible to stretch anymore, but I felt the painful pull once again from the people that I loved.

"Take her. Call 9-1-1." Ronin handed Anya to me. I knew the call wasn't for our daughter.

As soon as I turned to go find my phone, my dad rushed past me.

He knew too.

"I'm calling." Victor pulled his phone from his pocket.

Ling hurried toward me with a wad of tissues, pressing them to Anya's cut while I used my shirt to wipe the blood from her cheek.

Stretch.

Tug.

Pull.

I felt the cracks as Franz hugged my leg.

"Mommy! Anya bleeding!"

I couldn't let go of my little girl, but something happened to my mom, and I had no idea what it was. With my babies clinging to me, I couldn't go back to the room to find out.

Ling gestured to the wad of tissues on Anya's head. "Hold this here. I'll go see."

Fear strangled me, even a simple "okay" couldn't

make it out of my mouth. I nodded, holding the tissue to Anya's head as I tried really hard to not let out the tears pooling in my eyes. Dread snatched my ability to think coherently. Heart palpations stole my breath, making it hard to find enough oxygen. But I *had* to find that next breath. I knew at some point I would no longer have to be strong for anyone else, and I would crumble into a cloud of despair. Until then … I moved like a wave, miles off the shore, waiting for my turn to crash … break … and disappear.

My grandma told me God never gave us more than we could handle. Either she was wrong, or I was right— God didn't exist.

Closing my eyes, I let everything slow down until all I could feel were my children's arms—Franz around my leg, Anya around my neck. What if they were the only ones I could keep with me? Could I lose my mom, my best friend, and my husband and *still* be okay? Could I be the wave that changed courses in the storm, carrying them with me to avoid crashing … breaking … disappearing?

Yes.

I knew it the moment I held Franz in my arms. My love would always be strong enough to last *my* whole life. If *my* heart had a beat, I would be there for Franz and Anya. I never wanted it to beat alone. I'd always imagined it beating with Ronin's heart, a union as beautiful as the one that brought our children into the world.

"I love you." I found my voice as I kissed the skin beside Anya's head. She hiccupped with a few more sobs.

"I love you both so much." I squatted down, dropping to my backside and bringing Franz into my embrace too. "And *we* will be okay."

My internal reconciliation had nothing to do with me giving up on my mom, on Lila, on Ronin … It was me building a shelter in my heart for my children—one that would weather every storm.

"She had a seizure." Ling rested her hand on my shoulder.

My body gently swayed side to side with my world wrapped in my arms.

A seizure.

Knowing *we* would be okay no matter what, I was able to file that information into the right place in my mind.

My mom had cancer.

My mom was dying.

My mom was going to experience seizures, dizziness, vomiting, headaches, numbness, and possibly paralysis in parts of her body.

A seizure.

She would be fine … for the time being.

One moment. One breath.

I couldn't undo the past. Nor could I change the future.

My babies are okay. We are okay.

Victor moved from watching out the window to opening the door for the paramedics.

Two of them ushered past me down the hallway following Ling. A third one, a fair skinned woman with a soft smile, squatted next to me while slipping on her blue gloves.

"I'm Janette. Can I take a look?" she asked.

I eased the wad of tissue away from Anya's head.

She covered it with a gauze square. "We'll make this all better, sweetie."

"Grandma!" Franz jumped out of my lap and tried to run after the two medics taking my mom out to the ambulance.

"Anya ..." My mom's weak voice echoed.

"Your grandma will be fine, Franz. They just need to have a doctor check on her. You can see her later." Victor picked up Franz just before he made it out the door.

"Evie, let's go, baby." Ronin took Anya from me. "I'll take Anya in the ambulance with your mom. You take your dad and follow us in the Jeep." He held out his other hand to me.

I didn't take it. I didn't need his help to stand up. *He* was the one who needed help.

"Ronin, you can't—"

"I'm fine." He kissed the side of Anya's head.

He wasn't fine. Ronin's usually warm beige skin was whiter than mine. He had dark circles under his eyes, and his cheeks were sunken beneath his cheek bones more than usual because he hadn't eaten much in days.

"We'll stay with Franz. Call if you need anything." Ling handed me my coat, phone, and purse as I stood.

Ronin wrapped a blanket from the sofa around himself and Anya before heading out to the ambulance.

"Grandma and Grandpa are going to put you to bed, Franz." I hugged him. "We're going to let the doctors fix

Grandma and Anya. I love you *so* much. We'll be back soon."

I saw the unease in his eyes. Ronin's parents visited several times a year, but Franz wasn't as comfortable with them as he was with my parents whom he saw almost every week. But man, oh man ... did I ever *love* how my little boy put on his best brave face for me when I absolutely needed it more than anything else.

"Okay, Mommy. Goodnight."

Sheesh ...

That brought tears to my eyes more than had he tried to argue with me or beg me to stay.

CHAPTER TWENTY-TWO

Ronin

THEY ADMITTED MADELINE for the night, put three stitches in Anya's head, and gave me an IV because I had low blood pressure and appeared to be dehydrated. I refused to be admitted for the night too, much to Evelyn's sour-faced displeasure.

"I'm going to check in with my parents," I whispered, leaving Evelyn, her dad, and Anya in Madeline's room as she started to drift off to sleep.

Instead of calling my parents, I wheeled my portable IV to Lila's room. Graham had to go back to Denver earlier that day, leaving Lila's personal assistant to stay with her. I couldn't imagine leaving my wife just a few days after a major accident, but I wasn't the governor of Colorado. However, she was being transferred to a Denver hospital the following day. They wouldn't attempt the transfer until they felt she was stable.

Fiona glanced up from her computer when I opened the glass door to Lila's room. On a smile, she pushed her red-framed glasses up her nose before curling her dark blond hair behind her ears. "Hi," she whispered, which made Lila turn her head and open her eyes.

"Can we have a few minutes?" I asked Fiona.

"Sure. I might go grab a bite to eat if you'll be here for a bit."

"Sure." I wheeled my IV into the room and eased into the seat Fiona had occupied.

"You look like shit." Lila attempted to grin with half of her face bandaged. "I thought you were the one who rescued me. Who rescued you? And I thought you went home this morning."

I grunted, trying to at least match her half-ass smile. "Madeline had a seizure after dinner."

"Oh my god! Is she okay?"

I flinched as Lila tried to sit up. She flinched too because it hurt to move.

"Relax. It's fine. An expected complication of her condition. Unfortunately, she was rocking Anya to sleep when it happened. Anya fell from her lap and cut her head. But everyone is fine."

"Oh baby Anya ..." She closed her eyes for a brief moment. "You, Ronin ... earlier Evelyn told me your heart stopped. Please tell me it wasn't from the stress of trying to save me."

"No."

Truth.

It wasn't the trying part. It was because I succeeded, and more specifically, because she went into cardiac arrest a second time at the hospital. And fuck my life because at the exact moment her heart stopped, so did mine. It was complicated, and yet a rather simple explanation that I'd come to expect—and accept.

As a child, I envied the superheroes in all the books I stashed under my bed. Even when I decided to go through the long and rigorous training to become a paramedic, the young boy in me couldn't wait to be the person—the superhero—who saved lives.

"I hope you're feeling better than me," she murmured. "I'm so scared of getting addicted to pain medications. I've been making them give me the bare minimum and only toward the end of the day ... just to sleep."

While I appreciated her concern, which was a real one, I needed her to take a few more pain meds because they wouldn't prescribe them to me for a heart condition that shouldn't have caused me that much pain.

Yes. I needed *her* to take pain meds for *me*.

"Everything hurts ..." She closed her eyes.

Her head.

"My head."

Her right arm.

"My right arm."

But her leg ... it's the worst.

"However ... my leg is driving me crazy. I think amputating it would have been a better option. I can't imagine ever using it to walk again."

Was it selfish of me to want Lila to do whatever it took to take away the pain? Strong people pushed through and worked hard. They didn't pop pills and wither away in the corner. The problem was ... this wasn't my battle.

267

No matter how hard I worked or fought, it wouldn't make a difference. It was like running marathons in my dreams. Eventually, I would wake to the grim reality that I didn't move an inch. Dreams could be vivid and memorable, but that didn't make them real. Not moving an inch made it hard to be strong. It made it incredibly easy to want to crawl in that corner and pop pills.

Still ... I could do this. I *would* do this. Lila would recover, and I would recover.

"There are many ways to manage pain that don't involve medication. Acupuncture. Acupressure. Herbs. Hypnosis." I had tried all of them; they weren't as effective for me because I didn't own the source of the pain—the negative and blocked energy. But for Lila, they were worth trying.

"Okay." She sighed.

Okay was good. Okay gave me hope.

"Graham won't like the alternatives. He'll encourage me to take the medications."

Graham ... I would handle Graham through his biggest weakness—Evelyn. I liked Graham. We were friends. And part of my fondness for him was in fact his loyalty to my wife and the wellness of her family. Beneath all the money and political power, I honestly felt Graham had his feet planted on a solid base of good morals and an instinct to do the right thing. However, he looked at Evelyn in a way that kept me *aware*. It was hard to explain. Evelyn said they tried and failed at being more than friends, but Graham had never said those actual words. That was what kept me *aware*.

He worshipped my wife, and I had a feeling he did so as much if not more than his own wife. It didn't make me happy, but I needed to use the leverage that Evelyn unknowingly had over him to make the upcoming weeks—maybe months—more manageable. Lila might not stand up to Graham, but Evelyn had no issue with putting him in his place, no matter how much money he had in the bank or what title came before his name.

My wife was pretty fucking awesome like that.

"Your pain meds for the night are kicking in; I'll let you get some sleep." I eased out of the chair, using my IV pole for support.

"How do you know that? Did I yawn?"

"No. It's just a feeling."

"Well … you're very empathetic. I am feeling drowsy and a little numb in all the right places."

Me too.

It was time to go. "Sleep well, Lila."

Anya was asleep by the time I returned to Madeline's room.

"Ready to go home?" I whispered to not disturb either Madeline or Anya.

Evelyn nodded, rubbing Anya's back. "Dad's staying here."

I grinned, glancing over at Corey wedged into the hospital bed with his wife. "I figured." That would have been my dad too had it been my mom in the hospital. It was what made me sad for Lila. Governor of Colorado or not … Graham should have been there with her. Nothing would have taken me away from my wife in that same scenario. *Nothing.*

"Where's your IV?" Evelyn asked.

"I removed it."

"I'm not sure patients are supposed to remove their own IVs."

"Probably not." I shrugged.

"Can you carry Anya?"

I could barely carry my head on my shoulders. The adrenaline had worn off. The pain subsided, but I felt so groggy. "Of course." Lifting my pint-sized pixie from Evelyn's arms, I hugged her to me. She felt like a two-hundred-pound bag of dead weight. Evelyn kissed her mom and dad goodnight and followed me to the elevators. By the time we made it to the Jeep, I was drenched in sweat despite the thirty-degree temperature outside.

After easing Anya into her car seat, I closed my eyes and took a few slow breaths before my hands found the energy to fasten the straps.

"Roe ..." Evelyn stopped me after I shut the back door, resting her hand on my chest. "You're sweating like you just ran a race."

I did ... in my dreams or more like my nightmares.

Swallowing, I wiped my brow. She didn't need this, not with everything else crowded onto her shrinking plate. "I'm fine."

Evelyn shook her head slowly, eyes narrowed into a palpable concern as she held up the keys and opened the passenger door. "Get in. You're not fine."

I didn't argue. In fact, I didn't say a single word because as soon as I climbed into the Jeep and fastened my seatbelt, I fell asleep. When we got home, Evelyn nudged my arm. The inside of my eyelids felt like sandpaper rubbing over my eyeballs as I forced them open. She climbed out and carried Anya inside. It took that super-human strength I so desperately wanted just to drag my own ass inside the house. My parents were asleep on the Murphy bed, so we kept the lights off and made our way to the bedroom, depositing Anya in her bed on our way.

My wife looked the way I felt. We moved through an abbreviated bedtime routine in slow motion.

No showers.

Ten seconds of running toothbrushes over our teeth.

I managed to peel off my shirt and jeans. Evelyn pulled off her leggings and climbed into bed in her panties and a long-sleeved tee. There wasn't much strength left in my body. It took what little strength I had left to step up after Madeline's seizure. Still ... this woman—who gave me two beautiful children, who was the ultimate game changer in my life, who personified the truest meaning of life—needed my arms. She didn't have to say it. I felt it.

Amid my superhuman curse, the incurable pain of another human's physical suffering, and the anguish of explaining it to my wife, I could still *feel* her, like some-where along the way she'd woven a piece of her heart—a fragment of her soul—into me. I knew from those two perfect children on the other side of the wall that Evelyn and I were destined to come together in this life and make something beautiful that would let our love live on forever.

As weak and pain-ridden as I felt, nothing could have kept me from reaching for my lifeline and pulling her into my arms. Her body shook as I buried my face in her hair, kissing her neck.

"I…" her voice cracked "…had to…" more silent sobs "…tell myself we'd be okay without you."

That cut so fucking deep I feared my heart would stop just from the pain of reality. I was supposed to be the rock, the *one* person she could count on no matter what. I promised to carry *her*.

Her breathing slowed as the sobs subsided. "Roe … I don't want to be okay without you."

"Then don't. Be okay *with* me."

She turned in my arms to face me. After gazing up at me for several silent seconds, she sat up and shrugged off her shirt. I didn't know how to tell her that I honestly wasn't sure if I could make love to her. *Everything* hurt and my level of exhaustion was not like anything I had ever felt. Before I could say anything, she wrapped her body around mine, wearing nothing but a pair of white panties—her bare chest pressed to mine.

"My heart wants to beat with yours," she whispered in a sleepy voice.

CHAPTER TWENTY-THREE

Ronin — Age 27

AFTER SIX HOSPITALIZATIONS in five years, zero diagnoses, and weekly visits to a psychiatrist—that bore no fruit—my father sat idle with his tongue planted in his teeth while my mom showed me a website.

"Don't judge the content by the design." She smiled at me before pinning Dad with a scowl.

I grimaced. "That's hard not to do. What content? It's … a black page with a tiny light, like a pinpoint in the middle of the screen, and an email in the upper right corner. No navigation bar. A light? Have I mentioned at least a million times that I didn't see a light?"

"Athelinda is in California … Berkeley. I think you should go talk to her." Mom rested her hand on my back.

"Athelinda, huh? Well, I'm in France … Chamonix. I don't think I need to fly to California just to visit another psychiatrist." I plopped down into the desk chair.

"Her name means *one who guards and is immortal.* She's a parapsychologist."

My dad coughed, earning himself another scowl from

my mom.

Dad was a smart man, which made him cautiously skeptical. He was also a loving husband and father, which made him supportive and loyal. I couldn't blame him for his skepticism, but god, I loved him for *being there*.

Mom demanded more, seeing his skepticism as judgment. I never saw it like that. When I focused on his eyes, I saw the pain—his pain for me and my pain, the pain of not understanding it or being able to solve it. He could have voiced his judgment, but he didn't. My mom advocated for me with a loud voice. Dad supported me with a silent presence.

Sometimes *being there* was everything.

"How did you come across this website?" I distracted her from Dad's untimely coughing that she misread as more judgment.

"Dell."

I tapped my index finger on the mouse. "Dell the florist?"

"Yes."

"She's deaf." I narrowed my eyes. At least it had always been my understanding that Dell was deaf.

"Yes. But she hasn't always been deaf. Eight years ago, she drowned. They pronounced her dead. An hour later, she expelled a bunch of water from her lungs—in the morgue. Had it been summer, she wouldn't have survived—the cold temperatures preserved her or something like that. Anyway, she had a near-death experience that left her deaf."

"How would a near-death experience leave one deaf?"

Dad asked. Some things piqued his curiosity enough to ask questions.

Mom smiled. "Funny you should ask. No one can prove that she had a near-death experience, as we know all too well. But doctors can't figure out why she can't hear. Drowning doesn't cause one to go deaf. There were no signs of trauma. Her eardrums were intact. All tests and scans came back normal. Still, she can't hear. The last thing she remembers hearing was a voice. A voice!"

Swiveling in the desk chair, I laced my hands behind my head. "You have my attention."

Her wide eyes shifted to my dad. Yeah, she had his attention too. "I can't remember the exact words she heard, but the gist of it was that she had a choice. Cross over or go back and never hear the whisper of man again. Which ... not a deal breaker to a florist, right? But she wasn't a florist at the time. Dell was an opera singer. She knew a lot of famous musicians and people in the industry. I've been sworn to secrecy, but I can tell you a *very* famous pianist, who also had a near-death experience, told Dell about Athelinda. Only the most connected, highly prestigious individuals seek her wisdom and advice on near-death experiences."

"Then why the website lacking any sort of prestige?" I asked.

Mom shrugged. "Only those who seek feel the need for validation. I don't think Athelinda is seeking anyone or looking for validation. I think she's just allowed those who do seek her to find her."

TWO WEEKS LATER, I stood at the entrance to the address Athelinda sent me. The door read, "Psychic. Walk-ins welcome. Estimated wait time is eternity."

"Are you fucking serious?" I mumbled. Had I not taken three flights to get there, I would have turned around and headed right back to the airport.

"Come in." I glanced up at the camera mounted above the corner of the door.

A click followed a buzz. I pushed open the door, cringing as my head whipped backward from the pungent odor of incense. I coughed a few times and waved my hand in front of my face.

"Welcome, Ronin." A woman with straight silver hair to her waist bowed, hands folded at her chest. Tiny brown-stained teeth peeked out from behind thin dry lips on her gaunt face.

I coughed again.

Her croaky voice fit her brittle body. She probably did know the meaning to life after a hundred years on Earth—my best guess of her age.

"No need to worry. I haven't burned anything hallucinogenic since this morning. It's mostly sage and Frankincense you're detecting at the moment."

Under a black ceiling and a million stars and moons hanging via fishing line from said ceiling, I surveyed the situation. And by situation, I mean the *whole* room.

Creaky wood planks covered the floor with no furniture except two round velvet pillows the size of a car tire and the color of a cat's vomit after eating too much grass. Hand-painted white clouds covered the light blue walls.

"It's 10:00 a.m." I coughed again. "What do you consider morning?"

"Nine. Unless you book the early bird slot, but that's an extra hundred dollars." Athelinda lifted the floor-length skirt to her white cotton dress that may have been an actual sheet sewn into a frock. "Shoes and socks off, please." She wiggled her crooked toes, some smooth like they never had a toenail and others with thick yellow nails. "We need to access all of your energy. In fact, I encourage you, if it's in your zone of comfort, to remove all of your clothes and slip on a loose gown like mine." She tugged on the wide sleeves.

"You know … I think removing my socks and shoes is where my comfort zone is today."

"As you wish." She folded her hands and bowed again.

I removed my socks and shoes and took a seat on the pillow facing her lotus-posed body. Pulling my long limbs toward me, I crisscrossed my legs, certain if I sat in that position too long, I'd never get them uncrossed.

"Let's close our eyes, take a few deep breaths, and go through some questions."

The tacky room.

The terrible odor.

The witchy woman.

Why was I there? It took me a full second to answer that question as I followed her lead, taking several deep breaths.

I died.

Heard a voice.

Made a deal.

Lived to tell about it.

I was in no position to judge anyone or anything.

"Tell me about the voice. Was it a familiar voice?"

My eyes shot open. Hers did not.

I emailed Athelinda, asking to discuss a near-death experience. That was it. No details. She sent me a basic medical form. I listed the date of the accident and the six other visits to the hospital since that time. Medications ... allergies. All very basic.

"What makes you think I heard a voice?"

"Your date of birth. You were born on a Tuesday in September. A child born on a Tuesday in autumn will never see the light, only hear the voice."

O ... kay ...

Closing my eyes, I focused on memories of the voice. "It's indistinguishable. Unisex. Like a computer speaking, only softer. The words flow with perfect timing. They are neither angry nor compassionate. Factual. Consistent."

"It wasn't your fault."

"It was an accident," I whispered.

"But you feel punished."

I peeked open one eye. "Yes."

"Then it was partially your fault. Shared blame. Who do you blame?"

"I don't. I mean ... I was young. My parents were focused on my younger brother. It was my uncle's house. Maybe he should have warned my parents of the hazards.

And I should have known to not snoop around when they told me not to touch anything. But they always told me that. Isn't that a pretty standard parental warning?"

"So it's a trade." She opened her eyes, tawny and owlish in their inspection of me. "What did you agree to do in exchange for continuing in this life as Ronin Alexander?"

How did she do that? Know that? Why did I find her knowledge so unbelievable?

Again ...

I died.

Heard a voice.

Made a deal.

Lived to tell about it.

How insane and ironic that I maintained such a critical mind when it came to anyone who could help me understand my situation. Was the possibility of them knowing the meaning of the voice any more unbelievable than me hearing the voice in the first place?

"I'm not sure what I agreed to, but I think it involved not becoming a paramedic. I did it anyway."

"Oh ...." Athelinda held up her shaky twig of a finger, leaned to the side, and retrieved a book from under her pillow. It had the same hundred-year weathered appearance as the hands that held it. The brown-stained cover read "I AM" followed by an ellipsis. The binding creaked as she opened the hardcover. "I think we can narrow this down."

"I'm not looking to narrow anything down per se but rather completely remove its power over my life."

She glanced up, eyes narrowed into catlike slits. "Young man, your life is contingent on its power. I fear you don't have a true respect for *it*."

"I don't understand it. That makes it hard to respect it."

"Is that not why you're here? To shed the light of wisdom on this beautiful gift?"

"Curse." I shook my head. "Not a gift."

"You lived. That's a gift." She thumbed through the worn pages with curled corners and smudged ink spots and spewed off a string of questions. Some I knew the answers to, others I didn't *want* to know the answers.

What was my first solid food?

How many permanent teeth did I have when I died the first time?

How do I picture God? Man, woman, beast? Vengeful, kind, both?

Recurring dreams?

Biggest fear?

After a series of nods and "I see's," Athelinda stopped on a page toward the back of the book. Stroking her palm over the wrinkled page several times, she smiled. "Hinder not the soul's intended path unto the light, lest shards of darkness shed upon thee."

"H-how did you know that?"

"I wrote the book."

That didn't answer my question. Writing a book and reading my mind were two different abilities.

"Was it you? Was it your voice I heard?"

Her chest vibrated with a tiny chuckle. "That's a first.

I've never had anyone ask me that before. I was twenty-one at the time of your accident. Believe me, I had better things to do than counsel the in-betweeners. Third year of college." She shook her head. "My poor liver. I spent a full decade drinking myself into a coma. The twenties were brutal."

I did the math in my head, and it didn't add up. I was twelve at the time of my accident. If she was twenty-one at the same time, that meant she was only nine years older than me.

No.

Fucking.

Way.

The fragile woman before me could not possibly be thirty-six years old.

"I know what you're thinking." She winked with a wry grin on her face.

I no longer had any doubt that she knew all of my thoughts.

"I've had thirteen near-death experiences. That shit ages a person. I've seen many lights, heard many voices. The Keeper hasn't been as generous to me. Not all of my deaths have been accidental." She shrugged, scrunching her already wrinkled nose.

"The Keeper? You mean God?"

"The Keeper is definitely not God. If you ruled the world, would you seriously spend your days filtering through the dead? Hell no, you wouldn't. You'd assign that shit to someone else. Delegate. Delegate. Delegate."

"I'm …" I inched my head side to side.

"It's confusing. I know." She gathered her hair over one shoulder and began braiding it. "NDEs, OBEs, reincarnation, Heaven, Hell, eternal enlightenment ... the possibilities seem endless. It's easier to believe in the Big Bang Theory and resign yourself to the idea that the earth's creatures will devour your remains when you die. The circle of life makes the most sense. Yet ... here *we* are, knowing there's some other factor, some other force. Such a small percentage of people come back. I mean ... when the heart stops ... that's it. But humanity has messed with that. We like to swoop in and save lives— Hinder not the soul's intended path unto the light."

My brain hurt. It made no sense. Why would it be wrong to save a life? It was what I'd suspected the proverb or curse meant, but I didn't want to believe it.

"I'm *not* supposed to save people?" I laughed.

She replied with a sharp nod. "Think of those words as the original DNR (do not resuscitate). Once you get past the mass of flesh that is the human body, you'll have a greater respect for the eternal soul and the importance of not disrupting its journey."

"*Shards of darkness* ... I feel their pain until they die."

Her head bobbed side to side. "It's a little more complicated than that, but if that deters you from interrupting the soul's path, then sure ... you share their pain until they die, and all is released."

"But that's my job."

She closed the book. "Find a new one."

"I don't want a new job." I refrained from telling her my superhero dreams.

"Then accept the darkness. Listen ... you're looking at the queen of darkness, the ruler of rebellion, the obstinate soul who just can't get enough of this one life. You still have free choice, but with a new set of consequences."

"So this is what happens to everyone who saves a life?"

"Everyone? No. Most people in your position don't see anything wrong with saving a life. They're heralded as heroes. But knowledge imparts accountability. Those who know better must act better. Now, you know better."

CHAPTER TWENTY-FOUR

W ITH SWEAT BEADING along my brow, I forced myself to get out of bed the next morning. *Never again* would I take for granted the gift of mobility. Ten steps to the toilet shouldn't humble anyone. Yet, it robbed years of self-esteem as my ribs protested when I twisted my torso to wipe my ass.

After the marathon of a simple shit and hand washing, my leg tried to reject all attempts to walk into the other room. Closing my eyes, I reminded myself that *my* leg was fine. Still, it hurt. The injury wasn't real to me, but the pain was incredibly real.

Evie.

Franz.

Anya.

I had *every* reason to keep going, to push through. This wouldn't last forever.

"Good morning." Mom smiled from the kitchen. "Tea? Coffee?"

"Coffee." I limped to the sofa. "Where'd they go? The hospital?"

Keeping a smile on her face, she handed me a mug of

coffee. "Your family?"

"Uh-huh."

"Yes. Evelyn didn't want to wake you, but she wanted to go see her mom, and she thought it would cheer Madeline up to see the kids. So your dad went with her to help out. Also, she wanted to see Lila before they transferred her to Denver." She sat next to me on the sofa, angling her body toward me as she sipped her tea. "You're going to have to tell her."

Grunting a laugh, I gazed at the steam from my coffee. "I tried, but we got interrupted, and then everything just ... happened. It's not exactly a quick thing to explain."

"Ronin ..." Emotion filled my mom's eyes. She had been strong for everyone else, but I knew she saw the fear in my eyes. I knew it at the hospital. It was my fear too. "Your heart stopped."

"I know," I whispered.

"That's ..." She shook her head, blinking back the tears. "That's not how it works. You *feel.* That's it. You don't live it. You don't actually die. Why did your heart stop beating?" She cupped her hand to her mouth, choking back a sob as the tears fell down her cheeks.

I didn't know why my heart stopped. I felt the cracked ribs. My ribs didn't break. My leg wasn't broken. My face wasn't lacerated. The bruises were tender, but they weren't visible. I just *felt* things. I would *live* to feel an eternity of deaths, not actually die. That was the deal. So why the fuck did my heart stop when Lila went into cardiac arrest the second time?

It wasn't like before, when I was electrocuted. Again, no light beckoned me, and I wasn't given a choice to live more days as Ronin Alexander.

A blip.

Same voice.

Two words: "Not yet."

Okay, it wasn't my time to die, *yet*. That didn't answer the question—why did my heart stop?

"And Lila ..." Mom left her name hanging in the air, wiping her tears.

My brow furrowed. "Yeah," I whispered. I couldn't get her out of my mind, out of my body.

"She's still alive."

I nodded once. "For now."

"You think she's going to die?"

"We're all going to die."

"Ronin, you know what I mean."

Leaning forward, I set the mug on the coffee table. "She survived the surgery. They're moving her to Denver because she's stable. I'm sure she's on blood thinners to keep her from throwing a clot. Still ... things happen."

"What if she doesn't?"

Sitting back, I ran a hand through my wet hair and grunted a laugh. "What if Lila doesn't die? Wow ... that's pretty messed up. Her *living* shouldn't be a problem. It's not supposed to be this way."

"She was supposed to die?"

"Yes." I clamped my mouth shut and rubbed my temples. "I mean ... No. She wasn't supposed to die. She wasn't supposed to fall off the cliff. She wasn't supposed to cross the barrier. She wasn't supposed to go off on her own."

"Why didn't you wait for someone else to tend to her?"

I shook my head. My entire life at that moment felt like a perpetual headshake. Total disbelief. Massive confusion. "Because she wasn't breathing."

"But you knew you couldn't save her at that point. You knew the rules."

"Fuck the rules! It was Lila!" Tears burned my eyes as I gritted my teeth. "I couldn't *not* try to save her. Graham was right there. I couldn't look him in the eye and just ... do nothing. My wife's best friend. *My* friend. It was ..." I rubbed my hand down my face. "Lila ... It was Lila," I whispered.

"What are you going to do?" Mom rested her hand on my leg.

I didn't have a clue.

"Wait."

"For her to die?"

Staring unblinkingly at my mom, I shrugged. "Or live."

"When Madeline gets home safely and Lila's transferred to Denver, you need to tell Evelyn everything."

"What if I don't know what *everything* is anymore?"

"Then tell her exactly that. Give her honesty every step of the way."

"What if she doesn't believe me?"

"Then you make her see it."

If she didn't understand, it left only one option—I

was crazy. Who lived their life with a crazy person?

"Your dad doesn't believe it like I do, but he knows you're not crazy. There's a middle, Ronin. If you can bring her to the middle, that's good enough. She doesn't have to believe it like we do to accept you. And she's already halfway there. You know this. Every time you end up in the hospital and they can't figure anything out, Evelyn loses it. She hasn't been given a logical explanation, so at this point, I think she will latch on to anything you give her if you can show her it's *your* truth."

I cringed, leaning forward.

"What is it, Ronin?"

"Lila ..." I blew out a long breath to release the tension that gripped my body. They were doing something to her at the hospital, maybe getting her out of bed. Whatever it was, she was feeling serious pain.

"How are you going to go back to work?" She stroked my hair.

"I don't know yet." I leaned back and closed my eyes. Sometimes giving all my energy to the worst area of pain actually lessened it, but it wasn't easy when so many parts of my body vied for that top spot.

COREY TOOK MADELINE home the next day, a day after Lila was transferred to Denver. They anticipated she would be in the hospital two more weeks. I requested a few more days off work, hoping by some miracle I could do my job by then. It wrecked me to think that miracle had to be Lila dying.

With the help of little things, like celebrating Franz's fourth birthday, the pain started to subside; that was good for both of us. However, I had a feeling that Graham was encouraging Lila to stay on her pain medications, which meant the reprieve was temporary.

Among all the other chaos, Sophie got the flu, so Evelyn had to go back to work. My parents agreed to stay as long as we needed them. My dad thought that meant until I returned to work, but I knew my mom figured it meant until the funeral ... because she believed Lila's fate had already been determined.

I didn't know what to believe anymore.

"Ronin!" Evelyn glanced up from the half-constructed display toward the back of the store. No one else was in there at the moment. She brushed off her hands and quickly found her way into my arms. "What are you doing here? You're out on your own. You must be feeling better." Pulling back just enough to look up at me, she grinned.

I wasn't feeling on top of the world—yet. However, I knew I'd pretend that was the case if it meant making my wife deliriously happy.

"I am." Okay, I wasn't feeling better, but I was out on my own, testing the waters to see just how functional I could pretend to be.

If Evelyn could go back to work, in spite of her dying mom, best friend in the hospital, daughter with stitches in her head, and me with my fucked-up issues, *and* pull her shit together enough to keep going, then I had to make the same effort.

"Lila messaged me. She's feeling a little better today too."

Of course, she was feeling better; otherwise I wouldn't have been able to drag my ass to the shop.

"They probably have her drugged up."

Evelyn kissed the angle of my jaw. "No," she murmured. "Per your suggestion, I talked to Graham about alternative treatments for pain."

I narrowed my eyes. "Yes, you told me that. You also said he seemed pretty skeptical."

On a shrug, she released me and turned back toward her display, arranging bars of soap into tidy little rows. "Well, he must have had a change of heart because he arranged for her to have acupuncture this morning, and she said it cut her pain in half."

Her revelation and the optimism over Lila's recovery made it easy for me to second-guess telling her the truth. Why mess with a good thing? Maybe Lila was an exception to the rule.

"That's great."

"It is." She sighed, glancing over her shoulder at me. "I think I'm ready to finish our conversation."

"Our conversation?" I knew what she meant, but if there was a one-percent chance I was wrong, I wasn't going to shit all over her good mood by addressing something that maybe ... just maybe no longer needed to be discussed.

"The voices in your head."

I rubbed my eye. "That uh ... makes me sound crazy,

Evie. Do you think I'm crazy?"

She laughed. "Of course not. I just want to understand, and we got interrupted, so now I want you to finish telling me everything."

Understand.

She wasn't going to understand. *I* didn't understand it. I thought I did, but then my heart stopped beating.

"I fear *understand* isn't the best word. I'm not sure you'll be able to truly understand."

"Well, try me. Make me understand." She clasped her hands behind her back, waiting for my magical explanation.

I cleared my throat. "O … kay. Just go with me for a second. As an example, if you saw a pig flying, you wouldn't be able to dispute what you saw, nor would you be able to explain it. But it wouldn't mean that the pig didn't fly. Right?"

Evelyn laughed a little more, returning her attention to the display. "Yes. I suppose. Did you see a pig fly?"

"If I did, would you believe me?"

"Sure."

"No!" I laced my fingers behind my head and paced back and forth. "You wouldn't believe me. I can tell from your laughter you wouldn't believe me."

When she faced me again, her smile was gone. I didn't mean to take away her smile. After days of tragedy and grief, she had earned the right to have a moment that wasn't so damn depressing. "I'm not laughing at you."

My chin dropped to my chest on a long sigh. "I know. I'm sorry. It's just so hard to tell you this because it's not going to make sense. It's going to be completely unbelievable and utterly confusing." I glanced up at her again.

"Then don't try to explain *the voice*. Just tell me what it means for your life now. Tell me if you know why your heart stopped beating, and I promise I will believe you."

"I don't know what it means anymore. I didn't know what it meant for many years after the accident. Then I performed CPR on an actual person for the first time. I heard a ringing in my ears that intensified as I compressed the person's chest. And I heard that voice telling me the same thing. *Hinder not the soul's intended path unto the light, lest shards of darkness shed upon thee.*

"The person never regained a heartbeat. Once I stopped CPR, the ringing in my ears stopped. The next time I performed CPR, the same thing happened, only we did revive the woman. I heard the ringing, the voice, and I felt her injuries from the accident, her pain and suffering. She died less than twenty-four hours later. But that was the first time I ended up in the hospital too—feeling like I was dying, but having no signs of injuries or ailments. Come to find out, I miraculously recovered at the same time the woman died."

My brain told me to keep going, but my heart told me to let her take over and decide where she was ready for me to go with the rest of this revelation.

Lines formed along her forehead. "That man you tried to save in the restaurant with Graham, you felt his pain after he was resuscitated? That's why you were so sick?"

"Yes."

She kept her gaze somewhere between our feet, maybe the smudge on the wood floor. "Then your pain just … stopped?"

I didn't respond. She knew the answer.

"Because he died?" Blue eyes made their way to meet my gaze.

"Yes," I whispered.

Evelyn nodded in tiny increments as her eyes narrowed a little more. "Lila didn't die."

"True."

She cleared her throat and curled a few stray hairs behind her ear. "So what happens when they don't die?"

"I don't know."

"Why?"

I started to say it, but the words wouldn't come out. They raked along my throat like razorblades, burning my eyes and suffocating my lungs. I didn't know the real answer, just a few guesses mixed with my worst fears.

"Why?" she repeated with a hard edge to her demand.

"Because they all die."

CHAPTER TWENTY-FIVE

Evelyn

I KNEW I would never forget the look on Ronin's face when he said those four words.

The pain.

The regret.

The love …

Without love, there can be no pain and regret.

Taking a step toward him, I smiled, resting my palm on his cheek. "Don't you see what this means?"

He squinted, intensifying the anguish on his handsome face.

"It's over. This *curse* is over. Lila lived. She's getting better. You're getting better." Lifting onto my toes, I feathered my lips along his jaw to his ear. "You're free," I whispered.

"Evelyn." He grabbed my shoulders, holding me at arm's length. "It feels like a curse, but it's not actually a curse."

"You know what I mean."

Ronin nodded. "Yes. I know what you mean, but you

don't know what I mean. Lila could still …"

I waited. There was no way I was going to say it for him. Lila wasn't dying. She was getting stronger every day.

"I know you're scared, baby." I tried to infuse as much sympathy as possible into my voice.

Ronin had clearly been through a lot, not just from recent events, but during the span of most of his life. The accident he suffered as a child changed him. Even if I didn't fully understand it, or wholeheartedly believed all of it, I stood by him. His physical pain and emotional suffering emanated from every inch of his body.

"*Today* Lila is alive. *Today* you are feeling better. You don't need to prepare me for tomorrow or any day after that. How many times do I have to tell you I'm stronger than you think I am?"

"Evie …" He covered my hand with his and turned his head a fraction so his lips pressed to my palm. "*You* are the strongest person I know. But that will never stop me from dedicating every breath, every second, I have on this earth to keep you from having your heart broken. I said I'd hold our family together."

I wrapped both arms around his neck. He leaned down instead of picking me up off my feet like he usually did when I hugged him. His vulnerability chipped away at my emotional armor. "*We* will hold our family together."

"We …" he echoed me while wrapping his arms around my waist.

I slipped on my favorite—but rather weathered—

brave face and sent Ronin home to spend time with the kids and his parents so I could finish setting up my displays. At least ... that was my excuse.

After he made it across the street toward his car, I locked the shop door and stuck up our "Be back in 15 minutes" sign that we used in a pinch when only one person was manning the shop. Then I retreated to the back room to cry my eyes out.

Either my best friend was dying, or my husband was crazy.

TWO WEEKS LATER, I drove to Denver to visit my mom and Lila. Mom seemed to have rebounded since the seizure. We ate lunch before I headed to Lila's and Graham's house. They rarely stayed at the governor's mansion. It was subpar to the Porter estate, and no staff were provided. Lila needed help doing everything at the moment. She'd been released from the hospital that morning, so I was excited to see her and Graham.

"You look like you could use a manicure." I peeked my head into her massive bedroom. Seriously, the ceiling was two stories with mammoth windows and lavish coverings, all imported from some place I couldn't remember and hand-stitched by someone really important, also whom I couldn't remember. My window coverings were from Target.

"Evie!" She grimaced for a split second, pushing herself up in bed.

I hugged her so tightly; I feared I might hurt her, but I couldn't help it. After the accident and Ronin's revelation two weeks earlier, it felt amazing to hug my best friend and see her on the mend. "You look good, so good."

Lila gave me the stink eye as I climbed onto the other side of the bed, crossing my legs while facing her. "Really?" She pointed to her face. The four-inch gouge showed signs of mending nicely, but I realized all she saw was the potential scar. Graham brought in the best plastics guy to work on her face. I knew there wouldn't be much of a scar after it completely healed.

"Yes, I see it. And I see you. And you're alive! Please don't focus on the little things that don't matter." I glanced around. "Where's Graham Cracker?"

"D.C."

"What?" I drew my head back.

Lila lifted her good shoulder. "He'll be home in a few days. I have a gazillion people waiting on me and checking up on me." She smirked. "Besides you. So it's fine."

"He's your husband. No one replaces him. He should have been the one to bring you home. Who brought you home?"

"Fiona."

"Your personal assistant? You mean his parents couldn't even take it upon themselves to pick you up in Graham's absence? Are you kidding me?"

"It's fine, Evie. They're out of town. Besides, Fiona is my friend. She's become family of sorts."

I wrinkled my nose, not out of jealousy. No. It was

the memory of Lila telling me how Fiona would wait outside of Graham's office with clean underwear and a cloth for Lila after Graham fucked her in his office. I knew what it was like to be that kind of friend to Lila, so it made me sad for her. Who wants to need that from a friend?

"I'm glad she was there for you. Had I known, I would have picked you up. I was visiting my mom this morning, but we both would have picked you up and brought you home. I just assumed it was Graham, and I didn't want to step on his toes."

"I'm alive." She winked. "No need to focus on the little things that don't matter, right?"

I shook my head, trying to fight back my grin. "Touché."

Lila's gaze shifted to my bag. "Did you seriously bring stuff to give me a manicure?"

"Yes." I tipped my chin up. "And a pedicure."

She chuckled. "You realize I can order that sort of pampering anytime I want it, right?"

I grabbed her hand and inspected her nails and the peeling red polish. "Yes. But I knew you wouldn't do it today, so I jumped at the chance to go back twenty-five years to when we used to give each other manis and pedis." Crawling off of the bed, I padded to the bathroom to find a few things. "I bet these are expensive towels, huh?" I ran some hot water.

"Of course," Lila replied.

"Well, they're going to get fucked-up today." I returned with a wicked grin and fine linens to ruin with nail polish.

"Go for it. Graham has been extra nice to me since the accident. I don't think he'll sweat over towels."

I wet a cotton swab with fingernail polish remover and scrubbed at her nails. "Graham should be extra nice to you every single day. That was the deal."

"What deal?"

I glanced up and winked. "The deal we made when I said I'd be his advocate to get you to fall in love with him. You're on loan ... from me. Wedding vows or not, he knows the deal that was made."

"So if he breaks the deal, you get me back?"

"Yes."

"And I'll come live with you and Ronin?"

"Yes." I focused on her nails and the stubborn polish.

"Will we have a threesome?"

"Hell to the no fucking way."

She giggled. "Why not?"

"Because Ronin is a one-woman man."

"How do you know? Have you asked him?"

"No."

"Why not?" Lila cocked her head to the side.

"Because he's not Graham. I don't have to have threesome conversations with him. We're married. We have two kids. That's not our life."

"But you did it with us in Vancouver."

I paused and glanced up again, brow furrowed. "Seriously? That was *years* ago. And we didn't 'do it.' We ... messed around. Then I left. And you two 'did it.' No one was married. No kids. And it wasn't my idea."

"But you went along with it."

I sighed. "Why are we having this conversation? You were the one who said we should never discuss it again."

"Have you told Ronin? Does he know just how close your friendship is with Graham and me?"

Wiping her hand with the expensive white towel, I shook my head. "No."

"Why not?"

"Grr …"

Lila giggled. I hated that stupid conversation, but I sure did love her giggle. It meant so many things—she was alive, feeling better, and happy.

"Did you just growl at me?"

"Yes."

"Why?"

"Because I think you're on something. Did you start taking more pain meds?"

"No."

"Marijuana?"

"Nope. I'm just high on life and feeling nostalgic, and I'm in the mood to walk down memory lane because my BFF is here and doing something really sweet for me."

"I know … I'm pretty amazing."

"You are. Let's talk about your amazingness *and* why you didn't tell your husband about that night in Vancouver."

"Because it never came up. I'm not intentionally hiding it from him. I just haven't told him about every thing I've ever done in my whole life. Remember when we went horseback riding in sixth grade and I fell and broke my arm?"

"Yeah."

"Well…" I shrugged "…I don't think I've ever told Ronin about it. If we got on the subject of broken limbs or horseback riding, I'm sure I'd tell him the story. But … we haven't."

"Maybe I should bring up that night in Vancouver sometime when we're all together. I'd love to see the look on his face."

"Why?"

"Because I think he would find it pretty hot."

"No. He wouldn't."

"How can you say that?" she asked in disbelief.

"Because I'm his wife, the mother of his children. Maybe … just maybe he might have found humor in it or found it … slightly erotic before we got married. But not now. Graham is his friend. I think it would change their relationship."

"You mean he doesn't know that you slept with my husband in college?"

Again, I shot her a glare, giving her an incredulous look. "That just sounds horrible, Lila. Like Graham was your husband and I slept with him."

"You know what I mean."

"Yes, I do. But if you said those words to anyone else, they would *not* know what you meant."

"Do you think …" Her words faded.

"Do I think what?" I moved to her other hand, scrubbing off the polish.

"Do you think Graham will be attracted to me

again?"

I stopped, unable to look up at her because I didn't think I heard her correctly. "I don't understand what you mean."

"How long do you think it will take for him to want to have sex with me again?"

"Well," I resumed, "I think he *shouldn't* expect that until you're healed, and that could take a while."

"What do you think he'll do in the meantime?"

"Jerk off more."

Lila snorted. "I'm serious."

I shrugged. "So am I."

"Do you think he'll … wander?"

I snapped my head up. "What?"

Her lips twisted for a few seconds. "He has needs."

"Lila Rae Porter … you had better be joking or dealing with some sort of PTSD. Why would you think for one second that Graham would cheat on you?"

Her gaze dropped to her lap. "I don't know. I just … I don't know," she murmured.

"When he saw you in the ICU right after your surgery, he broke down. I had never seen that side of Graham. He sobbed over your broken body. *Sobbed!* It shattered my heart to see him like that, but it also erased any doubt, I mean *any* doubt I might have had about his love for you. So even if I think it's a little douchey of him to not have brought you home from the hospital, I don't let it dissuade me from trusting his love for you."

"I hope you're right."

"I'm right."

God … I hoped I was right. If I wasn't right, Graham was a dead man.

"So … how's Ronin feeling?"

"Fine."

"Is he back to work?"

I nodded.

"Did they figure out why he went into cardiac arrest?"

"No."

"And that doesn't bother you?"

I shook the bottle of nail polish, contemplating telling Lila about Ronin's theory … his past. We hadn't discussed it since that day in my shop. Lila continued to get better and so did Ronin. He wasn't back to himself, singing in the shower yet, but he was working and helping out around the house. It was hard to determine if his residual issues were really related to Lila's accident.

"Of course, it bothers me. But I hit this point, you know? No solid answers, but also there was nothing else I could do. He's supposed to be wearing a monitor still, but half of the time I find it tossed aside on the nightstand. He doesn't think it's his heart."

"Then what does he think it is?"

Forever. That was how long Lila and I had been friends, or at least as long as I could remember. We didn't keep secrets. All the things Ronin had yet to learn about me … Lila already knew.

Still, I couldn't bring myself to tell her about Ronin's near-death experience. I felt protective of him. As much as I loved and trusted Lila to keep an open mind and not judge him for what he believed, I found myself struggling with it. So if I still couldn't wrap my head around the idea that Ronin had this highly sensitive empathic power with people whom he tried to save, then how could I possibly expect her to understand?

"He thinks it was a fluke. A strange, unexplainable incident that probably won't ever happen again."

"I hope not, for both of your sakes. How about your mom? Is she doing better since the seizure?"

"Yes. It's..." I shook my head, brushing the pink nail polish onto Lila's nails "...weird. I know she only has so much time left, and her seizure was a very hard reminder of that. But today she looked good. Healthy. It was hard to believe that there's this cancer spreading through her body, stealing her life."

"And your dad? How's he holding up?"

"I'm scared for him. After she had that seizure, I was sitting on the floor in my house, holding my kids, Anya with a bleeding cut. And Ronin wasn't doing well. Mom was on the floor in the bedroom waiting for the paramedics, and you were still in the ICU. Something inside of me snapped, causing me to take a step back and reevaluate what would be left of my life if I lost my mom, you, and Ronin. And I knew ... I knew Franz and Anya would be enough. More than enough. I just don't know if my dad will be able to step back after Mom dies and see that he still has enough left in his life to ... *live*."

The second I finished that thought, my heart sank to the pit of my stomach. "Lila ... I ... I didn't mean—"

"It's fine."

I looked up from her hand. It didn't feel fine. "I

wasn't thinking. I was feeling, and—"

"Evelyn, it's fine." She nodded, maintaining her best reassuring smile.

After Lila's parents died, she had a rough time. I wasn't enough. My family wasn't enough. The only thing that filled that void in her heart was a flood of never-ending grief. She talked about that time as a black hole with no exit. She took a whole bottle of prescription pills that a friend from school sold her, and I found her in her car passed out later that afternoon in the school parking lot.

"I'm proud of you." I continued painting her nails.

"Proud of me?" She laughed. "For trying to commit suicide?"

"Once. You tried once. Then you got help. And your situation hadn't changed. You were still an orphan. You still missed your parents. You still thought life was unfair. But you never tried to check out again. And you could have."

"Thank you, Evie. That actually means the world to me," she murmured with soft sincerity.

"You're a survivor."

"Ha! I don't know about that. Look at me. I'm at the mercy of other people to do the most basic things like go to the bathroom."

"But you're feeling better."

"Yes. But I'm not without pain."

"Where do you hurt?" I capped the nail polish and gave it a few more shakes before doing her other hand.

"My ribs are still sore and my leg. But my lower back

has started to really ache at night too. I think it's just from being bedridden. I'm hoping the physical therapist will help that by getting my body moving, so I can heal quicker."

My hand shook, so I had to cap the polish again and flex my fingers a few times to keep it from shaking again. "Your lower back, huh. When did it start hurting?"

"About two days ago. It's sciatic pain, shoots down the back of my good leg. Talk about two steps forward, one step back. But, on the flip side, this has been the best day *emotionally* that I've had since the accident, and it's all because of you, Evie. My heart is full right now. I can't believe you're here, painting my nails like we used to do so many years ago."

Taking several deep breaths, I held the nail polish brush with a firmer grip to steady my stroke. "I'm happy to do it," I whispered, but not to Lila, more to a voice … *that* voice.

CHAPTER TWENTY-SIX

F ROM THE DRIVE, my house looked like one of those lit villages people put on their mantels at Christmas time—the windows aglow with soft light, the roof covered in snow, and smoke wafting from the chimney as if breathing out a long exhale on a cold evening.

Sue's car was gone, and the Subaru was parked in the garage. I anticipated takeout waiting for me and the kids in need of baths. On the nights Ronin got home before me, which wasn't often, he picked up dinner so at least everyone was fed. Since the accident, work took everything out of him. I was appreciative of his efforts. Takeout was fine.

I slipped off my boots and opened the door. "Sorry, I'm so late—"

"Shh ..." Ronin put a sudsy finger up to his lips.

With wide eyes and an unhinged jaw, I stood unmoving at the door. The house was quiet. My husband stood at the kitchen sink doing dishes in his thermal shirt and jeans that he wore over his base-layer pants to commute to and from work.

I slid off my jacket and padded into the kitchen in my

wool socks.

"Your dinner is in the oven, keeping warm," Ronin murmured as he rinsed the last dish.

"You made dinner?" I wrapped my arms around him, resting my cheek on his back.

"I need a shower, babe. You might not want to hug me. But yes, I made dinner."

"It's eight-thirty. Are the kids really asleep?" I slipped on an oven glove and retrieved my dinner.

"Yep, or at least they're probably close."

"Bathed?" I set my plate on the counter and glanced at Ronin, giving him a raised brow.

He dried his hands and hung the wet towel over the dishwasher handle. "Yes. Bathed. Any more questions before I shower?" Ronin crossed his arms over his broad chest.

I loved the way he looked after a day on the slopes in his fitted shirt, messy hair, and the perfect shadow of stubble covering his handsome chiseled face.

"No more questions." I grinned, grabbing a fork from the drawer. "You seem to have a bit more energy today."

"It's been an okay day. I'm not sure I have *that* much more energy, but I've been in a good mood all afternoon, and that goes a long way."

I nodded slowly, taking a seat at the little nook by the window. "Lila was in a good mood today too."

"I figured." Ronin turned and disappeared down the hallway.

I poked around at my dinner, no longer feeling hungry. *He figured.* What did I expect? He told me everything. I let him think I believed him, even when I knew my doubts overshadowed the true conviction I fed to him at the shop two weeks earlier. The worst part? I think he knew. Disappointment took up residence in his eyes when he looked at me ... when I couldn't hold his gaze.

He figured.

Lila had a good day. Ronin had a good day. Coincidence? God ... I hoped so. After forcing several bites of food, I covered my plate and put it in the fridge. Tiptoeing into Franz's room, I gave him a kiss on the head. He didn't even stir. Then I did the same to Anya. She released a heavy sigh, which made me smile. Ronin had not only made dinner; he wore the kids out, bathed them, and had them asleep before nine.

As I sneaked out of Anya's room, Ronin's voice stopped me. Tears filled my eyes. After two weeks of silence, he was singing Sinatra in the shower again. My lips curled into a much needed smile. The whole day had been filled with smiles.

Lila had a good day. Ronin had a good day.

Releasing a slow breath, I pulled my sweater over my head while instinct guided me to the bathroom. One by one, my clothes dotted the floor like crumbs on a trail.

"Evie." Ronin grinned as I opened the glass shower door.

I stepped inside, closing my eyes as he retreated to let me under the shower head. When I opened my eyes, Ronin was just ... gazing at me like he did that day in the little cafe in Vancouver. It made my heart feel light, like it had wings, exactly like that day in Vancouver.

He didn't touch me. He didn't have to.

"I'm glad you had a good day." I moved behind him, kissing along his back.

Ronin pressed his hands to the tile wall, bowing his head. My fingers massaged his back, inching lower until he moaned.

"Yes ... god that feels incredible."

He mentioned a bit of back pain the previous day. I didn't think much of it, until Lila said she had lower back pain.

It's sciatic pain, shoots down the back of my good leg.

Her words replayed in my mind as my thumbs kneaded lower, working to his left side and down over the tight muscles of his buttock.

"Evie ... god ... right there. How did you know I needed that *right* there?"

I hoped his question was rhetorical because I couldn't answer. Too many tears falling down my face mingled with the water as a hard lump formed in my throat.

You feel her ...

What did it mean? If I acknowledged it, what was I supposed to do? What would happen next? Was Lila dying in spite of her great strides toward recovery? Or would she live, leaving Ronin to be a voodoo doll enduring every painful moment of her life ... for the rest of her life?

We stayed in the shower until the hot water evaporated into a lukewarm stream. Ronin shut off the water and turned toward me. Water clung to his thick eyelashes as he blinked. We weren't the only ones in that tiny space. All the unknowns wedged their way between us—my mom's cancer and Lila's recovery.

The voice.

Weeks without making love.

Days of going through the motions to keep our family functioning.

We were merely existing, until that day. Hope peeked its head over our horizon. She wasn't blindingly bright quite yet, but that didn't stop us from feeling her warmth.

"Lila's having lower back pain. On her left side. Sciatica."

Ronin nodded slowly, blinking away more droplets of water. "Why the tears, Evie?" He brushed his thumb along my cheek below my eye.

"I wanted to believe you, but it was just … hard."

His other hand landed on my neck, gentle yet possessive. He bent down and kissed me, delivering his love with complete patience, unbroken trust, and a never-ending passion. That kind of love shouldn't have evoked regret or guilt, but it did. I think I could have told him I saw a pig flying and he would have believed me. I felt certain Ronin loved me in a way that reached far beyond the simple definition of unconditional.

"Roe!" I gasped as he lifted me up, guiding my legs around his waist. "I'm too heavy. Your back …"

His open mouth swallowed my protests as he carried me to the bedroom. I sucked in a breath, turning my head to the side as my wet back hit the sheets.

"Cold!"

He grinned at me, leaning back to grab the blankets, completely covering us under their tent.

I giggled. It felt incredible.

"Evelyn Alexander … you are my favorite." He kissed his way down my body, pausing at my breasts just long enough to make me moan and arch my back, slowly threading my hands into his wet hair.

"Your favorite what?" I murmured as my eyes closed.

He dragged his tongue down the center of my body achingly slow while his strong hands gripped my hips. "Everything." He dipped his tongue into my navel. "You're my favorite *everything.*"

"Roe …"

He excelled at wringing every possible emotion out of me. I needed a few minutes to just bask in his words. They were really incredible words, maybe the best words a man had ever spoken to a woman. However, my mind wandered to his back. I knew it hurt. "Your back." I made another protest.

"Fuck my back." He lifted my left leg, resting my foot on his shoulder, opening me up to him.

I clawed at the head of the bed, desperate to find a pillow to put over my face because things were about to get loud.

THE NEXT MORNING, I woke up before Ronin and made him an English muffin with peanut butter and filled his thermal canteen with hot coffee, feeling extra generous after his night of being *so* generous to me. After I had his breakfast lined up at the end of the counter for him to grab on his way out the door, I retrieved a pen and notepad from the junk drawer and wrote him a note.

Roe,

You're my favorite everything too. Xo

~E

I heard the creak of the bathroom door, so I quickly folded the note and shoved it into the pocket of his jacket so he'd find it when he reached for his keys. Feeling a bottle next to his keys, I pulled it out of the pocket. It was a prescription bottle, but I couldn't read the label in the dim light, so I took it over to the single light that was on above the sink.

"What did I do to deserve this?"

I jumped at Ronin's voice, hugging the bottle to me as he pressed his chest to my back and wrapped his arms around me.

I cleared my throat, smiling past my surprise and confusion. "I think you know exactly what you did."

He nipped at my neck. "In that case, I might have to do it more often." His right hand slid under my short nightshirt, splaying out over my stomach. I felt so small molded against his tall frame with his possessive hand warm against my skin. "Think I can make a case for you making homemade pizza tonight?" His sexy, gravely morning voice seduced me as that possessive hand breached the waistband of my pink panties.

I swallowed as he teased my clit. "Probably ..." My response came out as a labored breath.

"Do you remember what this used to lead to before Franz could walk?" He slid two fingers into me.

I closed my eyes and dropped my head back against his shoulder, widening my legs.

Yes. I remembered how good it felt to have Ronin fuck me against the kitchen counter from behind, our hands interlaced on the edge of the counter. I remembered how we couldn't keep our hands off each other, how every touch, every fleeting glance led to clothes being ripped off and him impaling himself inside of me on a guttural "fuuuck ... Evie ..."

Those days were over, but the tradeoff was so much better. It made the stolen moments that much more intense and quick, maybe embarrassingly quick.

"Harder ..." I whispered.

He chuckled, kissing my neck. "Only *you,* baby, would ask me to *finger you* harder."

I didn't respond. I didn't have to.

Ronin obliged me while his left hand slid up my shirt to my breast, pinching my nipple.

"Roe ..." my knees started to buckle.

He moved his left hand across my chest to my other breast, but it bumped my hand clutching the pill bottle. With a soft rattle and a *clunk*, it landed in the sink. We stopped, frozen in place with me a little breathless and him ... well, Ronin didn't move an inch for several seconds.

I blinked at the bottle, internally scolding myself for

letting him distract me, but it wasn't a big deal. At least I tricked myself into believing it wasn't a big deal because the pill bottle for oxycodone didn't have his name on it.

His fingers slid out of me, and his hand on my chest released me. I picked up the bottle and stepped to the side, re-inspecting the label, wanting so desperately to give him the benefit of the doubt. At that point in our lives, trust felt like everything.

Forrest Johnson, it said on the bottle.

Ronin didn't acknowledge the bottle or me as he hit the pump on the soap and washed his hands while staring straight out the window. He shut off the water, grabbed the towel, and turned toward me. After a few seconds of his head bowed toward the towel, he swung his gaze up to meet mine. That look said it all.

The pills weren't in his name, but they were his pills.

Good doctors didn't give opioid prescriptions without a legitimate source of pain, I assumed. Ronin's pain wasn't his own, but it was real.

My pain was real too, the pain I felt when he looked at me with so much guilt and anguish. I returned my attention to the bottle in my hand. "These are some strong pills. Forrest Johnson must be in a lot of pain. I …" I shook my head. "I just hope he doesn't get addicted to them. Lila had a friend, a boyfriend toward the end of college, who had a football injury. He got addicted to pain meds, and he eventually overdosed. That's why she's so opposed to taking them if she absolutely doesn't have to take them."

Biting my lips together, I narrowed my eyes, feeling

an ache in my chest. There wasn't a right answer. An easy solution. Those little pills allowed Ronin to go back to work. It made sense, even if it broke my heart. Lila would be utterly crushed if she found out—if she could wrap her head around the fact that Ronin felt her pain and was taking opioids to deal with it.

With one hand, I took Ronin's hand, and with my other hand I put the bottle of pills in it. "I trust you."

He closed his fingers around it, making a tight fist. "Evelyn …"

I shook my head a half dozen times. "It's fine. It will be fine. She's getting better. You won't need them very long. Everything will be fine." Glancing up at Ronin, my lips attempted a smile. "Right?"

I didn't ask where he got the pills.

I didn't ask about Forrest Johnson.

I didn't ask the things I didn't want to know, the things that would chip away at my trust in him. Those answers weren't going to change our situation. They were just going to drive a wedge between us.

"Right," he murmured halfheartedly. "I have to get to work. Thanks for breakfast." He slipped on his jacket and boots by the door and leaned over to grab his canteen and the English muffin wrapped in a paper towel sitting on top of it. With his other hand, he reached into his pocket for his keys, first pulling out the note I left.

After he read it, he glanced up at me.

I shrugged.

He knew how I came across his pills. I could see it in the tension that gathered along his brow. More guilt.

Shuffling my bare feet to him, I took the canteen and muffin from his hand, setting it back on the counter. Then I lifted onto my toes and wrapped my arms around his neck, hugging him to me tightly. He hugged me back, burying his face into my neck.

I was so close ... so damn close to saying it, and I think he was too.

I love you.

We didn't. We weren't there. Not yet. There were still too many ways to say it without actually saying it.

Before I released him, I batted away a few stray tears on my cheeks. He didn't need any more guilt.

CHAPTER TWENTY-SEVEN

Ronin

I FELT LIKE a failure. As a husband. As a man.

The pain and fear in Evelyn's eyes when she glanced up at me after telling me about Lila's boyfriend, who died from his opioid addiction, was almost too much to bear. Before I asked a friend to get me the pills, I tried high doses of over-the-counter medications. I tried all the things I suggested Lila try like acupuncture, but it wasn't cutting it—not enough to get back to my physically demanding job.

We weren't the Porters. Since having children, we experienced what it was like to live paycheck to paycheck. Even with not having a mortgage, the cost of living in Aspen was insane. Was I too proud to ask for help from Graham? Hell yes.

I didn't even have the guts to ask my parents for help so I could spend more time healing right along with Lila. The thought of my skeptic father handing me money, for a condition he questioned, made me nauseous. I just … couldn't.

TWO MONTHS PASSED without major incident.

Madeline fought more frequent headaches, but she managed to stay out of the hospital. That gave Evelyn hope. I worried about that hope, and so did her parents. Lila made a near-full recovery. Her leg had fractured in more than one place, requiring a longer healing time, but she managed to use crutches and occasionally a scooter to get back to her daily duties as First Lady.

With the end of the ski season, I opted out of working as a paramedic with the fire department (per Evelyn's request) and stayed on with the resort, providing safety services for bikers and hikers, as well as organizing tasks to improve safety for the next ski season. We spent as much time as possible taking the kids on the trails and enjoying all the facets of mountain living.

"How do I look?" Evelyn turned in a complete circle, showing off her new strapless red dress. Her birthday dress.

"Like you won't be wearing that dress long." I adjusted my black tie, giving her a conspiratorial look in the full-length mirror opposite our bed.

"So I look hot. Forty is the new thirty, right?" She slipped on her matching red heels.

I wasn't kidding. That dress was minutes away from finding a new home on the floor of the bedroom, next to the black thong I saw her slip on minutes earlier and those shoes. On second thought … I decided the shoes could stay on.

"You look stunning." Satisfied with my tie, I brushed past her to get my shoes from the closet.

She grabbed my tie to stop me. "I don't want to look stunning. I'm forty. I need more from you."

I chuckled, prying my tie from her death grip before she wrinkled the hell out of it. "Evie, I'm not sure I can find a word better than stunning. I mean … it trumps beautiful. Or were you thinking more along the lines of sexy." My gaze swept along her lithe body. She was definitely sexy. And as I adjusted myself, she grinned.

"More than sexy." She rubbed her glossed lips together, batting her mascara-covered lashes at me.

Smokey eyes.

Red lips.

And some sort of aphrodisiac as her perfume. I was ready to eat her alive in every way imaginable.

"More than sexy?" I raised a brow at her.

"If I were standing here naked, what would you call me?"

"Evelyn … I'm seconds away from tearing that dress off you. Why are you teasing me with these questions?" I took a step toward her.

She took a step back, her backside hitting the wall. I rested my hands on the wall above her head, caging her in with my body.

"Evelyn Alexander."

"Yes," she whispered, mid-swallow.

"You look so damn fuckable."

The sexiest grin crawled up her face as I said the words she needed to hear. "Thank you."

I shook my head, failing to hide my own grin. "You're one depraved woman."

"Thank you." She pushed against my chest until I surrendered, letting her escape.

The only reason she made it out of the bedroom with that dress still on her body was because it was her birthday, and Graham had a jet waiting to take us to Denver for a surprise birthday party at the Porter estate. She thought we were just meeting Graham and Lila for dinner.

"You should open your gift now." I pulled it out of my nightstand. "I don't want to forget to give it to you later when I have you tied to the hotel bed, wearing nothing but those heels."

She turned. Lips parted. Cheeks extra flushed. Still ... after years of marriage, I could make her blush. I could make her bend to my will with one look, make her scream, make her beg, make her *mine* a million times over again.

After I straightened my tie a bit more and winked at her, she rubbed her lips together again and swallowed. "A gift, huh?" She picked up the small box and opened it. "A ... soap dish." She inspected it carefully. "How ... nice."

"I carved it out of wood from that broken branch, the one where your grandpa hung the tree swing for your grandma."

Her hand flew straight to her chest. "Oh my god ..." she gasped. "Ronin ..."

"Kidding ... I got it from the gift shop at the lodge.

Someone hand carved it. But I thought it would have been really amazing of me to have done it with some wood from that branch. Then I remembered I have no artistic talent and a terrible gift-giver reputation to uphold, so I bought this one from the shop. After the fact ... I noticed you have a whole display of soap dishes at your shop." I shrugged. "Go figure."

Her hand moved from her chest to her mouth. She snorted and shook her head. "Only you, Roe ... only you would give the owner of a bath and body shop a soap dish." She tossed the dish over her shoulder, clearly not impressed with Walter Greenfield's hand-carved creation, and then she grabbed my tie again and pulled me in for a long kiss. "Let's go." She nuzzled her nose against mine.

"Be right out. Let me grab my jacket."

After slipping it on, I filled the cup by the bathroom sink with water.

"Forgot my lipstick—" Evelyn's gaze locked onto the pill bottle in my hand as I swallowed the water and the pills.

I didn't try to hide them because I knew she saw them. Hiding them would have felt like an admission of guilt. She reached over and plucked the bottle from my hand. I blew a breath out my nose, clenching my teeth.

"Ronin ..." Her blue eyes met mine, a sea of disbelief. "What are you doing with these? You ..." She shook her head. "You told me *one week* ... just one week after I found the bottle in your pocket. You said you were tapering off. It's been months. *Months!* Ronin ... what are you doing? Th-these are addictive drugs. Are you—"

"Addicted?" I snatched the bottle from her hand and slipped it into the inside pocket of my suit jacket. "No. I'm not addicted."

She mirrored my posture with a clenched jaw, eyes unblinking as she stared at me with an unrelenting anger. "Did someone else not die? Did you save another life? Bring back the dead?"

"No. But in case you hadn't noticed, Lila is still in a cast." I angled my body to slide past her to make my escape. "We need to go. We're going to be late, birthday girl."

"Lila's leg doesn't hurt." Evelyn followed me out to the living room.

I held up her cream wool coat like a gentleman to help her put it on. She stood there with her arms crossed over her chest, no intention of sliding those arms into the coat.

I sighed, draping the coat over her shoulders. "Did I ever mention I went through a lot of schooling to become an EMT? I have to take additional training to keep up my license. I know a thing or two about pharmaceuticals. Now, *please*, baby … can we talk about this later if you feel the need for more talking? Your friends are waiting. We don't want to be late." I grabbed our overnight bag. Since we had Sue watching the kids all night, we were staying in Denver—at Porter Suites.

Champagne.

A huge room with a city view.

And my naked birthday girl.

The longer I stood there engaging in her stare off, the

guiltier I looked. So I opened the door and waved my hand, shooing her out to the car. She narrowed her eyes but obliged. I hadn't heard the end of that lecture, but I hoped it was dropped for the night.

As expected, she gave me the silent treatment on the way to the airport. We were greeted on the Porter jet with an open bar and privacy. Graham told me I should use that opportunity to join the Mile High Club if I hadn't already.

I took Evelyn's coat from her and handed it, along with mine, to the flight attendant.

"Anything else I can get you, sir?" he asked.

"We're good. Thank you."

"I'll give you some privacy. Push this button here if you need anything."

"Great. Thanks." Even *he* knew I was supposed to be doing the Mile High Club activities on the way to Denver. As we took off, Evelyn gripped the arms of the seat, leaned her head back, and closed her eyes. Once we were in the air, I unfastened my seatbelt and reached forward for her foot, pulling it onto my lap, removing her shoe, and massaging her sexy foot, admiring her newly painted toenails.

She ignored me, tipping her chin to her chest, focusing on her phone.

After massaging both of her feet and getting the cold shoulder the whole time, I poured two glasses of champagne. "You look like you could use a drink." I tried to hand her the champagne flute, but she ignored it.

"Dizziness, mental confusion, nausea, vomiting, apathy, and difficulty breathing ..." She read from her phone screen. "Those are just a few short-term effects of mixing opioids with alcohol. Long-term effects include impaired vision, mood swings, liver disease, and increased risk of overdose and *death*." Evelyn glanced up from her phone, pinning me with a hard look. "But surely you know this since you've had extensive medical training and know a thing or two about pharmaceuticals. Right?" She canted her head.

Leaning back in my seat, I set the two glasses of champagne aside and folded my hands in my lap. "Fine. I won't drink. What will it take for you to let this go for *one day*?"

She grunted a laugh as her eyebrows slid up her forehead. "One day? My husband has an opioid addiction that he's been hiding from me, and I'm supposed to let it go for one day? What's one more day? I don't know ... maybe when I see Lila, I'll ask her if one more day is reasonable to give someone with a drug addiction."

"Jesus ..." I rubbed my face, closing my eyes. "I'm not a fucking drug addict, Evie."

"That's what all addicts say until they hit rock bottom—if they live to hit rock bottom—and check themselves in for treatment."

"Treatment?" I dropped my hands *and* my jaw, agitated we were having such a ridiculous conversation. "You're blowing this way out of proportion."

Tears reddened her eyes as she clenched her jaw. "I am a scientist with a background in chemistry. Do you know how fucking insulting it is for you to look at me like I'm crazy? Like I don't know what I'm talking about? The very day I found that first bottle of pills in your pocket, I poured through every bit of research I could find on opioids. I guarantee I know more about them than you do by this point. I knew there was a chance you were already addicted that day, even after only a week. But I know that there is a one hundred percent chance that you have an opioid addiction after taking them for *months*."

"That is not true." I shook my head.

"Lila's pain is gone!" She slammed her fists on the armrests and the tears won over. "What are you doing?" Her words broke apart as her tears painted black mascara lines down her cheeks. "My ..." She swallowed hard. "My mom is dying. You're going to leave me too, and I will *hate* you for letting this end our life together. I will *hate* you for leaving me to explain to our kids why they no longer have a father."

I kneeled on the floor in front of her, grabbing a tissue and wiping her face. "I'm not leaving you," I whispered.

"You check into treatment, tomorrow."

"Evie ..." I continued to shake my head. She was overreacting.

"You check into treatment, tomorrow."

"I'll taper off. I can do it on my own."

"You check into treatment, tomorrow." Every time she repeated that line, her words lost emotion, like she was losing any sort of feeling, shutting down, and putting up this indestructible wall around her heart.

I fucking hated it. Where had my wife gone? The

woman who looked at me like I was her king? "Please … just listen to me." I squeezed her hands. "This isn't a prob—"

"Over 70,000 people die every year from opioid overdose, including really well-educated—well informed—healthcare professionals like doctors, nurses, and *paramedics.* You check into treatment … *tomorrow.*"

"Give me a week … just a week." I rested my forehead on her shoulder. "Please … one week."

"You check in for treatment, tomorrow … or you move out of my house."

I sat up, shaking my head over and over. I didn't hear her right. There was no way a few pills could end our marriage. Before I could try harder to make my case, the pilot announced we would be landing in Denver soon. I knew Lila and Graham would be waiting for us the second we stepped off the plane.

Flowers.

Balloons.

Presents.

They planned a luxury ride to her surprise party with all her favorite foods and lots of champagne—champagne I was clearly not going to drink.

I hated lying to my wife. And I hated that she mistook truths for lies. I didn't have a problem. I wasn't addicted to drugs. There was no reason to check into treatment. But … it was her birthday. I needed to salvage what I could of it before a misunderstanding ruined the whole thing. So … I lied.

"Tomorrow, I check in for treatment." I forced a

smile and wiped the rest of the mascara from her cheeks.

Her body melted on a long sigh as she pressed her palms to my face and rested her forehead against mine. "Thank you," she whispered.

After she fixed her makeup, we slipped on our coats and I took her hand, leading her off the plane.

"Surprise!" Lila held up her arms, both hands holding balloons as part of her body poked out of the moonroof of the limousine.

I laughed, knowing it was the best she could do with a broken leg.

A red rug stretched from the plane's stairs all the way to the limo where Graham stood in a tux holding a huge bouquet of roses. I released her hand, assuming she would run toward them, eager to leave behind her *drug addicted* husband. Instead, she turned her back to them to face me. Throwing her arms around my neck, she hugged me like she did the morning she first found the oxy in my jacket.

Emotion stung my eyes as my heart fell hard like a boulder tumbling down the side of a mountain. "You're my favorite everything, Roe," she whispered, her voice thick with emotion.

All I could do was nod in reply to keep from crying like a fucking baby in front of our friends. For a moment, I realized I didn't deserve her love. And that scared me to death.

She released me, took my hand, and tugged me toward the limo.

"Hey, old lady." Graham smirked as she walked into his arms.

I tried not to read into her smile, wondering if she smiled bigger for Graham, but I couldn't help it. For the first time in over five years of marriage, I felt like we weren't invincible. And that hurt worse than any pain I tried to numb with medication.

"Roses …" She took them from Graham and sniffed them. "My favorite."

He stepped aside so she could climb into the limo. "Did you have a *pleasant* flight?" Graham patted me on the shoulder and smirked.

I returned a stiff smile. No. I didn't nail Evelyn to the leather seat in the plane. She nailed me to the cross and informed me my only salvation involved checking into treatment for a disease I didn't have. Could he read all of that from my smile? Doubtful.

Lila and Evelyn giggled as they tried to maneuver Lila and the balloons back into the limo.

"Screw it." Lila let go of the balloons, sending them into the air.

"Brilliant, babe. We'll probably get fined for releasing balloons into the air at an airport." Graham grabbed her waist to guide her back into the seat as she lifted her casted leg, propping it up on the seat between Evelyn and the door.

Evelyn rested the long-stemmed roses on her lap and grabbed my hand. It felt like a fucking lifeline. She had no way of knowing just how emasculating it was to have her give me that ultimatum on the plane.

"Are you tipsy already?" Evelyn cocked her head at Lila.

"No." Lila jerked her head back, but at the same time she fell into a fit of giggles. "Maybe." She grabbed a bottle of champagne and poured a glass, miraculously without spilling it, and handed it to Evelyn. "For you, birthday girl."

Evelyn took a sip. "Thank you."

"And for you." Lila handed me a glass.

"Thank you." I took it, feeling the full weight of Evelyn's gaze on me, further emasculating me.

"Your dress, *dear*." Graham frowned, covering Lila's lap with his jacket.

She wore a short, black dress that hit just above her cast which ended pretty close to the top of her leg.

"Yes, my husband doesn't need to see *all* of you." Evie rolled her eyes.

"Such prudes." Lila sipped more champagne, probably the first time she'd had the chance to kick back and throw caution to the wind again since the accident. I couldn't blame her.

"Besides ..." Lila shot Evie a mischievous look. "We're all *friends*." She slid her drunken gaze to me for a second while rubbing her glossed lips together. "Well, except Ronin. We really need to bring him into our circle. Don't you think?"

"Lila." Graham said her name like a warning.

She had too much alcohol in her blood to heed any warnings at the moment.

"So where are we going for dinner? I'm starving." Evelyn changed the subject, or so I thought.

I wasn't sure. Lila seemed to have a secret she was dying to share, while Graham and Evelyn exchanged a few uncomfortable glances with each other.

Yes, I knew they had sex in college. Surely, Lila knew Evelyn shared that with me.

"Evie, you're forty!" Lila leaned forward, resting one hand on Evelyn's knee while taking another sip of champagne with her other hand. "Carpe the fucking diem! We should all get deliriously drunk later and replay Vancouver with a plus one. Ronin really should have stayed that night." Lila winked at me while sliding her hand up Evie's leg a few inches beneath the flowers *and* her skirt.

What … the fuck?

Evie grabbed Lila's hand, stopping its ascent and squeezing it while smiling past her gritted teeth. "I thought the four of us were already having dinner tonight … like we did in Vancouver." She pushed Lila's hand away.

"Time to sober you up before the—" Graham caught himself before saying party as he took Lila's champagne from her hand and shoved a bottled water into her hand instead. "Dinner. Time to sober you up before dinner, Mrs. Porter."

"Humpf!" Lila stuck out her lower lip.

It was actually quite funny. I'd seen Evelyn do it a few times over our years together. It must have been a move they perfected together as young girls.

After a few seconds, as if everyone else was waiting to see what would come out of Lila's mouth next—because we were—she smirked at Evelyn. "I bet you still think of me when Ronin sucks your nipples." Lila slid her tongue out to show us her tongue ring and tapped it against her teeth a few times while looking at my wife in a way I had never seen her look at Evelyn.

"Jesus ..." Graham leaned his head back, closing his eyes and massaging his temples.

"You're so drunk," Evelyn murmured.

I was the odd man out, left with nothing but a drunk woman's confessions to spark my wild imagination since no one else offered to elaborate or clarify anything. Evelyn wouldn't even look at me, so I took a nice long drink of my champagne, nearly emptying my glass all at once.

That got her attention.

She tore me apart with a look. Evelyn made me feel more vulnerable than I ever thought humanly possible. She was the beginning and the end, the mother of my children, the keeper of my heart, the reason my lungs took breaths, my absolute favorite ... *everything*.

Wanting her felt like an honor. Needing her felt like a failure.

Silence took us hostage until we reached the Porter estate. Evelyn didn't wait for anyone. She didn't ask why we were there instead of at her favorite restaurant. Letting the roses fall to the floor of the limo, she jumped out and ran toward the front door.

Lila cringed, giving me a regretful frown. Graham completely avoided making any sort of eye contact with me as he helped Lila slip on her black coat. I climbed out of the limo, taking long strides after Evelyn.

Everything in my chest ached as she opened the front

door before I could stop her.

"Surprise!" echoed from the crowd of guests.

Her body froze, like hitting a wall. I made it to the threshold just as her mom hugged her.

"You look beautiful, baby." Madeline smiled at me from over Evelyn's shoulder.

Had she only known how her baby's husband and her friends shit on her birthday before ever getting to the party, she wouldn't have been smiling. I couldn't get to my wife. The crowd of guests swallowed her, showering her with hugs and birthday wishes.

"Forget everything I said ..." Lila mumbled to me as Graham helped her into the house. "It was the alcohol."

Graham finally looked at me as Lila followed the crowd toward the great room filled with more people and catered food and drinks. "It's all good, buddy." He squeezed my shoulder before following Lila.

CHAPTER TWENTY-EIGHT

Evelyn

I DIDN'T WANT a surprise party.

It wasn't my thing. It was Lila's and Graham's thing. However, after the string of events that led me to the front door of the Porter estate, I felt for the first time that day like I could breathe.

My family and friends.

Ronin's parents were there after spending months in Singapore while Ling finished approving the final line of her summer collection.

Sophie.

Julien and his wife.

My sister, Katie, and her husband, Tanner.

Tami and Noah.

Even Graham's parents took the time to come wish me happy birthday.

The biggest surprise was my kids. Graham flew them to Denver earlier in the day. I thought Ronin was taking them to Sue's for the night. I was wrong.

However, Sue was there too. After dinner, she took

them upstairs to one of the bedrooms and put them to bed.

It was by far the most perfect *and* tragic birthday of my life.

Ronin followed me like a shadow all night. He stood by me with his hand on my lower back when it felt right to put on an act for the guests. He smiled on cue and laughed at the appropriate moments. I glued together that awful mask I'd owned for so many years and put it on—bent and ready to fall to pieces again if I let it slip as much as an inch.

Graham stayed out of sight most of the evening while Lila found a chair and ottoman to elevate her leg while people lined up to see how she was feeling since the accident.

"Andre said it's time to cut the cake," Mom whispered in my ear as one of Graham's old buddies from college talked my other ear off about the Yankees, not realizing I had two kids and zero time to follow sports like I used to.

And yes, Andre was the party planner. My fortieth birthday party was better planned, and probably more expensive, than most couples' wedding receptions.

"Time for cake," I announced with a smile to end the baseball conversation.

It was all too extravagant, yet I didn't take for granted a single second of it. After all, I knew it might be the last time I would get to share something like that while my mom was still alive.

I fought an onslaught of tears as everyone sang "Happy Birthday" to me. Then I blew out forty candles on a huge cherry amaretto cake as cheers and clapping filled the room.

"Speech!" Lila yelled from just a few feet in front of me, balancing on her crutches, much more sober than she was in the limo.

Silence swept through the room, leaving all eyes on me. My heart raced. I preferred attention in small doses where I didn't shake under the microscope of the large crowd.

Where was my rock?

He stood a few feet behind Lila and Graham, next to his brother, Julien. My best friend put me on the stage, ignoring my insecurities. I stood there as my mask started to crack. Words—what was I supposed to say?

"Thank me first. I paid for the party."

Everyone laughed, breaking the tension.

My gaze shifted to Graham and his signature smirk. So arrogant. In that moment, he gave me what no one else did. A lifeline.

He saw me drowning, and he saved me.

A few tears tried to make their way out, but I quickly wiped them away as I smiled. "Yes." I laughed as the room quieted again. "I have to thank my favorite Graham Cracker for proving, once again, that our friendship is truly priceless." I winked at him.

He mouthed, "I love you," and winked back at me.

"And speaking of friendships, I have to thank my best friend, Lila, for letting me be the one who has aged more gracefully."

She flipped me the bird and everyone laughed.

"I love you too, Lila. And I'm so *so* grateful you're here to celebrate this day with me."

A collective "aww" exhaled from the crowd. We all knew how incredibly lucky we were to have Lila with us. She smiled through her trembling lips and tear-filled eyes as she blew me a kiss.

"And I wouldn't be here to celebrate forty amazing years of life if Madeline Hayes hadn't let herself fall in love with the handsome and oh-so-dapper Corey Taylor. Thank you for being the best parents anyone could ask for. I think I speak for Katie and Lila too when I say it's a privilege to be your daughter."

A few sniffles broke through the silence as I left a pregnant pause, finding the courage and strength to look at my husband and say everything I wanted to say about him. "Last, but not least …" I choked on the words, biting my lips together and swallowing as I looked up at the ceiling, unable to let my gaze lock with his eyes.

I shook my head, clenching my jaw and holding back not only the words, but the sob that fought to escape. No one else in the room knew how seeing Ronin's truth that morning ripped open my heart, leaving me so scared and helpless.

No one else knew how my world shattered in that tiny heartbeat.

No one knew how I took his confessions and guarded them with my life for months.

No one knew how badly I wanted to say three simple words that might profoundly change the course of something so tragic.

No one knew …

Drawing in a shaky breath, I tried again. "I want to thank my—" My hand covered my mouth as I choked on the sob that escaped along with all the tears as I bled out in front of everyone.

"Evie …" Lila called my name as I ran out the side door, shouldering past a few of the servers and taking a quick left to the door that led to the pool and courtyard.

The cool air forced a full breath into my lungs as I stumbled out of my shoes and just … ran. The Porters had acres of grassy hills. Acres of space to run away from my troubles. I didn't stop until my lungs burned from exhaustion, and I couldn't feel my feet from pounding them against the cold spring grass.

I didn't stop until I was ready to surrender to reality—as beautiful as I thought my life was, it wasn't a fairy tale. And if it was, it would likely end in tragedy.

Slowing to a stop, I ripped at the pins in my hair, releasing the messy strands to fall all around my shoulders as I bent over, panting with my hands clenched to my knees. Then I dropped to my knees, moving my hands to my face as I cried, not holding back anything. I just … couldn't any longer.

His woodsy Clean Art scent announced his presence before the warmth of his suit jacket covered my bare shoulders. Then he scooped me up into his arms.

I let him, feeling too numb inside to protest the long walk he was about to make with me in his arms back to the house. Ronin kissed the top of my head and effortlessly retraced our steps with long, confident strides. I rested my cheek against his shoulder and closed my swollen eyes.

Birthdays were overrated.

Instead of going into the house, he slid into the back of a car with me still cradled in his arms. Someone shut the door and hopped into the front seat, shifting the vehicle into drive. I felt dead inside. So tired of trying to control … everything.

Mom would take her last breath before I was ready to say goodbye.

Ronin would live or die by his own mistakes, and there was nothing I could do to stop him.

Lila and Graham had their lives that were, in so many ways, a million miles away from mine.

But I had Franz and Anya.

Every. Single. Day. I had to remind myself that they were enough. And they were. So very much.

When the vehicle stopped, the driver opened the back door. Ronin lifted me out and walked into the hotel. A bellboy followed us with our shared overnight bag. When we made it to the room, the bellboy opened the door.

"Thank you," Ronin murmured, his first words since he retrieved me from the back of the Porter estate.

The door closed behind us as he carried me to the king-sized bed in the lavish suite. I felt the immediate loss of his arms when he set me down on the edge of the bed and loosened his tie. I picked the most handsome man in the world to break my heart. It was such a rare occasion that I got to see Ronin in a suit, looking like sex on a stick. Why did this one have to end with him picking up my broken pieces?

Disappearing to the bathroom, he turned on the water before returning, wearing nothing but a plush white towel tied around his waist. He didn't speak. *We* didn't speak. What was there to say?

I let him slide his jacket off my shoulders, unzip my dress, and work my panties off my hips while I sat idle like a rag doll. All I wanted was to close my eyes and sleep for a hundred years. Was that too much to ask for my birthday wish?

Again, Ronin lifted me up into his arms, completely naked, and carried me to the bathroom. He eased me into the tub of steamy water, discarded his towel, and wedged his body in the tub behind mine. I rested my hands under the water on his legs and leaned back, using his chest as a pillow.

Warm lips brushed my ear. Strong arms wrapped around my shoulders. When the water reached its limit, Ronin leaned over and turned it off. Grabbing a washcloth, he wet it and brought his face down next to mine so he could see to gently wipe the makeup from it. I closed my eyes.

"I'm not going to ask you what happened in Vancouver."

My eyes blinked back open.

"I failed you as a husband, as a friend, and as a father to our children. It was my job to take care of our family. But I couldn't, and I hated it. Getting out of bed was a monumental challenge. Carrying our injured child nearly made me pass out. So ... I looked for a solution, but nothing worked except …"

The pills.

He continued to wipe my face, rewetting the wash-cloth. "You're so damn smart, and it was wrong of me to act like you wouldn't know exactly what was happening. I was … I *am* so ashamed that I let it happen to me." Ronin blew out a slow, shaky breath. "But it did. And I hate that you had to find out like you did. I hate that I was too weak to ask for help. I hate that in my attempt to show so much strength, I bared my biggest weakness."

I traced my fingers over his leg muscles, closing my eyes again as he continued to clean my face. "I'm both."

After a few seconds, he kissed my cheek, letting his lips linger there as he whispered, "Both what?"

"*I* am your biggest strength … and your biggest weakness." I shifted in the tub, not caring about the water sloshing over the sides. Settling myself at the opposite end, I massaged his calves as he ghosted his fingers along the topside of my feet. "And I know this because *you* are my biggest strength … and my biggest weakness."

Ronin nodded slowly, bringing my foot to his mouth and kissing my big toe.

"I fucked up your birthday." He teased the pad of my toe with his teeth.

"You did." I shrugged. "But you had help."

A tiny line formed along the bridge of his nose as he let his gaze fall away from mine.

"Ronin, I'm not shaming you. Or Lila and Graham. It was a disaster. Emotionally draining. But like *life*, it had its beautiful moments. Our families all together for the first time." I smiled. "Franz in that tiny tux and Anya in that red dress and big bow in her hair."

That brought a real smile to Ronin's face too, even if he still couldn't look at me.

"So while it's tempting to want to forget this whole day, that would be a greater tragedy. There are too many memories I will cherish. I'll take the bad with the good. *That's* life." I bopped his chin with my toe, forcing him to look at me again. "When we exchanged those vows five years ago, we promised a lot of things, but we never said it would be easy."

He leaned his head back, closing his eyes. "I lied," he whispered. "Earlier today, when I told you I'd start treatment tomorrow, I lied. I just didn't want to argue on your birthday. This stubborn part of me was still in denial that I needed help. But when you couldn't even look at me during your speech…" he brought his head up, opening his reddened eyes a bit as his forehead wrinkled, like saying the words pained him "…I knew the bottle of pills in the pocket of my jacket was destroying us. And it was chilling … like being buried under the rumble of an avalanche. I couldn't move. I couldn't breathe." He shook his head, leaning it back again and closing his eyes. "I couldn't believe I didn't see it coming."

After letting his confession simmer between us for a few minutes, I pushed myself out of the water. "I'm getting chilly." Wrapping a towel around myself, I stepped out of the tub.

On top of the overnight bag by the door was a sack. "What's in the sack?" I set it aside and opened the suitcase to retrieve a nightshirt. Only … I didn't pack one. I packed a sexy black lace and satin nightie because we were going to do some naughty things on my birthday with a suite all to ourselves and no kids to wake us up. Given the detour that my day took and the gravity of our bathtub conversation, I decided to skip the nightie in favor of a soft tee Ronin packed to wear the next day.

"Did I give you permission to wear my shirt?"

I turned, stepping into my panties. "You love me in your clothes."

He eyed me playfully as he retrieved a pair of boxer briefs and slipped them on. "You're staring, Mrs. Alexander."

I snapped my gaze to meet his smirk. Yes, five years later, I still loved looking at his naked body. "What's in the sack?"

He shrugged, plopping onto the bed. "I don't know. Graham put our bag into the car from the limo. The sack was there too."

I peeked into the sack and grinned, pulling out a clear container with a huge piece of cake inside of it. My birthday cake. He even packed a fork. Although … my bet was on Lila. She told him to send cake. Traipsing to the bed with my cake—my last bit of birthday joy—I took a seat with my back against the headboard.

"You're not going to share?"

Mid-bite, I glanced over at Ronin as he turned onto his side, head propped up on his bent arm. "It's *my* birthday cake. I didn't get any at the party."

"Neither did I."

"And whose fault is that?"

He frowned. "Fine."

I took the bite and hummed. It was so good.

"I'm not sharing cake with you on my birthday … just so you know."

Sliding my gaze to the side as I eased the fork from my mouth, I snickered. "I make your birthday cake. I always have the first piece, right out of the middle, then I fill it with frosting and nobody is the wiser."

He opened his mouth as wide as possible, nose wrinkled. "That is truly horrible!"

I scooped a dollop of frosting onto my finger and stuck it in his open mouth. "You've never made me a cake; *that's* the truly horrible part."

Ronin grabbed my wrist before I could pull my finger out of his mouth. Closing his lips, he sucked all the frosting from my finger. I liked it, but I told myself I wasn't allowed to like it. Not on a ruined birthday. There was no way birthday girl was giving her fun-spoiling husband sex on *her* birthday. Also, I convinced myself that reasoning it all out via third-person in my head was the way to go … the way to hold strong.

Evelyn was *not* having sex with Ronin.

With his other hand, he grabbed the entire piece of cake.

"Ronin!" I jerked my finger from his mouth, but not before he smeared cake down my face and neck.

"Stop!" I tried to squirm away, but he stuck his cake-covered hand up my shirt … well, his shirt. I gasped, eyes wide as he smeared the cake and frosting over me. "Not cool! Not cool at—"

That sticky hand cupped my jaw, and his mouth covered mine, kissing me hard, passionately, and with a clear purpose—getting his fair share of the cake. He licked down my face, lapping the sticky mess while humming his pleasure.

"Ronin ..." I claimed two fists full of his hair and tried to jerk him away, but he kept going.

Lower.

And lower.

Until ... I lost my resolve.

Birthday girl had sex with Ronin.

CHAPTER TWENTY-NINE

FORTY WAS SUPPOSED to be the true age of independence—the essence of youth still a glint in one's eyes with the wisdom of experience keeping that chin tilted high.

Yet ... we found it quite unwise to eat cake off each other while having sex in a hotel bed. That was how you ended up standing in the corner of the hotel suite, chins bowed, showered bodies wrapped in plush white robes (because you nearly ran out of clean clothes) while watching housekeeping change *all* the bedding because they wouldn't allow VIP guests to change the bedding on our own.

Ronin handed the lady a generous tip as she exited the suite with our dirty sheets and an awkward goodnight smile.

"TV?" Ronin took my hand and led me to the bed.

We discarded our robes and snuggled naked in the clean bedding, hair wet, grins rather mischievous. As he turned on the TV and scanned the channels, he stopped on a cable network with some late-night *adult* entertainment. In over five years of marriage, we never watched *adult* entertainment short of a few R-rated shows with some explicit sex scenes.

This was different.

I waited for him to click past it, as if he accidentally stopped on it. He didn't click past it. Nope, he set the remote down beside him and cocked that arm behind his head while hugging me to him with his other arm.

It was a threesome. Two women. One man.

Okay. He wasn't going to ask me about Vancouver. We were just going to watch a porn movie with two women and one man in bed together.

"Um …" I cleared my throat. "I'm not sure this is what I'd choose to watch on my birthday."

"Noted. I'll remember that for next year. But it's past midnight, so technically it's no longer your birthday."

Girl one sat on single guy's face. Girl two settled into cowgirl position.

Girl three—me—hid my face in the crook of Ronin's neck, hoping he might switch the channel or find some interest in me again and just shut off the television.

No luck.

I slid my hand down his stomach, going for a new distraction. My hand paused, not expecting him to be so turned on when I had just started to make my move. Yet, he was totally erect.

"You're …" My voice shook a bit. Five years of marriage … my voice had no reason to shake. That was the power of that little thing called the comfort zone. Stepping outside of it made voices shake and cheeks fill with embarrassment. "You're enjoying this?"

I had to ask, even though I knew the answer. We talked sex while having sex. We experimented with sexual positions without watching demonstrations. What was wrong with me that I felt so uncomfortable? What was wrong with him that he didn't?

"Yes. Aren't you?"

I crawled over his chest and grabbed the remote, pressing the *Power* button. "No. I'm not enjoying that. Why don't you just ask? I'd rather tell you about Vancouver than watch that shit. Is that what you want?"

He moved his other hand behind his head, lacing his fingers. "Well, you shut off *that shit*, so I assume you're ready to tell me—five years after the fact."

I sighed, sitting straight while facing him, pulling the covers up to my chest. "When I was in elementary school, I fell off a horse and broke my arm. It was in a cast for six weeks, and everyone in school signed it and drew pictures on it. I bet the cast is still in an old box in my parents' garage."

Ronin quirked a single brow. "That's why Lila was sliding her hand up your leg in the limo?"

"No. It's just a random thing about me that you didn't know and doesn't really matter in our life together. Just like that time in Vancouver when Graham and Lila invaded my hotel room and tried to drag me into a threesome—a random event that doesn't really matter in our life together."

Ronin narrowed his eyes. "Well, I disagree. Did this threesome look like *that* threesome?" He nodded toward the blank TV screen.

I sighed. "No. Not even close. And the reason I never told you is because you know all the parties involved, and I don't want you to get these images in your head. It could affect the way you look at me, or Lila and Graham too."

"Well, in case you missed the subtle hint I just gave you by stopping on that channel, if you don't clarify what Lila alluded to earlier in the limo, then *that...*" he nodded again to the screen "...is what I imagine happened between the three of you. And that makes me pretty fucking unhappy."

I bristled at his comment. How dare he be upset about *anything* after the debacle of my birthday sparked by his hidden drug addiction.

"Why would you be *fucking* unhappy?" I narrowed my eyes. "I felt you, and you were clearly turned on by what was happening on that screen."

He jackknifed to sitting, putting our faces six inches apart. "Getting a goddamn boner from watching a porn star doesn't mean I'm okay with my wife being a porn star!"

"Excuuuse me? Did you really just call me a porn star?"

"I don't know ..." He tilted his head to the side, eyes narrowed. "Did you sit on Graham's face or his cock the *very same day* we met?"

I opened my mouth to spit more venom, but nothing came out. Instead, I deflated. "Oh my god ..." I whispered. "What are we doing?"

That was easy—we were pissed off about other uncontrollable circumstances in our lives, and instead of facing them, making plans to survive them, we were throwing stupid punches over something as frivolous as Va-*ness*-uh karaoke. It was on me. I was the one in control of the situation. Ronin was simply reacting to jumbled pieces of the unknown.

I knew better. I had all the pieces.

Crawling onto his lap, I ran my fingers though his hair. He stiffened. I couldn't blame him.

"I'm so sorry." I kissed the corner of his mouth.

His head made a tiny jerk away from me.

Fair.

He had every right to feel upset and confused. Had the tables been turned, I would have been a tornado of emotions throwing shit like cell phones at his head.

"Graham didn't touch me, and I didn't touch him. He threw out some ridiculous idea about having a threesome as we were all in my bed in our pajamas. For the record, I didn't invite them into my room. They came over and just piled into my bed when all I wanted to do was go to sleep and dream about this sexy guy I met that day."

Ronin's lips twitched, but he managed to keep them from bending into a smile.

"I was hugging the edge of the bed with my back to Lila and Graham on the other side of her when he—out of the blue—suggested a threesome. I said nothing because I didn't take his stupid suggestion seriously. Then the next thing I knew he was touching Lila and Lila was touching me."

Ronin's right eyebrow worked its way up his forehead.

"She fondled my breasts and teased my nipples with her tongue ring; then I made a quick exit into the hallway before things went any further," I spewed out the words as fast as I could.

Nodding slowly, Ronin narrowed his eyes. "What was Graham doing while Lila was doing this to you?"

I wrinkled my nose, not wanting to replay that night. "I … I don't know. Touching her, touching himself." I shook my head. "I don't like to think about it."

He wet his lips and scraped his top teeth along his bottom lip several times. "How did it feel?"

I choked out a laugh. "No. We are not *discussing* this. It's not therapy. You now know it was nothing like what you were just watching. It was a weird moment between friends."

"Lila seemed to recall those memories with a sort of fondness. I think she liked your nipples." He took a quick glance at said nipples.

I grabbed the sheet to cover my chest. "So…" I squinted "…me sitting on any part of Graham's body nearly sent you into killer mode, but Lila messing with my breasts simply makes you curious? Had it been Graham's tongue on my nipples, why would that have not been okay?"

"I'm a guy." He shrugged; a boyish grin climbed up his face.

"That's such a pathetic excuse."

He tugged on the sheet, pulling it away from my

351

chest. "Let's be clear …" His hands slid from my hips, over my ribs to my breasts.

"Clear about what?" I framed his face with my hands, brushing my thumb over his lips.

He smiled, following my thumb with his tongue. "*I'm the only one who touches you.*"

"You …" I replaced my thumb with my lips, seeking the familiar taste of my husband, the comfort of his hands, the shelter of his body pressed to mine.

Life wasn't easy. It wasn't always beautiful. Some days it was flat-out cruel.

But … it was undeniably worth it.

The next morning, I woke before Ronin, feeling the dawn of reality crushing against my chest. My birthday was over. Our bubble would burst any second. Life would test us once again.

"It's too early to lift the weight of the world."

I grinned, glancing over my shoulder as Ronin stretched. My feet dangled from the side of the bed, daring me to touch the ground. After a night of remembering all the reasons I said, "I do," it was hard to take that next step. So … I just let my feet dangle for a few more minutes.

"It *is* a heavy burden, but I think I'll lift one thing at a time." I bit my lower lip and wrinkled my nose, not wanting to name that thing.

"I'll take a few days off, just to get through the initial withdrawal. There's no reason I shouldn't be able to do this on an outpatient basis. As long as I take the meds they give me, attend the suggested counseling, and join a support group, it should go smoothly."

Ronin made me so proud. Even in his weakest moment, he proved he was still my rock. Perfection wasn't strength. Righting your wrongs took more strength than anything. You were lucky to dodge the hits. Getting back up after being knocked down showed immeasurable strength and courage.

"You're my superhero."

He returned a sad smile, sitting up and dangling his feet from the opposite side of the bed. "We have a few rough days ahead of us."

Us.

Ronin knew it was, had been, and always would be *us*.

"We've got this. Just let me ski backward until you find your balance."

CHAPTER THIRTY

Ronín

One month later …

MADELINE DIED.

I got better, and then she died. It was as if the universe was waiting for me to be strong enough to take care of my wife during her grieving. I knew it would hit her hard, even with having so many months to emotionally prepare for the loss. However, no one imagined Corey's reaction.

Evie's dad didn't shed one tear.

Not. One. Single. Tear.

Until … she stopped breathing.

That was why his reaction knocked everyone back a few steps.

Graham made sure Katie got to Denver in time to be by her mom's side along with Corey and Evelyn.

"I wouldn't change a thing." Those were Madeline's last words.

Corey spent years being strong for her. So when he buckled over her lifeless body and wept, Katie and Evie left the room to give him his moment. They stood in the hallway and held each other, crying for him. Not for their mom—for him.

That was what we did. We grieved for the living, for those who still felt the pain, for those who would spend the rest of their lives desperately missing the ones who left us behind.

A week after the funeral, Corey packed one bag.

One. Single. Bag.

He left for California to be near Katie because she and Tanner were trying again to get pregnant, and he knew Madeline would have wanted him to help Katie the way they had helped us when Franz and Anya were babies. We felt certain he went back to California too because his parents were still alive, and he needed them. We *never* stopped needing our parents.

"You should take a few days and go through your mom's stuff," I suggested, playing on the floor with Anya and Franz while Evie did some bookkeeping on her laptop.

She shook her head. "I'm not ready. Dad said he's in no hurry to put the house on the market. Besides, I want Katie to do it with me, and she has her mind on other things right now. Maybe if she gets pregnant and feels okay, we can go through everything. Maybe Dad will change his mind and decide to go through stuff with us."

Madeline wanted her family to bury her and move on. I knew she never imagined them moving on by just abandoning her house and everything inside of it. But … it wasn't my place to push anyone.

"Okay." I perfected the agreeable husband role. We had survived a lot of monumental stuff, the other stuff just had to slide.

"Are you going to a meeting this afternoon?"

"Yes, dear." I continued to do the work—followed doctor's orders, never missed therapy, and attended group meetings once a week.

"I might take the kids to the library while you're at your meeting. Then we can meet for dinner. How does that sound?"

"Oomph!" I grunted as Anya jumped on my stomach and squealed, "Da-eee!"

"Sounds like a plan," I replied as I tickled my little wrestling princess. "I'm going to take a hike first. Who's in?"

"It's supposed to rain." Evie gave me a narrow-eyed look over the screen of her computer.

"Is that a no?"

She laughed. "It's a you're crazy and we're not. Have fun getting wet."

"Mommy's no fun." I nuzzled my face into Anya's tummy as Franz jumped onto my back, wrapping his arms around my neck. He continued to hold on as I stood. "Looks like I might have a tagalong after all." I walked toward the bedroom to change my clothes as Franz hung from my neck like a cape, making it a bit challenging to breathe.

"Franz can't go anywhere until he picks up the toys in his room," Evelyn called.

"Told ya … Mommy's no fun," I whispered, and it

made Franz giggle as I dumped his monkey body onto the bed.

AFTER THREE MILES on my favorite trail, I turned around just as it started to sprinkle. The trip down was always quicker, unless the terrain got too slick from the rain. I glanced at my watch, keeping an eye on the time so I didn't miss my meeting. Then I took a quick swig from my canteen.

Spitting the water out, I coughed. But when I tried to catch my breath, it felt like I couldn't breathe. Yet ... I was breathing. I clawed at my nose and mouth as if something was suffocating me, but nothing was there. Panic set in, and I felt a sense of fear ... not just physical fear, but emotional fear.

What was happening?

I rubbed my face and clawed at my neck. My head felt like it was ready to explode while my lungs caught on fire. Then it hit me as I collapsed to my knees on the verge of passing out ... *borrowed time.* My second chance had expired. I brought back the dead when I was warned to let lost souls pass.

Hinder not the soul's intended path unto the light...

The pain ... it was excruciating, by far the worst pain I had ever experienced because I couldn't breathe.

Evie would be at the library, reading books to the kids while I took my last breath.

And it ... would ... destroy her.

The very best moments of my life flashed before me—when Evie turned around at the cafe in Vancouver and first smiled at me, the snowy Christmas Day she said, "I do," the first breath Franz took, the moment we let him hold his newborn sister.

Every smile.

Every touch.

Every breath.

Madeline's words echoed in my ears, and they gave me peace because I felt them too. "I wouldn't change a thing."

Not a single life I tried to save.

In spite of the pain, I knew I'd do it all again.

I collapsed onto my side, clutching my neck, and gasping until I started to black out. The end. My time had come.

...lest shards of darkness shed upon thee.

Only, I was no longer alive—no more suffering.

To be continued ...

Also by Jewel E. Ann

Jack & Jill Series
End of Day
Middle of Knight
Dawn of Forever

Holding You Series
Holding You
Releasing Me

Transcend Series
Transcend
Epoch

Standalone Novels
Idle Bloom
Only Trick
Undeniably You
One
Scarlet Stone
When Life Happened
Look the Part
A Place Without You
Naked Love

Jersey Six

Perfectly Adequate

jeweleann.com

Receive a FREE book and stay informed of new releases, sales, and exclusive stories:

Monthly Mailing List

jeweleann.com/free-booksubscribe

About the Author

Jewel is a free-spirited romance junkie with a quirky sense of humor.

With 10 years of flossing lectures under her belt, she took early retirement from her dental hygiene career to stay home with her three awesome boys and manage the family business.

After her best friend of nearly 30 years suggested a few books from the Contemporary Romance genre, Jewel was hooked. Devouring two and three books a week but still craving more, she decided to practice sustainable reading, AKA writing.

When she's not donning her cape and saving the planet one tree at a time, she enjoys yoga with friends, good food with family, rock climbing with her kids, watching How I Met Your Mother reruns, and of course…heart-wrenching, tear-jerking, panty-scorching novels.

Made in the USA
Monee, IL
24 July 2020

36950374R00203